THE LEGEND

300 Brave Men *and* Lord of the Royal Umbrella *are two fascinating tellings of history of India's most inspiring political figure in the last 1000 years. There are books on Shivaji and there is this series - this one stands head and shoulders above anything written on Shivaji Maharaj in historical fiction. Well researched yet written in a lucid story-telling style that brings to life every character and the lifestyle of that period beautifully. Strongly recommend this series to everyone. Truly an inspiring read!* Mandar Ghatnekar

Too many books have been written on the Maratha King so 'one more book on Shivaji...huh?' was my reaction when I picked this one. But as I began reading, I realised this was not just the usual tale of Shivaji. This is the Book 2 of the trilogy, but despite not having read book 1, I understood every bit of it. Gautam Pradhan is a gem of a storyteller. Lucid language and maintaining pace is his strength. I don't know whether author has time-travelled or not but he sure has penned a time machine to the 17th century. The Regular Reader

This book is even better than the first book, 300 Brave Men. It is also hard to put down. Can't wait for the third book. Ernst van der Lingen

Shivaji is a true giant slayer... The gripping storytelling captures our imagination beyond fantasy. Must read book to understand how one man changed the course of history... Ranjan Keshava

This is the best book for non-Marathi readers who were [ignorant] of their own history due to partial NCERT *books which favour the Mughal [narrative]. This was a real treat. What happened after this is still in*

question though. The book finishes at the coronation of Maharaja Chattrapati Shivaji Maharaja. Arsh Dixit

A book which gives you a view of the time of Chhatrapati Shivaji Maharaj. The writer has narrated the history in a storytelling manner. The book keeps the reader interested till the end. Paritosh Dere

This book has to be read by everyone. In fact, the life history of the superman Sri Shivaji Maharaj has to be in our history curriculum. Heard lot of stories in my childhood, which were not sequenced. [Am] much more confident [now]. Jai Bhavani. Jai Shivaji. Nikhil Raj Yadav

This was my second history-based book. Gautam's book does not [seem] historical. It's like watching a movie in your head. It's a live story. The only issue is I can't locate the third volume. Reji Rajan

It is great to see such a good book on the Marathas, who played a great role during an important phase of Indian history in the 17th, 18th and 19th centuries. The book is very detailed and engrossing. Shiv Sharan

Great story writing by the author. Eagerly waiting for the final chapter. Gourav Bhattacharya

300 Brave Men, *based on the early life of the iconic figure of Chhatrapati Shivaji of Maharashtra, is most engaging. Written in lucid language, it recreates the sequence of events in an easy conversational style that compels the reader to become part of the narrative. It maintains a good balance between historical fact and fiction. A book in English on this subject was long overdue... the book makes very interesting reading and is certainly un-put-downable.* Dr Prof. Sonali Pednekar, Head, Department of History, V G Vaze College, Mumbai

300 Brave Men *takes you back into 17th century India. This truly captivating story, written in a simple yet appealing manner makes it hard to imagine it is the work of a debutant author. This book should be read by everyone so more people know Shivaji's story. I am waiting for volumes II and III to be released soon.* Rohit Raut, Goodreads

300 Brave Men starts slowly and grows upon you. The palaces, the forts, the large cannons, the pomp and splendour, all come alive as one is transported to that era. …Midway through, the book gains speed and becomes un-put-downable. Even when you know what is going to happen, every page makes you want to read on in anticipation. Meghdoot Karnik, Author, Blogger, Corporate Executive

300 Brave Men is nail-biting to say the least and succeeds in instilling a great sense of pride in this Maratha king. It makes you feel you are watching the action unfold live! …One of the best books I've read this year. Neeti, Goodreads

An exceptionally well written and captivating recounting of Maratha history. Such a rush reading this book! Gautam's captivating and action-packed writing helped me visualize the details of Shivaji's life and the events of Maratha history. The details of the hold-off by the 300 is breathtaking and heart wrenching at the same time. I am dying to read the next one! Chetna, Goodreads

A great admirer of the Greatest King of India, I have read the story of his life by many an author, including translations of Marathi masterpieces. But I was mesmerised by 300 Brave Men. *As Mr Pradhan wove his masterly tapestry, scene after scene kept playing in my mind's eye. Now I am like a man thirsting for more water on a hot day, having drunk the first glass in a great hurry, waiting for the next volume, and the next.* G Raghavan

Great confluence of research and imagination. A highly engrossing novel which is difficult to put down. Ajay Tendolkar

Despite the many historical books I have read, I have a special mention for Sri Gautama Pradhan. The narrative is so real and authentic that it is difficult to see where history meets imagination, until described in his own words at the end. The language and style are flawless and the flow of events gripping and dramatic. S. Gopalakrishnan, Amazon

THE LEGEND

Book III: 1674—1680

GAUTAM PRADHAN

ISBN: 978-93-5559-222-4
© Gautam Pradhan, 2022
Maps recreated by the Author
Printing: Print Plus Pvt Ltd

Published in India 2022 by
Leadstart
A Division of One Point Six Technologies Pvt Ltd
119-123, Building J2, Shram Seva Premises
Wadala (East), Mumbai 400 022, Maharashtra, INDIA
T + 91 96 99933000 **E** info@leadstartcorp.com
W www.leadstartcorp.com

DISCLAIMER: Though based on real events and individuals, this is a work of fiction and should not be taken as an accurate historical account. The author does not claim that all incidents and descriptions in the book are historically exact or documented; they should not be used as references by scholars and students. Some incidents have been taken from folklore and cannot be proven. Clarifications appear in Author's Notes at the end of the book. All maps have been hand-drawn by the author from available sources with the sole objective of aiding the reader's understanding of the places described. They are not to scale nor are claims made as to the accuracy of boundaries, territories, provinces and places depicted; they should not be used as reference material for scholarly purposes. At no time has the author intended to hurt the religious sentiments of individuals or groups. References to religion or caste have been made solely in the context of 17th century Indian society, and the characters involved. The opinions expressed in this book do not purport to reflect the views of the Publisher.

*In memory of the greatest warrior-king
this country has ever produced;
a true inspiration for every Indian;
a thinker far ahead of his times:
Chhatrapati Shivaji Raje Bhosale.*

About the Author

GAUTAM PRADHAN is a Radiologist by profession. Educated in Mumbai, he has been in private medical practice for two decades. He lives in Thane, Maharashtra, with his wife Dipali, son Aditya and daughter Aryaa.

Passionate about history, Gautam reads voraciously on the subject and enjoys visiting places of historical interest. Possessed of an imaginative bent of mind, he felt caged within the restrictive confines of the medical profession and took to writing as a hobby. It seemed a natural choice to base his first book on historical events and the life and times of a man he has always revered. He has devoted a decade to researching and writing the Shivaji Trilogy, receiving valuable inputs through extensive discussions with eminent historians. The project on Shivaji's life, in three dramatized volumes, has been an emotional but intensely fulfilling journey. *300 Brave Men* (Book I), and *Lord of the Royal Umbrella* (Book II), were published to critical acclaim. This is the third and final book of the trilogy, covering a period of Shivaji's life that is not much known or written about.

Gautam's other interests include wildlife photography, music and the movies.

CONTACT
gautammpradhan@rediffmail.com
Insta and Facebook: booksbygautam

Contents

निश्चयाचा महामेरु । बहुत जनांस आधारु ।
अखंड स्थितीचा निर्धारू । श्रीमंत योगी ॥

*The epitome of determination, a protector of his people,
firmly resolute in intent...*

Wealthy, yet detached from his opulence; an ascetic…

या भूमंडळाचें ठायीं । धर्म रक्षी ऐसा नाहीं ।
महाराष्ट्रधर्म राहिला कांही । तुम्हां करिता ॥

*Nowhere on this earth was there ever, a greater protector
of his people, culture and righteousness...*

*It is because of you, that the culture of
Maharashtra has survived...*

~ SAMARTH RAMDAS SWAMI

With a deep sense of fulfillment I present to you the third and final book in this series on *Chhatrapati*[1] Shivaji. In this volume, I take his story forward from his historic coronation in 1674, to his demise in 1680. This is a far less known period of Shivaji's life as it has not been much written about. Most authors and screenwriters stop their narrative with the coronation, a seminal event that marks the high point of his life. However, to get an in-depth knowledge of the man and his remarkable life, I felt I had to take it to its natural end, and narrate the story till the coronation of his son Sambhaji as the second Chhatrapati.

In these six years, we see Shivaji increase not just his land holdings, but also his military power and clout in the political scenario, like a King of old. Whereas, prior to 1674, there were just three imperial powers, there are now four, as Shivaji is no longer a local chieftain but a sovereign ruler himself. In spectacular, superbly planned military campaigns, he extends his kingdom southward, first into the Canara district, and later the Karnatak region. With the former, he establishes his hold on the western coast of the subcontinent, and with the latter, on the eastern coast, thus cutting off the Adilshah from all sea trade and travel.

During the Karnatak campaign, he clashes with his half-brother Vyankoji, who holds their father's estates in the South. When Vyankoji refuses to part with half the estates

---

[1] Lord of the Royal Umbrella; title of royalty

peacefully, Shivaji takes them by force, defeating Vyankoji in battle. Vyankoji then signs a treaty with his more illustrious brother. This period also sees the Maratha navy come of age, as Shivaji's Naval Commanders clash with the powerful English and Abyssinians at sea, albeit with mixed results. Shivaji attempts to fortify the island of Khanderi, south of Mumbai, to convert it into a naval base. All opposition, first by the English, and later by the Abyssinians, comes to naught, though at a heavy price for the Marathas. The Khanderi campaign has far-reaching consequences as it marks the first time an indigenously developed naval force has held its own against the established naval powers.

These six years of Shivaji's life see him struggle to come to terms with his own health as well as family strife. Shivaji appears, to me, to have been isolated by the growing discord between his eldest son Sambhaji, and his chief wife Soyarabai, and his ministers. While Soyarabai nurtures the obvious motive of seeing her own son Rajaram ascend the throne, the Ministers appear to disagree with the Crown Prince's tactics and decisions, and disapprove of his behaviour. The widening chasm appears to have driven Shivaji to despair, and toward the end, he appears to have lost hope that his beloved *Swarajya*[2] would hold its own after his death. Finally, with no solution to the domestic crisis in view, Shivaji suffers a serious illness and breathes his last.

As with my earlier books in the series, I have concentrated on portraying only the key characters around Shivaji. I have also attempted to give the reader some understanding and context about Shivaji's family issues, especially those

---

[2] Self-ruled state; in the context of Shivaji's struggle, a state ruled by a son of the soil; here, self-rule should not be confused with democracy

involving his Chief Queen Soyarabai, and his elder son Sambhaji. Sambhaji's character has always been a topic of much debate and hence was the most difficult to create. I have tried to remain true to my own understanding of him, while steering clear of controversies. The result may seem half hearted to some, but in the interest of maintaining peace, that was the best I could do.

Finally, as I have done in my earlier books, I would like to request the reader to treat this book only as a dramatized account of historical events involving *Chhatrapati* Shivaji between 1674 and 1680. Though, for my part, I have tried to remain true to documented historical accounts and timelines, this is by no means a scholarly work on the great man. Instead, my books attempt to present the reader with a near-cinematic depiction of Shivaji's life and work, while trying to portray him as a human and not a deity.

Cast of Primary Characters

Shivaji's Family

Chhatrapati Shivaji Bhosale/ Shivaji Raje/ Seevaji/ Seeva 19 February 1630–3 April 1680: Sovereign Maratha King and Founder of the Maratha Empire

Soyarabai: Shivaji's second wife (according to most sources), hailed from the Mohite family and became Shivaji's chief consort following the death of his first wife, Saee

Sambhaji Bhosale/ Sambhaji Raje/ Shambhuji/ Shambhu Yuvraj: Shivaji's eldest son and Crown Prince; born of Saeebai: 14 May 1657

Rajaram: Shivaji's younger son, born of Soyarabai (14 February 1670)

Vyankoji Raje: Shivaji's half-brother, son of Shahaji and Tukabai

Note: Shivaji had eight children, among them two sons. By Saeebai: Sambhaji [son], Sakhubai, Ranubai & Ambikabai [daughters]; by Soyarabai: Rajaram [son] & Deepabai [daughter]; by Sagunabai: Rajkunvarbai [daughter]; by Sakwarbai: Kamlabai [daughter].

Putalabai: One of Shivaji's younger wives; she bore no children

Note: Shivaji had eight wives. Polygamy was an accepted custom of the time, especially in royal families. It is noteworthy that Shivaji did not have concubines, a widespread practice then.

Shivaji's Ministers, Administrators & Diplomats

Moro Trimal Pingale/ Moro Punt/ Mukhya Pradhan: Shivaji's Prime Minister, and Chief of the Council of Ministers

Anaji Datto, Anaji Punt, Sachiv: Minister for Land Revenue

Hambirrao Mohite, Senapati: Shivaji's Commander-in-Chief

Niraji Raoji, Nyayadheesh: Chief Justice in Shivaji's Council

Ramchandra Trimbak, Sumant: Minister for External Affairs

Balaji Avji, Chitnis: Shivaji's Secretary for Correspondence

Pralhad Niraji, Pralhad Punt: Niraji Raoji's son, an administrator in Shivaji's government; he served as *Nyayadheesh*[3] in Sambhaji's regime.

Raoji Somnath: Administrator, served as Governor of Raigad in Shivaji's absence

Dattaji Trimbak: Governor of Shivaji's Central Province

Ramchandra & Janardan Hanmante: Administrators who served Shivaji's half-brother Vyankoji, but later left him to join Shivaji; Ramchandra Hanmante served as Shivaji's *Amatya*[4] .

---

[3] Chief Justice

[4] Finance Minister

SHIVAJI's COMMANDERS & CAPTAINS

HIROJI FARZAND, SARJERAO JEDHE, SURYAJI MALUSARE, YESAJI KANK: Shivaji's most faithful and trusted Captains; some of his earliest adherents

BAHIRJI NAIK: Chief of Shivaji's intelligence network

SIDHOJI NIMBALKAR: Captain in Shivaji's army; killed in a rear-guard action against Ranmast Khan

Maynak Bhandari & Daulat Khan:Shivaji's naval Commanders

FIRANGOJI NARSALA: Commander of Bhupalgad Fort

VITTHAL MAHADKAR: Commander of Panhala Fort; ordered by Soyarabai to restrain Sambhaji after Shivaji's death

SAKHUJI: Shivaji's errant Captain who was blinded as punishment for misbehaving with a woman

NETOJI PALKAR: Shivaji's ex-*Sirnaubat*[5], who returned to him after a decade

GANOJI SHIRKE & MAHADJI NIMBALKAR: Sambhaji's faithful adherents and kinsmen, the former his wife's brother, the latter from his maternal family

HOUSE OF BIJAPUR (ADILSHAHI)

SIKANDER ADILSHAH: The ninth Sultan of Bijapur, placed on the throne when he was four years old

KURSHEEDA KHANUM, QUEEN MOTHER: Sikander's mother

SHAHR BANU BEGUM: Adilshahi Princess and Sikander's sister

---

[5] Military Commander

KHAWAS KHAN: Abyssinian *Vizier*[6] and Regent at the Adilshahi court from 1672- 1675; murdered by Bahlol Khan

ABDUL KARIM BAHLOL KHAN: Pathani Vizier and Regent at the Adilshahi court from 1675 -1677

SIDDI MASUD: Abyssinian Vizier and Regent at the Adilshahi court from 1677

SHEIKH MINHAJ, SHARZA KHAN: Adilshahi Captains belonging to the Deccani faction

KHIZR KHAN PANNI, JAMSHED KHAN: Pathani Captains faithful to Bahlol Khan

MUHAMMAD KHAN: Commander of Phonda Fort

ABDULLAH KHAN: Abyssinian Commander of Vellore Fort

NASIR MOHAMMED: Abyssinian Commander of Gingee Fort

SHER KHAN: Pathani Governor of South Gingee District; faithful to Bahlol Khan

HAKIM SHAMSHUDDIN, ABD-UR-RAZZAQ: Bijapuri nobles who defected to the Mughals

VYANKATADRI: Siddi Masud's *Brahman*[7] administrator

HOUSE OF GOLCONDA (QUTUBSHAHI)

ABUL HASAN QUTUBSHAH: Eighth Sultan of Golconda

MADANNA: Abul Hasan Qutubshah's Brahman Prime Minister

AKANNA: Madanna's brother, an administrator in the Golconda government

---

[6] Prime Minister

[7] Brahmin, high caste among the Hindus

MUHAMMAD IBRAHIM: Qutubshah's Persian Commander-in-Chief

MIRZA MOHAMMED AMIN: Qutubshahi Military Commander

THE MUGHALS

AURANGZEB: Sixth Mughal Emperor

PRINCE MUAZZAM: Aurangzeb's son

JAFAR KHAN: Aurangzeb's *Wazir*[8] from 1663 -1676

ASAD KHAN: Aurangzeb's Wazir from 1676 -1707

MUHAMMAD AMIN: *Mir Bakshi*[9] of the Mughal Empire

BAHADUR KHAN: High ranking Mughal *mansabdar*[10]; served as *Subadar*[11] of the Deccan Province

DILER KHAN: A Pathan and a high ranking Mughal mansabdar; one of Aurangzeb's most trusted men

MALIK BARKHURDAR: Mughal agent at the Bijapur court

ISLAM KHAN, IKHLAS KHAN: Mughal Captains

RANMAST KHAN: Mughal Commander of Jalna

---

[8] Head of Revenue for the Mughal Empire; usually the highest ranking officer at court, on par with the Prime Minister

[9] High ranking military officer in charge of nobility, intelligence and information agencies

[10] A person (usually a court noble) holding a mansab (Arabic word meaning "rank"; a military post at the Mughal court specified by the number of mounted soldiers the person was allowed to maintain (ie: 5000/10,000))

[11] Presiding officer of a *suba* (administrative district), appointed by the sovereign; supreme in that *suba* but for the Emperor

THE ENGLISH

JOHN CHILD: Officer at the English factory, Mumbai

WILLIAM MINCHIN: Captain, Mumbai

FRANCIS THORPE: Lieutenant, Mumbai

NASH: Sergeant

OTHERS

SIDDI SAMBUL: Abyssinian Commander of Janjira; later General of the Mughal armada

PAM NAYAK: Chieftain of the Berads, headquartered at Sagar Fort

FICTITIOUS CHARACTERS

Mahadu: Shivaji's personal attendant

Ganpat: Sambhaji's personal attendant

Kaveri: Rajaram's nanny

Hari: Maratha soldier on Khanderi Island

Jalal: Professional assassin in Khizr Khan Panni's employ

Basheer Khan: Captain under Jamshed Khan

Ahmed: Jamshed Khan's spy

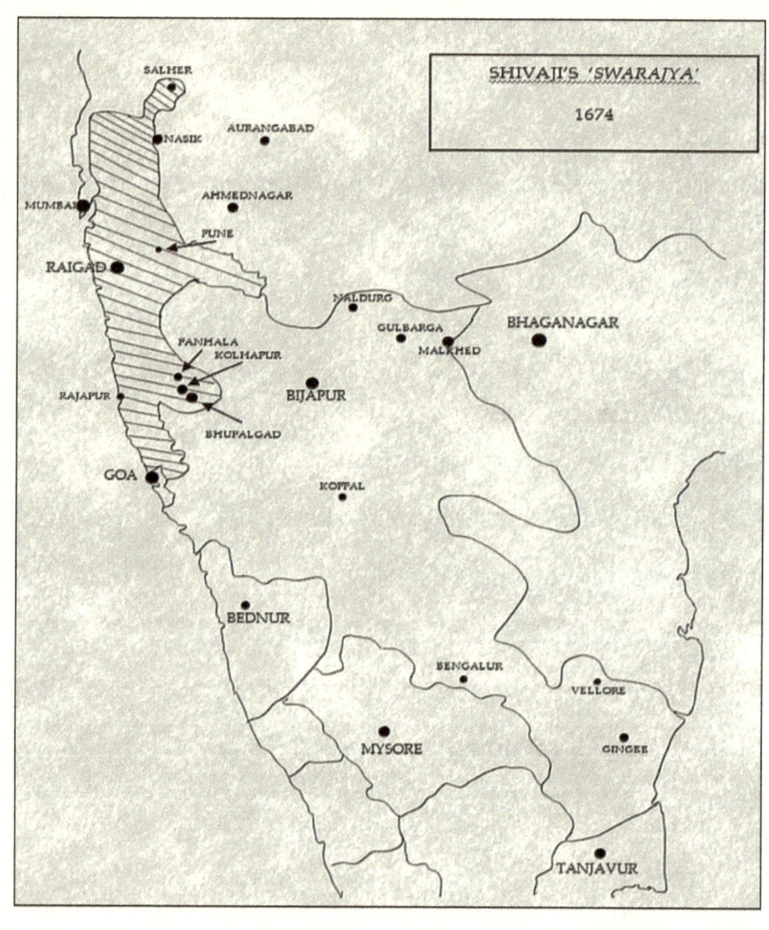

SHIVAJI'S 'SWARAJYA'
1674
SALHER
AURANGABAD
NASIK
AHMEDNAGAR
MUMBAI
PUNE
RAIGAD
NALDURG
GULBARGA
BHAGANAGAR
PANHALA
KOLHAPUR
MALKHED
RAJAPUR
BIJAPUR
BHUPALGAD
GOA
KOPPAL
BEDNUR
BENGALUR
VELLORE
MYSORE
GINGEE
TANJAVUR

Prologue

Maharashtra, Western India, Mid-17th Century

The Indian sub-continent is ruled by three imperial powers: the Mughal Empire in the north and the two Deccani Sultanates, Adilshahi and Qutubshahi in the south. But now a new power has risen in the west, a man they call Shivaji Bhosale. For the first time in three centuries, this incredible man unites the people of the Maratha homeland and leads a remarkable rebellion against the imperial rulers to carve out an independent principality. While his adversaries, who earlier ignored his growing power, now fear him, his bravery, heroics, generalship and foresight make him a legend in his own lifetime.

The Maratha homeland has experienced centuries of subjugation under foreign rule. Generations have suffered injustice and bigotry. The Maratha populace has long forgotten what freedom feels like, having resigned themselves to their fate and to their rulers. Now, at long last there rises a man who has a radically different mindset from those around him. He realizes that his fate lies in inspiring and leading his people to rebel against foreign rule to free their homeland. The journey is long and perilous, yet he embarks upon it, followed by thousands who believe in him.

Circa 1646

At the age of sixteen, Shivaji declares rebellion against the Adilshahi by usurping Torna Fort, inviting the Sultan's ire.

The infuriated sovereign first arrests his father, and then sends an army against Shivaji. As fate would have it, the Adilshah underestimates Shivaji's military and political skills, and not only suffers an ignominious defeat but is compelled to release Shahaji from prison, under Mughal pressure. A lull ensues in which the Adilshahi government is loath to initiate further action.

Circa 1656-58

Ten years after initiating his struggle, Shivaji commits his first brazen act of defiance against the Adilshah by killing Chandrarao More, a powerful chieftain of Jawali, in the Maval district of the Sahyadri Hills, annexing More's entire fief to his own. Shivaji's gains from this campaign are tremendous. Besides the fief itself, he gains control over several forts, key routes and mountain passes. He is now perilously close to Adilshah's coastal territory in the Konkan. The Adilshahi administration is rudely jolted from slumber but can do little as Sultan Muhammad Adilshah himself is terminally ill. The Sultan's demise later that year sees power pass into the hands of his widow, Badi Begum. No sooner does she place her young son on the throne and stabilizes her government, than the ambitious Mughal Prince Aurangzeb arrives at their doorstep with a large army, ready to swallow the Sultanate.

Shivaji takes full advantage of Bijapur's vulnerability to usurp as much territory as he can, rising in stature and power. Aurangzeb's plan to annex the Adilshahi receives a setback, however, as he receives news of Emperor Shah Jahan's illness and has to rush back to the Mughal capital to claim the throne. A bloody war of succession ensues between him and his brothers. Aurangzeb eliminates all challengers, imprisons his father, and ascends the throne as the sixth Mughal Emperor, assuming the title *Alamgir*[12].

Circa 1659-60

Having received a reprieve through Aurangzeb's departure from the Deccan, Badi Begum turns her attention to Shivaji, and appoints her faithful noble Afzal Khan, to lead the campaign against the Maratha rebel. The giant Khan, feared across the land, vows to bring back Shivaji dead or alive. Following Afzal Khan's march into his Swarajya with a large army, Shivaji shifts base to Pratapgad, and invites the Khan to a personal meeting in the Jawali Valley. Blinded by ego and overconfidence, Afzal Khan misreads Shivaji's tactics and demeanour and takes his army into the dense forests of the Koyna Valley. What ensues is the stuff of legend. In spectacular fashion, Shivaji manages to kill the massive Khan during their meeting and then flee to the safety of the fort, while his men attack the Khan's army from all sides, annihilating it. The Marathas follow up this victory with a whirlwind invasion of the Adilshahi territory, swallowing large tracts of land and annexing forts.

The Adilshahi is shaken by this collosal defeat. The young Sultan Ali decides to sideline his mother and assume control of the government. Hastily, he puts together a massive force and appoints the able Abyssinian officer, Siddi Jauhar, to head it. Jauhar follows Shivaji's movements, finally besieging him in Panhala Fort. The siege continues for four months, driving Shivaji to his wit's end. Finally, he makes a desperate escape from the fort on a stormy night, with six hundred chosen men, and his Captains Baji Prabhu and Fulaji Prabhu, two brothers who vow to take their King

---

[12] Conqueror of the World

to the safety of Vishalgad Fort. Their nocturnal adventure is discovered by Jauhar's spies, and Jauhar sends a force of three thousand in hot pursuit. The Bijapuris accost the Marathas in a mountain pass near Gajapur. Realizing they can no longer outrun the enemy, Baji and Fulaji stay back at the pass and block the enemy's advance with three hundred men, while Shivaji makes good his escape. A bloody battle is fought for over twelve hours in the Gajapur Pass, during which Baji and Fulaji perish.

CIRCA 1660

Mughal Emperor Aurangzeb has sent his uncle, the renowned noble Shaista Khan, to the Deccan to subdue Shivaji. Shaista Khan marches almost unchallenged into the heart of Shivaji's fief – Pune – and stations himself in Shivaji's childhood home. The Maratha lands and its people buckle under the impact of Mughal depredation. Shaista Khan's first military mission is to capture Chakan Fort, to the north of his position in Pune. He expects it to be a simple affair, but is surprised by the stoic resistance put up by the fort's small garrison. For well over two months the Maratha garrison resolutely fights Khan's large army. Though faced with hunger and fatigue, they refuse to surrender.

CIRCA 1663

Realizing his inferiority in numbers, Shivaji avoids direct confrontation and engages in a war of attrition to wear out his powerful opponent. But the Mughal depredation of his lands soon mounts to an alarming level and he is forced to plan a daring and audacious raid on the Mughal General himself. In a spectacular example of guerrilla warfare, Shivaji and four hundred hand-picked Maratha soldiers sneak into the large Mughal military camp in Pune, and launch an attack on the General's residence, slaughtering at will. In the melée, Shaista Khan escapes alive, albeit missing a few fingers, but is so shaken by the incident that he ceases all activity in the Deccan. The infuriated Emperor recalls him and hands over charge of the Deccan Province to his son, Prince Muazzam.

CIRCA 1664

Shivaji realizes that battling the mighty Mughal Empire requires him to cripple it not just in battle, but economically as well. With this goal in mind, as well as to forcibly extract remuneration for the losses incurred by his kingdom during Mughal campaigns, Shivaji raids Surat, the richest Mughal port, and carries away cash, precious stones and valuables worth over ten million rupees, a staggering sum in those days. The Marathas finally leave Surat, but not before they have burned down over two-thirds of the town, reducing it to ashes. The devastation is so complete that the Empire's entire income from Surat ceases for a prolonged period.

CIRCA 1665

Aurangzeb organizes another campaign to the Deccan; this time under the generalship of Jai Singh, the Rajput King of Amer. To safeguard against any treachery, he also sends the Pathani noble Diler Khan as Jai Singh's deputy. Jai Singh proves more than a match for Shivaji's guile and in just three months accomplishes what both Afzal Khan and Shaista Khan had failed to do earlier. The Maratha King is finally forced to surrender and accept a humiliating treaty in which he loses nearly two-thirds of his kingdom to the Empire.

Jai Singh now turns his attention to the Adilshah, aiming to annex his southern Sultanate. As per the terms of the recent treaty, the proud Maratha King is forced to march to Bijapur under the Mughal banner. Jai Singh's campaign against the Adilshahi fails miserably as Ali Adilshah manages to unite all factions in his court for the defence of his Sultanate. He employs the 'scorched earth' policy to such telling effect that the hapless Mughals are left scrounging for food and water in the hot Deccan. Jai Singh finally retreats, defeated not just by Ali's war tactics and the elements, but also by internal strife in his camp, between Diler Khan and Shivaji. Undefeated till then, Jai Singh is left humiliated in what turns out to be the last campaign of his life.

Circa 1666

Jai Singh manages to convince Shivaji to visit Agra and attend Aurangzeb's *durbar*[13], to be held to mark the Emperor's fiftieth birthday. Despite the inherent risks involved, Shivaji agrees to go, hoping to gain sufficient grants from the Emperor to launch a fresh campaign against the Adilshah. This is also Aurangzeb's best chance to either cajole the Maratha King into accepting his suzerainty by offering benefits, or arrest and kill him. However, both rulers fail to get anything worthwhile from the meeting, as one thing after another goes wrong during Shivaji's visit. Slighted by the Emperor and forced to endure the humiliation of bowing before him, the usually stoic Maratha loses his cool in the Emperor's durbar and walks out, a direct insult. The infuriated Emperor places him and his eight-year-old son Sambhaji, under house arrest. Faced with certain death, Shivaji counters every move of the Emperor, and finally

---

[13] The grand hall of audience at the royal court where the monarch conducts matters of State

flees Agra in a daring escape, leaving Aurangzeb seething in impotent fury.

Circa 1670

Shivaji has been at peace with the Empire for three years, biding his time while healing the wounds inflicted on his lands. He has no plans to submit his political ambitions to Aurangzeb, but waits for an opportunity to strike back. When Aurangzeb plans to arrest his officers, stationed peacefully in Sambhaji's *jagir*[14] of Varhad, Shivaji decides to put aside the treaty of 1665. In a spectacular campaign of reconquest, Shivaji takes back all the territory and forts ceded to the Mughals three years before. The Marathas then extend the limits of their Swarajya into Mughal territory to the north. Aurangzeb does his best to curb the Marathas, but is left frustrated by the incompetence of his Commanders.

Circa 1674

Three decades after he began his struggle against the imperial powers, Shivaji crowns himself King of the Marathas, assuming the title of Chhatrapati. He is the first indigenous ruler in three centuries to be crowned in accordance with ancient vedic customs, as King of an independent principality. Following his coronation, Chhatrapati Shivaji continues with his conquests, expanding his kingdom south, at the expense of the Adilshahi lands. His first major campaign as a sovereign King is in the Canara District. *The Legend* begins with this campaign.

---

[14] Fiefdom gifted by a sovereign, usually to a court noble

1

Master of the Western Coast

Raigad Fort, Early 1665

Chhatrapati Shivaji sat in council with his chief administrators and military officers in his private offices on Raigad Fort. It was early in the day and the air was still rather chilly. The Chhatrapati pulled his shawl closely around his torso as he listened intently to the middle-aged man seated on the far side. The man was dressed simply in a *dhoti*[15] and loosely fitting jacket. On his head he wore a cloth turban. Though of medium height, he was well built and the muscles of his arms rippled as he gripped his wooden shaft. He was not, however, the simple peasant he seemed, for he was none other than that mysterious individual of many parts, Bahirji Naik Jadhav, Head of Maratha Intelligence

He now updated the council on the latest developments along the Mughal front. "Your Highness, our forces successfully raided Dharangaon and other areas of the Mughal Khandesh province, right up to the walls of Burhanpur. I have received word from Hiroji Farzand's camp that they have collected a large booty."

The Chhatrapati smiled in satisfaction. Hiroji, his ever reliable Captain, had done his job.

---

[15] Unstitched length of cloth worn as a lower-body garment by men

"But there is a slight problem, Sire," Bahirji said, his face sombre.

The Chhatrapati merely raised his eyebrows in question.

"Hiroji's men burned down the English trading station in Dharangaon."

Shivaji Maharaj sighed. This would lead to yet another unending series of meetings and negotiations as the English were certain to approach him for reparations. But, deeming it unimportant at this time, he brushed the news aside and asked Bahirji, "What is the news from the Adilshahi?"

"Your Highness, the troubles of Bijapur grow by the day. Nobles of the Pathani and Deccani factions are at each other's throats. I have a feeling something is about to give."

"What do you mean by that?"

"Abdul Karim Bahlol Khan, the Pathan, and Khawas Khan, the Siddi, are at loggerheads. They haven't seen eye to eye for years, but now the struggle for control of the government grows ever more. I have a feeling one of them will oust the other for good."

Shivaji Maharaj sat in deep thought for some time and then turned his attention to Bahirji again. "What is the state of the Canara District?"

Bahirji's mouth quirked in what might have been a smile. Having worked for his Lord for decades now, he could read his thoughts. He instantly realized that his King aimed to use the impotency of the Bijapur administration for the benefit of Maratha Swarajya. "The Governor, Rustum-e-Zaman, is away in Bijapur. The district is scarcely protected," he said knowingly.

The Chhatrapati turned to his *Mukhya Pradhan*[16], Moro *Punt*[17] Pingale, who sat to his right. "Punt, I think it's time we entirely wrested control of the west coast from the Adilshah."

"Excellent thought, Highness," Moro Punt agreed. "If we can annex Canara District now and take control of the entire west coast, Adilshah's sea-trade with Arabia will be effectively finished."

Senapati[18] Hambirrao Mohite, who flanked his King on the left, said, "That will seriously hamper their supply of horses, which comes from the Arab lands to the west coast."

Maharaj nodded. "Exactly my thoughts," he said. "Then they will have only the east coast to get their goods and horses from." After a brief pause he added, "And of course, we shall do something about the east coast too, shall we not?"

Heads nodded around the room. The *Sachiv*[19], Anaji Punt, and Prince Sambhaji, were among those present.

"Bahirji," Maharaj said, turning to his chief spy, "set the campaign in motion. I want an unbroken chain of informers across the Canara. Decide on safe travel paths for our men."

Bahirji bowed. His heartbeat quickened at the prospect of another military campaign. Though rarely in the thick of battle, his job and expertise were crucial to the planning of each mission, and he knew it. Much depended on how

---

[16] Prime Minister (same as Peshwa)

[17] A suffix denoting a person's administrative function; usually from the Brahman or Kayastha castes

[18] Commander-in-Chief of the armed forces (*sena* [Army] and *pati* [Lord])

[19] Minister for Land Revenue

he and his men did their job of gathering intelligence and reconnaissance. He knew only too well how much his King relied on him.

"Senapati," Maharaj continued to his Commander, "get a force of fifteen thousand cavalry and an equal number of foot soldiers ready for the campaign."

"It will be done, my Lord," Hambirrao bowed his head.

The Sachiv moved restlessly on his seat. The newly proposed campaign sounded logical, but a thought was eating him. "Er, Your Highness, if I may…" he interjected.

"Yes Anaji Punt, what is it?" Maharaj asked.

"What about the Mughal, my Lord? Bahadur Khan sits in readiness at Aurangabad, ever ready to march on us as soon as we divert our attention elsewhere."

Prince Sambhaji smirked at the suggestion. "The Sachiv worries unnecessarily about the Mughal. Our Swarajya is not as helpless and powerless as he thinks."

Anaji Punt was irritated by this rebuke from the young Prince, but maintaining a straight face said, "Certainly not! I agree the *Yuvraj*[20] is more than capable of handling Bahadur Khan, but we are talking about avoiding or circumventing hostilities with the Mughal right now."

Maharaj thought for a while, then said, "Ananji Punt is right. We need to devise some tactic to mislead Bahadur Khan. Maybe the *Sumant*[21] can help us here."

All eyes turned to Ramchandra Trimbak, who sat bolt upright at once. "Does his Highness have some sort of

---

[20] Crown Prince

[21] Minister for External Affairs (same as *Dabir*)

temporary peace treaty with the Mughal in mind?" He was sufficiently well versed with his King's ways to guess his thoughts.

Maharaj nodded. "Meet the Mughal Subadar and beg for a pardon from the Emperor. Offer the services of our Prince under the Mughal banner in return for peace. That should divert his attention from us at least till we wind up the Canara campaign."

"I shall begin working on it at once, my Lord," said Ramchandra Punt.

With that, the Chhatrapati rose, and amid salutations from the men, left the chamber.

"His Highness must spare some time for his family on *MahaShivratri*[22]."

Maharaj smiled as Queen Soyarabai made this demand of him. Post his night meal, he was relaxing in her chamber. "Soyara, you are aware that we are planning a major military campaign into the Canara district. I do not have time for festivities," he replied.

"Highness, it is an auspicious year for us."

Maharaj, momentarily unsettled by the remark, hastily tried to figure out what he had missed. The Queen threw a sideways glance at him, knowing instantly that he had no idea what she was talking about.

"Our son turns five this year!" Soyara said, fixing her gaze on him.

---

[22] Festival to mark the marriage of Lord Shiva and Parvati

"Rajaram is five already?" Maharaj's eyebrows went up in surprise. "How time flies!"

"The festival falls in the month of his birth. I have planned an *abhishek*[23] to Lord Mahadev, and the Chhatrapati will perform the rites with Prince Rajaram."

Maharaj sighed in resignation. "As you wish, my Queen."

Soyara laughed. "His Highness' family also has some right to him. Swarajya can wait for a night."

Maharaj was quiet for a while. Soyara toyed with the idea of bringing up the topic she was eager to discuss with her husband. Realizing that she was hesitating to say something, Maharaj asked, "What is it, Soyara? What is on your mind?"

"Your Highness, Rajaram is growing up to be a wise boy. We must start his formal education soon."

"I agree, and I shall see to it once I am back from this campaign."

"Rajaram too, can grow up to be a worthy heir to the throne."

The Chhatrapati regarded his wife intently. She returned his gaze, trying to gauge if her remark had disturbed him. Maharaj realized Soyara was merely trying to turn his mind to favour her own son, over Shambhu. "Rajaram is too young to think about that, Soyara. But I agree with you. He *is* growing up to be a wise boy."

"Wiser than his much older sibling anyway!" Soyara permitted herself the liberty of criticizing Shambhu.

The door to the Queen's chamber opened just as Maharaj was about to say something. They could hear the maid

---

[23] Hindu offering to God in the form of a ceremonial ablution (eg: pouring water/milk over an idol or Shivling); also used to anoint a King

whispering to someone. "Do not go in without permission, Your Highness…" But before she could finish, the little boy ran in at top speed toward the royal couple. Maharaj's eyes lit up as he saw his younger son Rajaram leap into his mother's arms.

The maid followed him in and bowed low. "Forgive me, Highnesses. The Prince wouldn't listen to me… I tried stopping him… to announce his arrival…" she stammered.

"It's alright, Kaveri," Soyarabai said to her. Kaveri bowed and left the chamber, to wait outside for her charge.

Rajaram hid his face in his mother's bosom. Momentarily, he stole a glance at his father and then hid his face again. His parents laughed indulgently.

"Now Rajaram Raje, you must not harass your nanny like that," Maharaj said to his son.

"She no let me come to mother!" Rajaram said with a lisp, venting a long-held grievance.

"Well, it is past your bedtime. Why won't you sleep?" Soyara asked him.

"I wan' sleep with mother!" Rajaram said, throwing his arms around Soyara's neck.

Maharaj smiled indulgently. "What gift would you like for your birth day?"

The boy's face brightened. He regarded his father with sparkling eyes for a moment and announced, "I wan' holse, like *dada*[24]!"

"Oh, you want to ride a horse like your Shambhu dada?"

---

[24] Elder brother

Rajaram nodded vigorously. "I lide holse like dada!"

"Well then you shall get your own horse on your birth day."

The Maratha envoy reached the Mughal Subadar at Aurangabad with Chhatrapati Shivaji's petition for peace and servitude for the Maratha Prince. Subadar Bahadur Khan was quite eager to have this petition endorsed by the Emperor. For one, it would mean he could rest easy on the Maratha front at least. He hated campaigning in the Western Hills and hated going after the slippery Maratha King even more. Besides, if he could somehow engineer Seevaji's submission, his own prospects at the Mughal court would certainly be bettered. Bahadur Khan wasted no time in forwarding the petition to Emperor Aurangzeb.

The Emperor, however, was far more experienced in dealing with the Maratha King. He knew Seeva's old habit of engaging in false treaties and offering empty promises of subservience. "Seeva cannot be trusted this easily," Aurangzeb said thoughtfully as he sat on his plush *baithak*[25] in the antechamber, turning prayer beads in his right hand. "Bahadur Khan is an idiot if he trusts that rat!"

Jafar Khan, the Mughal Wazir, nodded in agreement. "His Majesty is wise. Seeva is unreliable."

"Write to Bahadur Khan immediately," Aurangzeb commanded. "Tell him to be careful of Seeva's tricks. He should send reliable persons to Seeva and draw up a formal document. Malik Barkhurdar who is in Aurangabad as an

---

[25] Floor level seating arrangement with cushions

Inspector of Branding should be sent to Seeva with some other men."

"It shall be done, Majesty." Jafar Khan kept to himself his own doubts about this proposed peace with the Marathas.

The MahaShivratri festivities were in progress on Raigad Fort. The Chhatrapati himself sat to perform the abhishek rites in the Mahadev temple to the south of the royal palace. With him sat his sons Rajaram and Sambhaji. The Queens, Ministers, and chief officers, gazed at the trio with admiration and pride. One person in the assembly however, was less elated. Soyarabai had objected when Maharaj had insisted that both Princes perform the abhishek with him. She would have preferred her husband to perform the rites with her own son, Rajaram. She was keenly aware of the fact that Sambhaji was the Crown Prince and had first right to the throne after their father. She also knew that somehow she would have to enhance her own son's reputation not only in the durbar and amongst the Ministers, but also in the Chhatrapati's heart, while damaging that of Sambhaji. And she would have to do all this without raising her husband's suspicions.

The *pooja*[26] was soon completed and the priests distributed the *prasad*[27] to all the attendees. The assembly soon shifted to the royal palace where an ensemble of bards sang *bhajans*[28], entrancing everyone.

---

[26] Religious ceremony

[27] Edible offering that had first been presented to the deities

[28] Spiritual songs

Chhatrapati Shivaji embarked upon his campaign in the Canara District of the southern Konkan, with ten thousand horse and foot, and thousands of camp followers. The advance guard had already begun leaving the capital a month earlier, preparing the ground for the King's march by procuring key military stations of the Adilshah. Dattaji Trimbak had advanced as far south as Kolhapur, capturing the town and arresting the Adilshahi Governor. Another Maratha force was operating in the eastern part of the Adilshahi. These forces not only laid the foundation for the campaign, but also diverted attention from the main force under the Chhatrapati, which marched in the direction of Phonda Fort.

Two weeks later, the Maratha forces halted for a breather in the shade afforded by a mango grove on the outskirts of a village called Vilawade. They were still some twenty four *kos*[29] north of their destination. Being almost mid-day, it was stiflingly hot, but a shifting breeze gave some respite. The Chhatrapati had just freshened up when Hiroji Farzand walked up to him and bowed. "Highness, the English Company has sent an officer to meet you. He requests audience."

Shivaji Maharaj took some time to settle down on the baithak prepared for him under the shade of a large mango tree. "What does he want?" he asked his Captain.

"They are experiencing some difficulty in restarting their factory in Rajapur. He has some petition regarding the same."

---

[29] An ancient measure of distance; used in India for over 3000 years; a *kos* was 2.25 miles

"But isn't Anaji Punt already in Rajapur? He should have looked into the matter."

"His Highness is right. But it seems the English are not happy with the way Anaji Punt has handled their problem."

Maharaj nodded permission to let the Englishman approach. At once his personal bodyguards flanked him, unsheathing their swords.

A tall and fair Englishman arrived, dressed formally in a tight-fitting red coat, black trousers, knee-high boots, and a tall red hat. He bowed, offering a warm greeting, "Salutations to His Highness, the Chhatrapati."

Maharaj acknowledged this with a brief nod. He couldn't help but notice the white hair under the man's hat. He looked far too young to have his hair turn white, he thought. He always found the Europeans strange.

The accompanying Brahman clerk introduced his master, "Your Highness, this is John Child, an officer of the English Company's Mumbai Council." Child then spoke in a clear firm voice, letting Maharaj know the purpose of his visit, while the clerk translated rapidly. Maharaj smiled and beckoned him nearer. The Englishman walked up to him and bowed. Maharaj extended his right hand and gently felt the locks of his white hair. Child threw a confused glance at his clerk, who was quick to offer an explanation to the Maratha King, "Your Highness, that isn't real hair. It is a wig; part of their official uniform."

The Chhatrapati nodded. These Englishmen were weird. He spoke for the first time, "We are sympathetic to your troubles. But it is much too hot to discuss your problems here under the noon sun. Meet me at Rajapur in two days' time, and I will personally look into the matter."

John Child bowed and retreated. Two days later, he was sitting before the Maratha King at his residence in Rajapur. The King heard his complaints and demands, granting most of them. Their difficulties in setting up a new factory would be looked into, he said. They would get remuneration in kind for losses incurred.

Having thus settled the issue of the English, Chhatrapati Shivaji left Rajapur the same evening.

Phonda Fort, 4 April 1675

"My Lord, the Marathas are investing the fort systematically. Our guns have caused them no damage thus far. They sit comfortably beyond our range of fire."

Muhammad Khan, the Commander of Phonda Fort, listened with dismay as the Captain of the Guard reported. Earlier in the day they had noticed Maratha contingents stationing themselves around the fort, closing off the exit routes one by one. He had ordered his men to fire immediately, but to no effect. He was now faced with the prospect of a long siege or a tough battle, or both. He did not relish the thought at all. Turning to his clerk, he asked, "What is the state of our supplies?"

"Khan-*saheb*[30], our grain, salt and other supplies can last some four months," the clerk replied diligently.

"But our ammunition reserves could run out much sooner, my Lord," the Captain of the Guard informed him.

Muhammad Khan pondered these details for some time. In the distance, he could hear guns booming as his men retaliated to the Maratha offensive. Finally, he said,

---

[30] Respectful form of address

"Surrender is out of the question. We must fight or die. We have no other option."

The Brahman clerk swallowed hard. Stories of Shivaji Maharaj were legendary by now. If he or his men decided to take a fort, they rarely failed.

Khan dismissed the clerk. Looking his Captain in the eye he said, "Double the watch on the ramparts. Change guard every two *prahars*[31]. That should keep the men rested. Watch out for mines. The Marathas are likely to try and blow up one of the bastions. I want reports every prahar. I will not let those Maratha swines have my fort, do you hear?"

"Yes, my Lord!" The Captain bowed and left. Muhammad Khan's face was lined with worry. He would have to send pleas for help to Rustum-e-Zaman and Bahlol Khan immediately. Things did not look good to him at all.

Maratha camp, environs of Phonda Fort

"The siege is tight, Your Highness," Hiroji Farzand informed his King the next day, having completed the deployment of troops around the fort.

"Good!" The Chhatrapati sat at the head of the war council in his command tent, pitched well to the north of the fort. His chief Captains – Hiroji Farzand, Suryaji Malusare, Sarjerao Jedhe and Sidhoji Nimbalkar – listened attentively. Bahirji Naik, his chief spy, who now accompanied him on all campaigns, was present. Anaji Punt, who had joined him at Rajapur, sat to his right.

"We must guard against either Rustum or Bahlol Khan succouring the fort from their respective headquarters in

---

[31] A unit of time used in India from the Puranic Age; one prahar was approximately three hours.

Canara and Dharwar. Send detachments into the *ghats*[32] and block the approach routes. Fell trees to block the passes. Position units in the hills to intercept any Bijapuri troops that may get across."

"It will be done, Sire," Hiroji said.

"Sarjerao, begin work on the mines immediately. We must try and get as near the walls as possible."

"Of course, Sire!" Sarjerao said.

The men discussed details of deployment for some more time and then were dismissed. As the men prepared to leave, Maharaj said, "Stay back a moment, Bahirji."

Maharaj waited till the others had left and then beckoned Bahirji near. "Send a trusted man to meet with Bahlol Khan," he said in a low voice. "Offer him gifts and money to stay out of our way. If he manages to land his troops here, we will have a sticky situation on our hands."

Bahirji nodded. "I will organize that at once, Highness."

LAST WEEK OF APRIL 1675

"The men have created a mud and stone bank five *guz*[33] from the fort ramparts, Sire. Under its cover, they have commenced work on digging a tunnel to the north-west bastion," Sarjerao Jedhe said, pointing to the map of the fort spread out before them.

"Good," Maharaj nodded in satisfaction. "How many days till we reach the ramparts?"

---

[32] Mountains

[33] A unit of length, still used in some parts of India; its exact length varied from region to region, but was roughly equivalent to twenty-eight inches

"Three days at most, Sire. It isn't too far to dig, but the Bijapuris have been firing at the wall incessantly. We have to work under the cross-fire."

Maharaj's forehead creased. "We have lost too many men. It has taken us longer than expected to take the fort. Muhammad Khan is a stubborn customer."

It had been over three weeks since they had besieged the fort. The Marathas had tried to assault the ramparts repeatedly but had been driven back each time, with heavy losses. Chhatrapati Shivaji had been so hard pressed that he had finally ordered his men to approach as near the ramparts as possible and build a bank, under fire. His loyal soldiers had done exactly that and would soon, he hoped, tunnel underground to mine the ramparts themselves.

"Any signs of desperation from the garrison?" Maharaj asked his Captain.

"None yet, Lord. They seem to have enough supplies for now."

Maharaj turned to Suryaji and Hiroji. "What have our mobile units been up to?"

"We have received news that our cavalry has raided the surrounding Adilshahi lands and have gone as far east as the Golconda territory. They should send us back quite some booty."

There was a suppressed cough. The men looked up to see Bahirji enter the tent. The Chhatrapati nodded to his Captains, dismissing them. "Give me good news, Bahirji," he said when they were alone.

"Bahlol Khan will not cross the hills, Sire. I have greased his palm. Even if he does, I doubt he will get across the blocked passes."

"Good. What about Rustum?"

"I received news that Rustum is marching in our direction. But he has a small force with him, no more than two thousand horse. In any case I have dispatched Sidhoji's unit to intercept him before he reaches the hills. Muhammad Khan will not get any help."

"You have never failed me yet Bahirji."

"I have word from Goa that the *firangis*[34] continue to help Muhammad Khan in secret."

Maharaj sighed in frustration. "These foreigners cannot be trusted. Send word to our agent in Goa that he should approach the Portuguese Viceroy and demand an explanation. Keep up the pressure on him. Meanwhile, order Hiroji to send fresh cavalry units to raid Portuguese territory to our north. That should warn the Viceroy not to double-cross us."

The stage was set for one final charge on Phonda Fort.

NIGHT OF 30TH APRIL – 1ST MAY 1675

Despite the late hour, Hiroji's face beamed as he announced to his King that the tunnel was ready and had been packed with gunpowder. The fuses were in place and the men had been moved away from the fort. Chhatrapati Shivaji ordered him to ready a unit of two thousand well-rested men for the assault.

By the middle of the third prahar, they were finally ready to blow up the fort ramparts. The Chhatrapati, clad in armour, watched as his artillery men readied the fuses. The assault

---

[34] Foreigner; a term used by the Marathas to refer mainly to the Portuguese

unit waited impatiently. Hiroji looked back at Maharaj for the signal. The Chhatrapati nodded firmly and Hiroji ordered, "Light it!"

With a sharp hissing sound, the fuses sparked up and progressed toward the fort wall. In a few moments the sparks disappeared into the tunnel. Deathly silence ruled as everyone waited with bated breath. Finally, after what seemed an eternity, a massive blast shattered the still night. The Marathas crouched low as stone, dirt and debris were thrown into the sky, only to crash to the ground. The air was filled with dust and gunpowder. As the deafening blast died away, they could hear the cries and shrieks of the garrison. The moment the air cleared enough for them to see their way across, Hiroji cried, "Charge!"

Two thousand Marathas began running to the breach, screaming for blood. Before the fort garrison could recover enough to set up a defense, the Marathas had assaulted the breach and cut through the enemy front ranks. The garrison buckled under the attack and the Marathas entered the fort.

The battle had lasted less than a prahar. The eastern skies had brightened when Muhammad Khan, the Bijapuri Commander, was dragged into the Chhatrapati's tent.

"The Commander of Phonda Fort, Your Highness!" Hiroji bowed, announcing his captive.

"On your knees vermin!" Suryaji hissed as he roughly forced Khan down.

"Salutations, Shivaji Raje," Khan said, falling to his knees.

"You will address the King as Chhatrapati, you swine!" Hiroji kicked the prisoner in the back.

"Chhatrapati Shivaji, I surrender the fort and myself to you. In return, I only ask for mercy. Spare our lives."

"Marathas never kill imprisoned soldiers, Muhammad Khan," the Chhatrapati said coldly. "We leave such actions to you. But in return for sparing your life, and those of your men, you will have to do something for us."

"Command me, Your Highness," Khan said, face downcast. He was a proud man and such humiliation roiled his soul.

"You will write to all the Fort Commanders of Raibag, Ankola, Shiveshwar and Karwar regions, to surrender to my men."

"They are not bound to abide by my letters, Your Highness."

"Which is why, you will instill fear in their minds by writing that our armies are vast and cannot be defeated and that we have already conquered most of the territory along the western shore."

Muhammad Khan remembered the months spent in repulsing attack upon attack by the Marathas, only to be overcome by gunpowder. "It will be as you wish," he said. Defeat felt bitter in his mouth.

Within the next month the Marathas had taken Ankola, Shiveshwar, Karwar, Kadra and Gokarna, completing their domination on the west coast. The southern boundary of the Maratha Swarajya now touched the northern limits of the Kingdom of Sonda, a vassal of Bijapur. The Adilshah had lost access to the west coast for trade, and more importantly, for importing Arabian horses for his cavalry. He now had only his trading ports along the east coast available to him.

Chhatrapati Shivaji had managed to seriously compromise the Adilshah's revenues from sea trade.

Agra, Mughal Capital, Mid-July 1675

The Emperor was furious. Yet again the wily Maratha rat had managed to fool his officers by proffering a make-believe treaty. Bahadur Khan, Subadar of his Deccan Province, had swallowed the bait, and following his recommendations, Aurangzeb had awarded a *mansab*[35] to Sambha, and gifts to Seeva. What's more, he had even sent a cash reward to Bahadur Khan himself, besides promoting him in military rank. But a few months later, Seeva the scoundrel, had banished the Mughal envoys Malik Barkhurdar and Muhammad Sayyid from his fort with the words, "Why should I give any of my forts to the Emperor? Be gone, else I will evict you in humiliation!"

"I expected that rat Seeva would do something like this!" Aurangzeb fumed to his Wazir, Jafar Khan. "We should never have trusted him in the first place."

"His Majesty is quite right. Seevaji never stands by his treaties," Jafar Khan simply echoed his sovereign's thoughts.

"Seeva! His name is Seeva. Do not add *ji*. He does not deserve that respect!" Aurangzeb flashed angry eyes at the Wazir.

"Of course, Majesty." Jafar Khan glanced helplessly at the *Mir Bakshi*[36] Muhammad Amin, who stood across from him.

---

[35] Arabic word meaning 'rank'; a military post at the Mughal court specified by the number of mounted soldiers the person was allowed to maintain (ie: a 5000 or 10,000 *mansab*)

[36] High ranking military officer in charge of nobility, intelligence and information agencies

"We must finish Seeva completely. Destroy his lands, his people and his forts!" Aurangzeb banged his fist on the cushions in frustration. "I doubt if Bahadur Khan can do that alone. We will have to join hands with Adil Khan for the time being. We will finish Seeva and then turn our attention to Bijapur."

"A clever strategy, Majesty," Jafar Khan said. "What terms should we propose to the Adilshah...er...Adil Khan?" Aurangzeb's displeasure at calling the King of Bijapur the Adilshah was known to all. The Emperor believed that only the King of Persia deserved the title 'Shah'. Here, in Hindustan, he himself was the *Shahenshah Alamgir*[37]. The Kings of Bijapur and Golconda deserved only the title of 'Khan', and no more. Jafar Khan had corrected himself just in time.

"Write to Adil Khan. Tell him the Emperor will forego the annual tribute from Bijapur if he agrees to join hands with us on a campaign against Seeva."

Jafar Khan and Muhammad Amin exchanged looks. The annual tribute from Bijapur was a hefty sum and foregoing it would make a dent in the treasury. These were tough times for the Empire, what with rebellions in the northwest and the perennial threat of Maratha raids in the south. Military expenditure was at an all-time high. The Empire needed every bit of tribute from its vassal states.

"Jafar Khan?"

Aurangzeb's stern voice jolted the Wazir from his thoughts. "His Majesty's command will be carried out immediately," he said.

---

[37] Shahenshah: Title for an Emperor; Literal meaning is 'King of Kings'
Alamgir: Seizer of the world.

Having tried to wipe out Shivaji Bhosale several times in the past, unsuccessfully, Aurangzeb had put into motion another ambitious plan to tackle the Maratha. Only time would tell if this time he would succeed.

"The Siddi has been hard-pressed for supplies these past six months, Sire." Bahirji Naik was briefing Maharaj on the situation in the coastal areas of Danda-Rajpuri. "I have word from my men in Surat that he has approached the Mughal Governor for aid."

The Chhatrapati smiled. The long protracted siege of Janjira Fort seemed to be working.

"The Siddi will not be able to hold out for too long now," Bahirji continued. "Help from Surat is unlikely to upset our plans very much. Surat is too far away for him."

"That may be so," the Chhatrapati said reflectively. "But the Siddi also gets help each year from the English at Mumbai. We have to convince the English to stop helping him."

"Apparently Sire, they help him unwillingly. The English are as fed up with the Siddis as we are. These freebooters create enough trouble for them at Mumbai, festering crime and violence."

"His Highness will remember that we recently lost an opportunity to placate the English," Anaji Punt, the Sachiv, chose to interject with a reminder of the Chhatrapati's last meeting with the English Ambassador.

Prince Sambhaji, who sat across from the Sachiv, raised his eyebrows at that comment, his face clearly showing his irritation. "Does the Sachiv wish to say that His Highness was wrong in his decision to refuse compensation to the English?"

"I merely meant that we had an opportunity to strengthen our relations with the Europeans." Anaji Punt felt flustered at the prospect of yet another spat with the Prince. Of late, he seemed to disagree with anything the Sachiv did or said.

"So you probably want to suggest that we should have paid the English plenty of money, which they did not deserve, in the *hope* that they would stop assisting the Siddi, and thus favour us?"

"That is not what I…"

"And what if the English continue to help him *after* we pay them?" Sambhaji interrupted.

"Yuvraj, I am but a servant of the Swarajya. My duty is not just to comply with His Highness' orders, but also to provide him with wise counsel about his political decisions."

"It would be better if the Ministers stick to their office duties and leave the decision-making to the rulers."

Several ministerial faces in the assembly expressed displeasure at this comment by the Prince. None spoke, of course.

The Chhatrapati raised his hand to calm things down. "I think we should negotiate with the English afresh. I have decided that the Yuvraj will deal with the Europeans now. That should free my mind for other issues at hand."

The Sachiv was crestfallen. He had brought up the issue merely to point out to his King that his hasty decision in turning the English down could impact them adversely. But the King had appointed the short-tempered Prince to deal with the wily foreigners, and that was unlikely to help their cause.

The fourth prahar of the day had ended. The lengthening evening shadows cast an eerie look over the southern courtyard of the palace complex. Soyarabai alighted from the palanquin and was immediately surrounded by her ladies. They had just returned from a visit to the Jagdeeshwar Temple. As they climbed the stairs leading from the courtyard to the palace and the Queen's chambers, they saw Yuvraj Sambhaji approaching from within.

He bowed to the Queen, as the other ladies retreated into the shadows, leaving the two alone. "Greetings, Mother," Sambhaji said. "I heard you had been to the Jagdeeshwar Temple."

Soyarabai regarded the Prince intently. "I was unaware you kept track of my whereabouts."

Sambhaji fumbled for a response. "I…I don't."

"Or perhaps you are more interested in the whereabouts of some of the ladies in my chambers?"

Sambhaji was silent.

"Your behaviour of late has been quite disturbing, Shambhu Raje. I have heard you have quite the roving eye."

"That is not true, Mother. You have heard wrong. Perhaps, people lie about me."

"Perhaps. I also heard you have had another altercation with Anaji Punt."

"If I state my views, it is always viewed by the Ministers as an altercation."

"There is a difference between stating one's views and forcing them upon others."

"Well, it happened in my father's presence, so you can get the truth from him. Or have you stopped believing him as well?"

"Shambhu, I am merely saying that the heir apparent must have a spotless character and display impeccable conduct. He must also learn to work *with* the Ministers."

"Lesson learnt, Mother! Now you must excuse me." Shambhu bowed and hurried away, leaving Soyarabi exasperated yet again.

2

Civil War in Bijapur

Mughal camp, Pandharpur, 19 October 1675

Bahadur Khan, Subadar of the Mughal Deccan Province, seemed quite relaxed as he sat with his back resting comfortably against soft cushions. His right hand lay on his folded knee, toying with a Jasmine flower. The sweet scent of the flower diverted his mind from the odour of sweat which was particularly heavy in his tent at the moment. He looked thoughtfully at the dark-skinned noble who sat to his right, and tried to read his mind. Politics was a dirty business, especially if you were merely carrying out the Emperor's orders. Nearly two months ago he had received the Emperor's *firmaan*[38], ordering him to conclude a treaty with the Adilshah and organize a joint campaign with the Bijapuris against Seevaji. It had taken him this long to finally get the Adilshah's Vizier, Khawas Khan, to come to his camp for the negotiations. The Abyssinian seemed reluctant to join hands with the Mughals, and had delayed responding.

"Do not think too much, Khawas Khan. The Emperor's terms are just and favourable to you. Seevaji has cost your government plenty. I hear he has recently driven away your officers from the west coast. That will affect trade grievously

---

[38] A royal communication from the ruling Muslim Emperor/Sultan, with his personal seal

I am sure. At such a time, the Emperor has decided to relieve you of paying the annual tribute. You should be grateful."

"And I am, Bahadur Khansahib." Khawas Khan smiled and bowed his head with mock humility. "The Emperor is kind. But if I organize a military campaign now, it will wipe out my treasury in any case."

"We will finish off the infidels, Khawas Khan. Then you shall have your share of Seevaji's lands."

"That is not so easy to achieve, Khansahib." Khawas Khan's face was sombre. "Remember how past Mughal missions against the Marathas have fared. Even after Mirza Jai Singh's successes, the Marathas bounced back and are now more powerful than ever."

"The past should be forgotten. We plan to finish Seevaji himself."

"Seevaji Raja sits in his castle on top of his mountain fort. How are you going to get your hands on him?"

"If we join hands, our forces will be enough to devastate his entire kingdom. This time we will not leave any of his people alive. He will then be forced to descend from his abode and fight us!"

"That strategy has failed in the past. His people do not break easily."

Bahadur Khan's patience with the Bijapuri Vizier was running thin. Persuasion was not working. He would have to use coercion. "Tell me Khawas Khan, would you rather have a war against the Emperor or a war against Seevaji *with* His Majesty on your side?" His message was clear: join hands with us or else...

Khawas Khan shifted uneasily in his seat. He had known for many years now that Aurangzeb ultimately meant to annex the Adilshahi. With a boy King on the Bijapur throne, it was his job to protect the Sultanate. He could not take rash decisions that would impact Bijapur's safety. He was in no position to fight the Mughal right now. Seevaji was no easy prospect either. Of the two, joining hands with the Mughal seemed more prudent at the moment. With the Mughal hordes with him, who knew but they might have some unprecedented success against the Maratha.

"I hear you do not get along too well with the Pathans," Bahadur Khan needled further, bringing up Bijapur's internal politics. "I hear Bahlol Khan swallowed a hefty bribe to stay out of Seeva's way in Canara."

Khawas Khan shot him an angry look. "Maybe you can reason with Bahlol Khan."

Bahadur Khan smiled. "Maybe I will. But for now, let us get this treaty done so we can begin planning the campaign."

The Bijapuri Vizier nodded reluctantly, though he knew the terms would benefit only the Mughal. Under the terms proposed by Bahadur Khan, Bijapur would have to launch a vigorous campaign against Seevaji. Obviously, Bijapur would have to finance that war. The accruing benefits to Bijapur were more intangible than real. His sovereign, Sikander, would officially get the title of 'Shah'. Sikander's elder sister, Shahr Banu Begum, would be wed to one of Aurangzeb's sons. But most importantly, this treaty would keep the Mughals away from Bijapur for some time at least.

"I have one more proposal to fortify the bond between us," Bahadur Khan said, glancing slyly at the Vizier.

Khawas Khan's brow creased on hearing this. Bahadur Khan fingered a ring on his left hand and said at length, "I ask for your daughter's hand for my son."

Khawas Khan was jolted by this demand. The Mughal Subadar was making sure he would not be double-crossed later. "My daughter, Khansahib? Why bring my family into this? The Bijapur Princess will be sent to the royal Mughal harem. Isn't that enough?"

"That may be enough for the Emperor, but not for me. I need a personal assurance from you, and what can be more personal than to give your daughter in marriage to my son?"

Khawas Khan agreed to this demand most reluctantly. He left the Mughal camp with more worries than he had arrived with.

RAIGAD, EARLY NOVEMBER 1675

"I have news of a treaty between Aurangzeb and the Adilshah. My man in Aurangabad informs me that Bahadur Khan and Khawas Khan met in person to plan a joint campaign against us."

Chhatrapati Shivaji looked at Bahirji Naik and sighed. "Does Khawas Khan have enough funds to launch a big campaign?"

Bahirji squatted on the floor before his King. The two were alone in the Chhatrapati's private chamber. "Maybe not, Sire. But with the Mughal behind him, he may just pull it off."

"Aurangzeb is forcing Khawas Khan to fight his battle against us. When will these Bijapuris realize Aurangzeb's true motives?"

"I think Khawas Khan is wary of Bahlol Khan's intentions. The Pathan harbours a desire to be Regent himself. Khawas Khan may have joined hands with Bahadur Khan merely to keep Bahlol Khan at bay."

The Chhatrapati nodded. "Keep a close watch on the political scenario in Bijapur. If the situation becomes favourable to us, we should be in a position to intervene at short notice. Is there any fresh news from Janjira?"

"Aurangzeb has appointed Siddi Qasim as General of his fleet. Sambul, the previous Naval Chief has been sidelined, though he does not seem to be in a mood to leave any time soon. Qasim and Sambul are brothers and I have a feeling they will have a fight soon. In the meantime, Qasim sailed to Janjira and tried to attack our ships."

Maharaj's eyebrows wrinkled. "And…?"

"He failed!" Bahirji gave a low rumbling chuckle that seemed never to leave his throat. His face became sombre once again. "Frustrated, the rascal landed at Vengurle, and plundered the town."

Maharaj rose and began pacing the chamber. "The Siddis keep harassing our people in the Konkan. Why are we so helpless to stop them?"

Bahirji had no answers. He merely looked away.

"Bahirji, send word to Maynak Bhandari and Darya Sarang, that they must do their utmost to stop the Siddi vessels from landing along the coast. Order them to increase surveillance along the shoreline. We must also move more cavalry into the Konkan and set up patrol units."

The tall well-built Pathan walked briskly to the entrance of Asar Mahal, located on the eastern fringes of the Bijapur citadel. The outer gates of the spacious mansion opened towards the eastern part of Bijapur city, while the inner courtyard overlooked a delicate pond. A moat surrounded the ramparts of the citadel. A bridge over the moat connected the mansion to a small private gate, which allowed direct entry through the fort wall into the citadel. Asar Mahal was the residence of the Bijapuri Vizier, Khawas Khan.

The Pathan announced himself at the gate and was let in by the Captain of the Guard. He was then ushered into a private office where, seated on a comfortable *asan*[39], he found the burly, dark-skinned Abyssinian Regent. The Pathan bowed and said, "Greetings, noble Vizier. I bring a message from my Lord, Bahlol Khan."

"Welcome back to Bijapur, Khizr Khan Panni," Khawas Khan said, regarding the Pathani Captain intently and trying to read his face. "What does my friend Bahlol Khan have to say?"

"My Lord has arrived within five kos of Bijapur. He should be here by sundown and wishes to see you as soon as he gets here."

---

[39] Cushioned seat on the floor

Khawas Khan was alarmed at this news, but did not show it on his face. "Bahlol Khan is riding to Bijapur? I had no news of his intentions. This is most irregular…"

Khizr Khan cut him short. "It's a matter of utmost importance, I was told. The Vizier would do well to meet him."

"I don't take orders from you, young man!" Khawas Khan snapped. "As for Bahlol Khan, he is always in a hurry, is he not? Tell me, how many men does your Lord bring with him?"

"Just the usual retinue and bodyguard," Khizr Khan lied.

Khawas Khan did not believe him. "What does he wish to talk about?"

"I have no knowledge of that, noble Vizier."

Khawas Khan dismissed the man with a wave of his hand, and summoned his *quorchi*[40]. When the man appeared, he said brusquely, "Send for Shiekh Minhaj immediately."

Sheikh Minhaj was one of Khawas Khan's faithful Captains. An Abyssinian himself, Minhaj hated the Pathans in Bijapur as much as his master and strived to do his utmost to keep them out of power. The Abyssinians and Pathans were forever at each other's throats in the Bijapur court. Though they served the same master and believed in the same faith, the differences in their cultures meant they could never see eye to eye. Heretofore, a strong sovereign on the throne of Bijapur had kept both parties at least nominally united to fight under one banner. Three years ago, Ali Adilshah

---

[40] Personal attendant

had died young, leaving behind his toddler son to take the throne. His Vizier, Khawas Khan, had automatically been named Regent. The Deccani Muslim nobles, as well as the Hindu nobles at court, had sided with the Abyssinian Vizier, effectively keeping the Pathans away from the seat of power. But the ambition of the Pathani Chief Bahlol Khan to seize control of the Bijapur government had never died. Khawas Khan was ever aware of Bahlol Khan's designs. The news that his adversary had suddenly decided to appear in the capital disturbed him deeply.

"Minhaj, I have news that Bahlol Khan has marched within five kos of the city," Khawas Khan said to Sheikh Minhaj when the latter appeared in the Vizier's chamber.

Minhaj's eyebrows shot up on hearing this. "Is this a regular visit? I had no idea he was expected."

"Neither did I. Send out your scouts. I want a detailed report of his position, his camp and his man-strength. Above all, I need to know his intentions."

"At once, my Lord," Minhaj said.

"Where is Masud?"

"Away in the eastern districts. There was some trouble regarding…"

"Send word to him. Order him to turn back immediately."

Siddi Masud was another of Khawas Khan's trusted Abyssinian Captains. Khan rued the fact that Masud was away from Bijapur. "Check the city guard personally," he continued. "If there are any Pathani Captains on duty, replace them with our men. Also, double the guard on Asar Mahal."

"Yes, my Lord." Minhaj left, worry writ large on his face.

Minhaj's scouts encountered Bahlol Khan's party advancing leisurely, some four kos from Bijapur. The party was small, just a few hundred horsemen. There was no heavy cavalry, no guns. In the centre of the unit was an ornate palanquin, being carried by eight men. The scouts assumed it to be the Pathani chief.

Messages were relayed back rapidly to the Vizier's mansion. "It's a small platoon, my Lord," the scout said. "They do not appear to be ready for battle. By the looks of it, Bahlol Khan could be on a diplomatic mission."

The scout was dismissed. Khawas Khan breathed a little easier. Unknowingly, he had dropped his guard.

The last prahar of the evening had begun. The sun had disappeared long ago. It was dark and Khawas Khan watched as his slaves lit lamps in the mansion. He had received news from his spies that Bahlol Khan's party had camped two kos from the city. Maybe the Pathan had changed his mind about entering the city at night, Khawas Khan thought. Nevertheless, he had moved his *zenana*[41] inside the citadel walls for greater safety. His mansion was guarded by nearly three hundred trusted bodyguards. Yet he felt uneasy. The Pathan was cunning, impulsive, unpredictable.

---

[41] Literal meaning: 'of the women/pertaining to women'; denotes the inner apartments of the house, meant for ladies (as opposed to the outer apartments or *Mardana*, for males and guests); also used (in the context of medieval society) to refer to the ladies attached to the principal male of a Muslim family.

Unknown to the Vizier, a few hundred black shadows were moving stealthily toward Asar Mahal. They surrounded the mansion systematically, and waited in the shadows for a signal from their Captain. Khizr Khan Panni assessed the situation. The mansion was quiet. He had no way of knowing if the guards at the gates, whom he had bribed heavily, would stick to their word. Neither was he sure if the Vizier was still inside. But he would have to take his chances. If all went well, he would march into the Sultan's palace with his Lord Bahlol Khan that night.

Khizr Khan gave the signal. A few of his men silently moved toward the mansion and lined up outside the walls. A bird call rang out. It was the signal for the defected guards inside. The Pathans waited. For a long time nothing happened. Khizr Khan moved forward from his position till he could see the gate. He cursed under his breath as the gate did not open for a long time. The lead Pathan in the assault unit looked to his Captain's position for a signal. There was none. He would have to wait.

Much later, the wicket gate opened slightly. The Pathans moved forward and stepped through into the courtyard of the mansion. In a few brief moments of struggle, the guards had been cut down and their places taken by the Pathans. The mansion was still quiet. Khizr Khan knew he had to make haste. They must seize the Vizier before the citadel garrison was alerted. He moved rapidly, followed by his men. Before the Abyssinian guard knew it, a few hundred armed Pathans had entered the mansion.

Khawas Khan was startled as a commotion broke out in the courtyard. He was on his feet instantly and seized his sword.

He parted the curtain to his chamber and peered out. The Captain of the Guard was demanding to know in a loud authoritative voice why there were strange soldiers inside the mansion. Though dressed in the Bijapuri army uniform, they sure as hell did not look like Abyssinians.

"We are here by order of the Vizier," a man said roughly.

"The Lord has not issued any such order," the Abyssinian Captain barked. "Get out of here!"

"Not so fast, you dark piece of shit!" The alien moved so fast the Captain felt the pain of the dagger buried deep in his abdomen before he realized the man had attacked him. There was bedlam. The Abyssinians and Pathans engaged. In the commotion, no one noticed two dark shadows enter the Vizier's chamber.

Khawas Khan was panic-stricken. He knew he had to get inside the citadel immediately. He shouted for his quorchi, but the man was already dead. As Khan tried to rush towards the rear entrance to the mansion, two shadows moved in on him. One grabbed his sword arm, while the other fastened a vice-like grip on his throat. The Vizier began to choke. The sword slipped from his hand. His tormentors kicked him behind his knees, forcing him to the floor. Within moments his hands were tied behind his back and a blade held to his throat.

From behind the curtains, Khawas Khan saw his executioner emerge. Bahlol Khan walked up to him, sword in hand. "Greetings, great Vizier!" he mocked as he touched the Vizier's face with the tip of his blade.

"Bahlol Khan! What is the meaning of this?" Khawas Khan tried to muster what courage and authority he could.

"Your reign as Regent is over, Khawas Khan," Bahlol said spitefully. "Your future is now as dark as your skin!"

"You will not live through this, Bahlol! The citadel is guarded by my men."

"Yes, and you will order them to stand down if you do not want your neck sliced."

"Kiss my backside, you swine!"

Bahlol smashed the hilt of his sword into Khawas Khan's face, sending forth a spray of blood and teeth. The Vizier collapsed in an unconscious heap. More Pathans had entered the chamber by now. They dragged the Vizier outside into the courtyard and dropped him there unceremoniously.

"Abyssinians! Lay down your weapons or your Lord dies!" Bahlol raised his voice over the din of battle. The guards stopped fighting. They knew they had been betrayed. In short order, they were disarmed and arrested. Asar Mahal was in Bahlol Khan's control.

The mansion was quiet again. Bahlol secured his position and moved his pieces rapidly. Messages were relayed to the eastern gate of the city. Guards at this gate had been bribed too. Bahlol's Pathans swiftly took over the gate. Shortly, his army of five thousand marched into the city and headed for Asar Mahal.

The first prahar of the night was half spent when Khawas Khan was dragged in chains across the bridge leading to the citadel ramparts.

"Who goes there?" the guard manning the small gate opposite Asar Mahal asked.

"Open the gate or the Vizier dies!" Khizr Khan said.

The guard lowered his torch to see the faces better. He was shocked to see the Vizier bound and held captive by alien soldiers. The Vizier's face was bloody and swollen; it was evident he had been attacked.

Khawas Khan looked up and said coldly, "Open the gates. Do as they say."

Within moments the gate was opened and taken over by Bahlol's men. The Pathans moved along the ramparts and soon took control of the eastern wall. Khawas Khan was marched into the citadel, sword to his neck, followed by Bahlol Khan, Khizr Khan, the other Captains, and thousands of Pathani troops. They marched straight to Gagan Mahal, the residence of the royal family. Guards at various checkposts and gates were swiftly overthrown. Bahlol Khan walked into the palace gardens. As their approach was discovered, a commotion arose within the palace. Small parties of palace guards tried in vain to stop the invaders, but were cut down mercilessly. The palace was surrounded by Bahlol's men.

With a hundred of his trusted bodyguard, Bahlol entered the palace itself. Sentries and guards at each entrance were cut down. Bahlol sprinted up the stairs to the upper level. Screaming could be heard from the zenana. Some eunuch guards stood firmly with drawn swords at the entrance to the zenana. Khizr Khan moved forward with some of his men and sliced through them. Bahlol stepped into the royal chambers.

Khizr grabbed a screaming slave girl who had tried in vain to hide behind the curtains. "Where is the Sultan?" he asked the girl, jerking at her hair. Sobbing, the girl pointed in the direction of the Queen Mother's chamber, begging him to let her go. Khizr released her. He was not interested in her anyway.

Bahlol and Khizr marched on. More eunuch guards were cut down. The Queen Mother's chamber erupted in tumult as the Pathans entered. "Silence!" Bahlol commanded. His men spread out and subdued the slaves while he advanced toward Kursheeda Khanum, the Queen Mother. She was obviously scared, but maintained a stoic expression and erect posture. "Bahlol Khan, how dare you insult His Highness like this?" she demanded.

Bahlol sheathed his sword at leisure and bowed to her. "Forgive my impudence, Your Highness. But there was no other way to remove the incompetent Abyssinian wretches from control. Khawas Khan's Regentship has brought nothing but misery and poverty to Bijapur. The treasury is empty. The Marathas harass our western borders and usurp our land. And now Khawas Khan has sold us out to the Mughal!"

The Queen was shocked at the last words. "What do you mean, Bahlol Khan?"

"He has signed a treaty with Bahadur Khan and agreed to fight a war against the Maratha at our expense. A war we cannot afford. He has also agreed to send Shahr Banu Begum to the Mughal harem to marry one of the Emperor's incompetent sons."

"He has *what*?" The Queen Mother was furious. "How could he do that without my consent?"

"Rest easy, Your Highness. Khawas Khan has been arrested. I will assume charge as Regent of Bijapur at once. The royal palace will be guarded by my men now. His Highness will come to no harm. I ask that you keep me informed about your movements."

Bahlol looked at the little boy who clung to his mother, and smiled. Kneeling before the Sovereign, he touched his head to the floor. "Long live His Highness, Sultan Sikander Adilshah!"

The Queen Mother breathed a sigh of relief when Bahlol and his men turned and left the zenana. She and her son were safe for now. But Bahlol Khan had made it amply clear the royal family was at his mercy.

BIJAPUR ROYAL DURBAR, A FEW DAYS LATER

Ba-adab ba-mulahizah hoshiyaar[42]... the quorchis announced the arrival of the Sultan of Bijapur. The assembled nobles bowed low, offering their salutations. The seven-year-old sovereign walked in, followed by his bodyguards, and seated himself on the throne as he had been instructed to do by his mother. The throne being too big for him, his bodyguard had to help him up.

Bahlol Khan, who stood next to the throne, smiled. Let the tiny Sultan enjoy his throne, he thought. I wield the real power here. Momentarily, he glanced up at the screen on the upper level, behind which he knew the Queen Mother would be seated. Then, with a flourish he began, "Nobles of Bijapur. The Regentship of the traitor Khawas Khan has ended. He has been arrested and, by the order of His Highness, will receive his just punishment. I have taken over the office of the Vizier with the consent of the Queen Mother. I expect nothing less than full co-operation from everyone."

---

[42] Ba-adab: with respect, ba-mulahizah: stand facing, hoshiyaar: alert

Placing his right hand on the hilt of his sword, Bahlol paused to look each noble in the eye. His expression said it all. The Pathani nobles beamed proudly at their leader. The Abyssinian and Deccani nobles had looks of resignation on their faces. With the Queen Mother behind Bahlol, there wasn't much they could do at the moment.

"Khawas Khan has agreed to a highly unfavourable treaty with the Mughal Emperor, a treaty which will push the Sultanate further toward financial crisis."

"But I heard the Emperor has exempted the Sultanate from paying the annual tribute," Sheikh Minhaj tried to object to the new Vizier's allegations.

Bahlol Khan shot him a look of disdain. "The military campaign Khawas Khan has agreed to will cost us many times more! Keep your mind on military duties, Minhaj. Let the Queen Mother and I think about running the Sultanate."

Minhaj fumed, but had to keep his mouth shut. Bahlol continued, "Certain changes have been made in the administration, with the consent of Her Highness." The nobles understood what that meant. Officers loyal to Khawas Khan had been replaced with those from the Bahlol Khan camp. "There will be fresh military appointments as well."

Bahlol looked hard at Minhaj and said, "We need a resourceful and brave Commander to lead our forces at the Maratha front. Seevaji and his men have usurped much territory in the Konkan and Canara districts. We must stop him from creating further trouble. I have decided to appoint Sheikh Minhaj to lead our forces on the western front."

Minhaj gritted his teeth. He had been in charge of security in the capital city. Obviously Bahlol wanted him out so he could appoint his own Commander in Bijapur.

"Sheikh Minhaj, you will lead your entire battalion out of Bijapur and proceed to Canara. Your job is merely to limit further damage. Remember, we cannot invest too much money in fighting Seevaji right now."

Minhaj bowed slightly, conveying his acceptance of the new position.

"Khizr Khan Panni will be in charge of the Bijapur city defences." Bahlol smiled at his faithful Captain. He deserved the promotion after what he had done for his master. "Siddi Masud will head another division of our forces and proceed north to the Mughal front. We must take care that Bahadur Khan does not try something new. Masud, you too, will remain defensive. We do not wish to engage with the Mughal. Leave Bahadur Khan to me. I will deal with him."

Masud, the Abyssinian Captain faithful to Khawas Khan, had half expected this. Bahlol Khan had secured his position by systematically evicting all nobles from the opposing faction lest they unite and create trouble for him. After discussion on a few trivial matters, the durbar adjourned.

Raigad, Early January 1676

Chhatrapati Shivaji's council was in session in the large durbar hall of the royal palace. The Chhatrapati sat on his throne, flanked by his Ministers, and chief Captains. The Senapati, Hambirrao Mohite, was away on campaign.

Bahirji Naik, Chief of Intelligence, was present as well. The news of the civil war in Bijapur had reached the Maratha court. Bahirji's spies had done an efficient job of keeping their King updated on the developments in the Adilshahi. The Chhatrapati had been thinking hard about how he could use the current scenario to his advantage. For a long time he had wanted to extend his kingdom in the South, so he could play a more decisive role in Deccan politics. A few days earlier, an opportunity had presented itself.

Two Brahman administrators sat respectfully to one side. They were not in the Chhatrapati's service and were new to Raigad. Their names were Raghunath and Janardan Hanmante, sons of Naro Punt Dikshit, who had been a faithful administrator to Maharaj Shahaji. Following Shahaji's death, they had served Vyankoji Bhosale, the Chhatrapati's half-brother, who had inherited Shahaji's estates in the South. Chhatrapati Shivaji knew this family of hereditary administrators well. Their loyalty and competence in handling government affairs were well known. The Chhatrapati was, however, curious to know the reason for their visit to Raigad.

"We are grateful to the Chhatrapati for granting us audience," Raghunath Hanmante said.

Chhatrapati Shivaji smiled. "Tell me Raghunath Punt, how is my brother? I trust all is well with him?"

"By the grace of Lord Mahadev, Vyankoji Raje is in good health," Raghunath Punt said.

"You brothers have been in Vyankoji's service since my father left the mortal world."

"Yes, your Highness, we have." Raghunath Punt paused. Glancing at his brother, he added, "But we are not in his service any longer."

The Chhatrapati reflected on this last sentence. *So that's why they are here. They are looking for employment.* "Why did you leave my brother's service?" he asked. He had to ascertain the reason for their defection.

"His Highness must pardon me for speaking frankly," Raghunath Punt said politely and bowed. The Chhatrapati nodded and raised his hand, signalling for him to continue.

"My King, you must be aware of the political scenario in the Mysore and Ginjee districts of the Adilshahi. But I would like to summarize the situation before I proceed. Two years ago, Chokannatha, the *Nayak*[43] of Madurai, invaded and annexed Tanjavur. Vijay Raghava, the Nayak of Tanjavur, and his entire family were murdered. Chokannatha appointed his foster brother Alagiri as Governor of Tanjavur. But this ungrateful brother declared his independence and shrugged off suzerainty to Madurai. Meanwhile, some of the old faithful ministers of Vijay Raghava found a young boy from his family who had somehow escaped the carnage. They took the boy to the Adilshah and secured his permission and help to reinstate the boy on the Tanjavur throne. The Adilshah ordered Vyankoji Raje to do the needful and Raje did it successfully. Alagiri and his followers were defeated in battle and fled. The young boy who became the Nayak of Tanjavur later proved to be an incompetent ruler and misbehaved with his Ministers. Once again Vyankoji Raje was invited to intervene. Raje annexed Tanjavur and held it in the Adilshah's name. A few months ago, with the Adilshahi civil war playing out, Vyankoji Raje declared his independence from the Adilshah and shifted his seat to Tanjavur."

---

[43] General term meaning Chief/ Headman of a body of men/soldiers/ labourers

"We did hear about these events, Punt," Maharaj said to him. "I am proud of my brother for finally declaring his independence from the Sultan. The Maratha hold on the South will be strengthened."

"Your pardon Highness, but that is exactly what will not happen," Raghunath Punt said pointedly. "Declaring his independence was a commendable act, but shifting the seat of power to Tanjavur was not. With Vyankoji Raje and his Ministers in Tanjavur, the Mysore district will be neglected. It will not be long before Vyankoji Raje loses control over his holdings in Mysore. The Chhatrapati will remember these are the very territories held by his late father."

Pensively, Maharaj analysed this information. Mysore district was the southernmost territory of the Adilshah. A part of it, including Bengalur, had been his father's estate, which had passed to Vyankoji. The rest of Mysore was held by the Nayak of Mysore, who was a feudatory of the Adilshah. With Vyankoji away in Tanjavur, on the eastern coast, the Nayak would begin usurping Vyankoji's lands.

"I see. With Vyankoji absent from Mysore, Maratha influence will, in fact, wane. I for one cannot allow my father's estates to pass into someone else's hands. Is my brother not concerned about this?" Maharaj asked Raghunath Punt.

"Sadly no, Your Highness. We did our best to make him see reason and avoid shifting to Tanjavur, but he did not heed our advice. We have worked hard for over a decade to establish Maratha rule in Mysore. Maharaj Saheb Shahaji Raje himself worked ceaselessly for it in his lifetime. But Vyankoji Raje has become negligent these past few years and has allowed things to simply drift away from him. It was too painful for us to watch. Hence we decided to come here. Both my brother Janardan and I are ready to serve you, Sire."

"If I may add something to what my brother has said, Highness?" It was Janardan who spoke. "We know the Mysore and Ginjee districts intimately. We can help His Highness plan a campaign there and extend the Maratha Swarajya in the South!"

There was a buzz in the assembly. Everyone had been listening intently to the two Brahmans. While the Ministers had understood the turn of events down south, the possibility of a campaign to extend their holdings was undoubtedly intriguing.

"Janardan Punt, tell me about Ginjee." Maharaj was eager to get as much information as possible before he committed himself.

"Sire, most of the Ginjee district is held by two officers under the Adilshah's banner. The northern part is held by Nasir Mohammed, an Abyssinian. He is Khawas Khan's brother. The southern part is held by a Pathan named Sher Khan, who is a confidanté of Bahlol Khan. The Pathan has invaded the northern district and made life miserable for Nasir, who is now walled in Gingee Fort. We have heard that he has approached the Qutubshah and offered to hand over the fort to him in return for a small fief and a job at court. If the fort passes to the Qutubshah, he will eventually gain control over the entire district. Sher Khan will not be able to hold out against the might of the Qutubshahi forces, especially as he is unlikely to get any help from Bijapur."

"Your Highness, the time is ripe for you to make your presence felt in the South. The Adilshahi is torn by war.

Your brother Vyankoji has moved to Tanjavur. The other Nayaks will hardly pose a problem to the Maratha forces," Raghunath summarized the situation.

"What about the Qutubshah?" Maharaj asked. "If he decides to intervene and take over Gingee, it could become difficult for us."

"Sire, the Qutubshah's Prime Minister is a Hindu Brahman named Madanna. He is certain to be sympathetic to the cause of the Maratha Swarajya."

The Chhatrapati was quick to understand what Raghunath was hinting at. If they could somehow influence Madanna, their job would be infinitely easier. The seed of a new campaign down south had been sown in the Chhatrapati's mind. He saw an immense opportunity not just to extend the boundaries of his Swarajya, but also to increase his influence over the two imperial powers of the Deccan.

Raghunath and Janardan were told a decision would be made and conveyed to them. Once they had left, the Maratha Council began to debate the pros and cons of the campaign.

Before the Council adjourned, Maharaj said to his Mukhya Pradhan, Moro Punt Pingale, "Punt, organize a diplomatic mission to Bhaganagar. I think we should send an able diplomat to meet with Madanna to turn him in our favour."

"Does His Highness have a name in mind?" Moro Punt asked.

"Who better than Niraji Punt to accomplish such a difficult task?"

"Minhaj is proving difficult," Bahlol Khan said. "He refuses to leave Bijapur. We have to take care of him."

Khizr Khan clenched his fists. He hated the African scum with all his heart. "Let me deal with him," he said.

"Kill him!" Bahlol urged. "Let us set an example. If we kill one, the others will fall in line."

Khizr Khan nodded. "I will send him to hell," he said unequivocally.

Sheikh Minhaj pondered the invitation he had just received. A messenger had arrived from Khizr Khan Panni's camp, requesting him to join his master for a feast that evening. Minhaj smelled a rat. He did not trust the Pathans one bit. The Vizier's arrest was still fresh in his mind and he knew Bahlol Khan would go to any lengths to secure his own position.

The quorchi entered and announced, "Siddi Masud is here, my Lord."

A moment later, a heavy-set Abyssinian in his mid-forties entered. Minhaj greeted his friend warmly. "Welcome, Masud! How's your progress on the campaign?"

"We can delay our departure somewhat," Masud replied, "but eventually we will have to go. Bahlol Khan is the Vizier now and he has the Queen Mother's approval. The firmaans have the Sultan's seal on them. We cannot disobey."

"Khizr Khan has invited me to join him for a feast tonight."

Masud looked up sharply. "A feast? There is no occasion for a feast. The Sultanate is in chaos. What does that Pathan wish to celebrate?"

"I doubt he has a celebration in mind."

Masud took a moment to realize what Minhaj was saying. "Do you think Bahlol and Khizr Khan are plotting to kill you?"

Minhaj nodded gravely. His expression changed to one of pure hatred. "But I am going to turn the tables on that bastard. I will kill him before he realizes what happened."

"We must be careful, Minhaj. Our Lord, Khawas Khan, is still in prison. His life is in danger."

"We cannot be defensive with these Pathans, Masud. I agree Lord Khawas Khan is in grave danger. But we must oppose the Pathans. Bahlol Khan must be taught a lesson or two."

Masud sighed. Minhaj had always been impulsive and difficult to control. Yet he might be justified in his actions if he had reason to believe Khizr Khan was planning to kill him. "Let me go with you," he said finally.

"No Masud, you get in touch with the other nobles faithful to Lord Khawas Khan. Let us form a unified opposition to Bahlol Khan. I will deal with Khizr Khan alone."

Pathani camp, outskirts of Bijapur, 11 January 1676

Khizr Khan Panni emerged from his tent and stretched, his arms held high. His bodyguards bowed as he walked past them to the grand *shamiana*[44] that had been set up to welcome

---

[44] A pavilion; a grand tent usually built for a military Commander, a Prince, or a person of consequence

the Abyssinian ex-Chief of the Bijapur City Guard. The power struggle between the two factions had gone on for too long, he thought. It was time to put an end to it and assert the supremacy of the Pathans in Bijapur. If he succeeded in killing Minhaj that night, the remaining Abyssinians would not dare stick their necks in. The Deccani Muslims would fall in line too.

Khizr Khan checked the deployment of his soldiers around the shamiana. He wondered how many men Minhaj would bring with him. If he decided to bring an entire battalion, Khizr Khan would have a battle on his hands, and he certainly did not want that. He had to finish off Minhaj swiftly and quietly. He returned to his tent and summoned his trump card. Moments later, a man entered, clad in black, his face half hidden behind the tail-piece of his turban.

"Jalal, are your men ready?" Khizr asked.

"Yes my Lord," Jalal replied curtly, bowing.

"He must not return alive!" Khizr growled.

"He will not, my Lord!" Jalal bowed once again and left.

Besides the regular guards, Khizr Khan had planted his assassins around the shamiana. Led by Jalal, these men usually did the dirty work for him. Everything was in order. The Abyssinian just had to show up.

The sun had set on the western horizon and the skies had darkened. Khizr Khan was getting restless. The Abyssinians were not expected for another half-prahar at least. He left his tent and began walking through his camp, accepting salutes along the way. His bodyguards followed at a respectful distance.

A while later, he heard the *azaan*[45] in the distance. Khizr Khan cursed himself for having forgotten all about the evening prayer. He ordered his guards to fetch him a prayer rug. The rug was set up for him between two guard tents. They were at the western boundary of the camp, with a dense orchard behind them. Khizr knelt on the rug and began to pray, touching his forehead to the ground.

No one noticed the Pathan archer who quietly emerged from the trees. He had been following his Captain for some time, looking for an opportunity to do his job. Seeing Khizr Khan kneeling in prayer, he smiled and cocked an arrow. The African would pay a handsome sum for this, he thought. Pulling the bowstring taut, he aimed and let go. The shaft pierced the back of Khizr Khan's neck and emerged from the front of his throat, under his chin. The Pathan slumped forward, choking on his own blood, still uttering the name of Allah. There was no better way to die.

It took his bodyguards a few moments to realize what had happened. They rushed to Khizr Khan, raising a commotion, but they were already too late. All was lost for their Captain.

The treacherous assassin melted away into the trees.

Bahlol Khan's eyes blazed with anger when he heard the news of Khizr Khan's assassination. The Abyssinian bastards had turned the tables against his most trusted Captain. In a fit of rage, he pulled out his sword and strode

---

[45] Islamic call to prayer, recited by a muezzin at prescribed times of the day

from his chambers, heading straight for the dungeons. His bodyguards rushed to keep pace.

"Send for the executioners!" he barked to the man nearest him.

The small party soon reached the underground prison cells where the ex-Vizier of the Adilshahi, Khawas Khan, was held. The air in the cellars was thick with fetid odours. Bahlol grimaced but ordered the guards to open the cell. Khawas Khan, who had been sleeping, was roughly roused. He was surprised to see Bahlol Khan towering above him.

"You rascal!" Bahlol fumed. "you plotted to kill Khizr Khan, did you not?"

"Wha…?" Khawas Khan could not understand what had happened.

"Your men murdered my best Captain!" Bahlol screamed. "You will pay for this!"

"I don't know what you are talking about, Bahlol Khan." Khawas Khan was tired and broken. He half wished he could just die and end all the humiliation and torture.

"Minhaj sent assassins to kill Khizr Khan in his own camp! How did you plan it? Which of my men have become traitors?"

"I have no knowledge of this," Khawas murmured again. "You should ask Minhaj." Inwardly, Khawas Khan smiled grimly. So Khizr Khan was dead. Served him right for plotting against the Vizier, he thought.

"There will be retribution, Khawas Khan! Your men will realize that Pathans do not take things lying down. An eye for an eye and a life for a life!" Bahlol stepped back. "Cut his head off!"

The executioner moved forward. Khawas Khan was forced to the ground. He did not struggle. The executioner raised his thick blade high and struck. The ex-Vizier's body trembled and shook. The executioner struck again, severing the head.

Satara Fort, early 1676

The Chhatrapati felt the evening chill as he gazed out of the window. He clasped his arms around his body and shivered. His personal attendant Mahadu stepped forward with a shawl and proceeded to drape it around his master.

"His Highness should step away from the window," Mahadu said with concern. "The evening breeze is cool now. His Highness has not fully recovered yet."

The Chhatrapati smiled at the man who stood with head bowed. Patting him on the back, he said, "Mahadu, my man, you fuss over me unnecessarily. Your King has endured many a battle. What harm can a mere fever do? It will pass."

"It will, Sire, by the grace of Lord Mahadev. Yet we must take utmost care, else the fever may relapse." Mahadu closed the window and urged his King to rest.

The Chhatrapati walked to a divan and sat down. Mahadu immediately squatted on the floor next to him and began giving him a leg massage. Presently he said, "The Sachiv visited here while His Highness slept. He requested a meeting."

"Anaji Punt was here? And when were you planning to tell me?"

Mahadu kept his eyes on the floor. "The Punt's visit will open the door to others through the day. If I let them all in, His Highness will never get to rest."

The Chhatrapati laughed out loud. "The Queen has trained you well to take good care of me," he remarked.

"That is my only job Sire; to take care of my King and see to all his needs…" Mahadu stopped mid-sentence. After a pause, he added, "and to keep the Punts away when His Highness needs rest.'

"You have made your point, Mahadu. But go now and summon Anaji Punt. Tell him his King waits for him. And send for Bahirji as well."

Mahadu rose, knowing he had lost the battle yet again.

"Anaji Punt, we have stayed away from Raigad too long. Urgent political matters await my attention. We must head back now." The Chhatrapati sat on the divan, sipping a herbal decoction sent by the *Vaidya*[46].

"Politics can wait, Sire," the Sachiv replied gently. "We will wait till you are recovered. Besides, all urgent matters will certainly be looked into as long as Moro Punt is present at Raigad."

The Chhatrapati sighed. "It seems all my people have conspired to keep me out of action."

Anaji Punt smiled affectionately. "Of what use are your Ministers Sire, if we cannot run the government while you are unwell?"

---

[46] Physician trained in the traditional form of medicine (Ayurveda)

"I have never doubted the capability of my ministers, Punt. I trust them completely. Besides, Shambhu Raje is now old enough to take decisions as well."

Anaji Punt looked away at the mention of the Prince. Displeasure was clearly visible on his face as he absently rubbed his palms on his thighs. The Chhatrapati sensed his unease and said, "Give him some time, Punt. Young blood runs through his body. Boys are often impulsive at his age."

"True, Sire. But impulsiveness never pays in politics. The Yuvraj rarely considers all the pros and cons before pronouncing a decision. Sometimes…" Anaji Punt stopped. As the Chhatrapati raised his eyebrows in question, Ananji Punt became restless, cursing himself for starting a sentence he could not finish.

"I am waiting for you to finish, Punt," the Chhatrapati prodded.

"Sometimes…it is difficult to work with the Yuvraj, Sire."

The Chhatrapati looked him in the eye and said firmly, "He is your future King, Anaji Punt. The Ministers must not forget that!"

The royal entourage halted outside the palace complex of Satara Fort. As the palanquins were placed on the ground, the maids alighted and hurried to the Queen. Soyarabai was helped out of her palanquin and led straight to the Chhatrapati's chamber.

"My Queen?" The Chhatrapati was surprised to see her. "I was unaware that you had left Raigad!"

"It is indeed strange that His Highness was in the dark about my movements despite having the most competent spy network in the land."

"Yes, it is surprising."

"When I heard His Highness was unwell, I could not bear to remain at Raigad."

"And who informed you of my health? I had given instructions not to spread word about it."

"Well, I too have my informers!" Soyara sat down beside him.

"It must have been Anaji Punt," the Chhatrapati sighed.

"How are you, Highness? Are you well now?" Soyara took his hand in hers.

"Yes Soyara, I am much better, and itching to get back to work."

"I shall not hear any of that!" Soyara snapped. "You will rest completely and stay away from work for a while. Now that I am here, I shall personally take care of your needs."

"I have rested enough, Soyara."

"His Highness must not argue with me over this. I was told the Vaidyas thought you had been poisoned. Is that true?"

The Chhatrapati laughed. "Your informers exaggerate, Soyara. Who would want to poison me here? I am surrounded by my own people."

"Danger often lurks within, Highness."

"Do not speak in riddles, Soyara."

"His Highness is well aware what goes on in the Mughal Empire over rights to the throne."

The Chhatrapati was startled by the remark. To suggest that someone in the family might want him dead seemed far-fetched indeed. But an even more disturbing thought was that his Queen actually considered it possible.

"My Queen, do not upset yourself over such matters. There is no such danger, I assure you," Maharaj said, dismissing the matter. "You must be tired after a long journey. Rest now. We shall speak again tomorrow."

Khawas Khan's execution changed the complexion of the civil war in Bijapur. Sheikh Minhaj, Siddi Masud, Sharza Khan and the other faithfuls of the late Bijapuri Vizier withdrew from the city and moved east, with the aim to re-group and fight back later. Masud assumed leadership of the faction. He led his forces away and camped at a place called Adoni, some seventy kos south-east of Bijapur.

Bahlol Khan, filled with spite and revenge, followed their forces, desiring to eliminate them once and for all. The two armies met on the plains near Shah Dongar, some twelve kos from Adoni. There, the Pathans inflicted a crushing defeat on Masud's forces and the latter withdrew further east to the Qutubshahi territory.

From relative safety, Masud began soliciting the help of the Mughals. He wrote to Bahadur Khan, pleading with him to intervene. Bahadur Khan was reluctant as he had insufficient troops and funds at his disposal to fight both the Marathas and the Pathans. He wrote to the Emperor for advice. Aurangzeb saw an opportunity to strike at the

Adilshahi while civil war raged, and ordered Bahadur Khan to march against Bahlol Khan.

Reluctantly, Bahadur Khan marched south and crossed the Bhima River, where he was joined by Masud's forces. Bahlol Khan had already marched north. The two armies met at Indi, a place twenty-three kos north-east of Bijapur. The Mughal forces were organized into a right-wing under Islam Khan and his Turks, with a left-wing and an extreme right-wing under the Rajputs. Bahadur Khan himself held the centre.

The Pathans charged repeatedly on the Mughal right, but Islam Khan's men repelled them twice. By then, however, their ammunition was exhausted and while a fresh stock of gunpowder was being distributed, it exploded in front of Islam Khan. His elephant stampeded forward into the enemy ranks and Islam Khan and his son were slain by the Pathans.

The jubiliant Pathans next charged the Rajputs at the Mughal left and extreme right wings. The battle was fierce, with heavy losses on both sides. The battleground was soon covered in dead bodies. When the fight halted for the day, the Mughals held their position and entrenched themselves, while the Pathans invested their forces and harassed them for three days. There was no respite even at night.

While Bahadur Khan was thus kept busy, a detachment of Bahlol Khan's men rode north, crossed the Bhima River, attacked and completely looted the Mughal base camp. The Mughal Subadar managed to extricate himself with great difficulty from this hopeless situation and retreated north of the Bhima River. There, he invested Naldurg Fort, which was under the Adilshah's control. He had to achieve some success before reporting back to the Emperor, who would certainly not be pleased to learn about his misadventure at Indi. He hoped Bahlol Khan would not cross the Bhima in pursuit. But the Bijapuri Vizier did cross the river, even in full spate, and attacked Bahadur Khan near Naldurg. This time the Mughals held out admirably and, after an indecisive battle, the Pathans turned back south.

By this time, Diler Khan, one of Aurangzeb's pre-eminent nobles, had arrived in the Deccan and joined Bahadur Khan. Diler, a Pathan himself, was sympathetic to Bahlol Khan's cause and tried to turn the Emperor in the latter's favour.

In this way, Bahlol held on to power in Bijapur. His grit and determination had neutralized the efforts of the opposing faction to oust him. But Masud and the others were far from resigned to their fate. They continued their political endeavours, trying to secure the support of a powerful ally. Having suffered two defeats at the hands of the Pathans, Masud had no heart left to fight them without help. But the political scenario was changing rapidly and the parties who had been foes not long ago, were soon to become allies in a new campaign

3

Master of the East Coast

Raigad, mid-1676

A special council was in session in the royal palace. The Chhatrapati sat at the head as usual, with Prince Sambhaji to his left and Mukhya Pradhan Moro Punt Pingale to his right. The other Ministers were also present, as were Senapati Hambirrao Mohite and the Chhatrapati's chief Captains. It was a day of great rejoicing for the Maratha Swarajya. Moro Punt had just returned from a successful campaign to the principalities of Jawhar and Ramnagar in the north. These fiefs had been annexed four years before by Moro Punt himself, and their chieftains had been evicted. But the fallen Chiefs had continued to harass the Maratha garrisons with guerrilla warfare from adjacent Mughal and Portuguese territories. This had prevented the establishment of a stable government. Moro Punt had taken it upon himself to rectify the situation, and in a whirlwind campaign, had led ten thousand troopers into the troubled areas and systematically eliminated the troublemakers.

"Our Mukhya Pradhan has returned victorious from Jawhar and Ramnagar," the Chhatrapati said, smiling warmly at Moro Punt. "And Niraji Punt has returned from Bhaganagar, having achieved a political milestone. It is a happy day indeed."

Niraji Raoji, the Nyayadheesh, had just come back from his diplomatic mission to the Qutubshah. After days of negotiation, he had managed to convince Madanna, the Qutubshah's Prime Minister, to join hands with the Marathas in a southern campaign.

"A much greater joy for us is that His Highness is in good health once more. We have all been worried, Sire." Moro Punt voiced the thought in everyone's mind.

"I am no longer as young as I used to be, Punt. There are bound to be some health issues. But I do feel well now and we should start planning our moves. Niraji Punt will first update us on the situation in Bhaganagar."

Niraji Raoji cleared his throat and began. "Your Highness, Abul Hasan Qutubshah is a man given to a life of pleasure and debauchery. He is not in the least interested in managing the Sultanate. The Qutubshahi survives because of Madanna, the Prime Minister. Ever since he assumed this office some years ago, he has worked hard to increase Hindu influence in the Qutubshahi. He has appointed his own kinsmen to various important offices. His brother, Akanna, assists him. Madanna cherishes the prospect of restoring the Karnatak region to its ancient Hindu dominance. He is enamoured by Your Highness' achievements and feels you are the only King who shares his dream."

"Nasir Mohammad has approached Madanna for help and has even offered to cede the Gingee Fort to the Qutubshah. After my meetings with him, Madanna has managed to convince the Qutubshah that the best way to take over Gingee would be to aid us in capturing it. I have laid the foundations, Sire. What remains is for you to meet Abul Hasan and sign a treaty with him."

"Is the Qutubshah likely to go back on his word if we go there with our troops?" The Chhatrapati had been listening intently thus far. He needed a few clarifications from his diplomat before taking a decision.

"The Qutubshah simply agrees to everything Madanna says, and Madanna is inclined to support us right now. So I do not think the Qutubshah will go back on his word."

"The fact that Madanna has increased his influence must not have escaped Abul Hasan's attention. How does he maintain the balance of power?"

"Highness, the Commander-in-Chief is a Persian named Muhammad Ibrahim. The Qutubshah has pitted a Hindu Prime Minister against a Persian Commander at his court. In any case Sire, Madanna is far too loyal to his state. He has decided to side with us because he sincerely believes that the Qutubshahi will benefit from a treaty between them and us."

"This Persian Commander you speak of... what kind of man is he? Is he likely to create trouble for us?"

"Very unlikely, Your Highness. I have met him in person and have greased his palm well. He will not obstruct us in our campaign in the Karnatak region. In any case he is not too ambitious, being given to a life of leisure."

The Chhatrapati was quiet for some time. The campaign into Adilshahi Karnatak territory was forming in his mind. Yet he wanted the opinions of his Ministers. "What do the others think?" he asked. "Should we proceed on this campaign?"

"Certainly we should," Moro Punt said. "This is a golden opportunity for us to set foot in southern politics. The Adilshahi is torn by civil war. If we conclude a treaty with the Qutubshah, no one can stop us from achieving our objectives."

"I agree with Moro Punt," Hambirrao said. "I will lead an advance guard to prepare the route for your march, Highness. I will make sure it is safe for you."

The Chhatrapati nodded. "A wise thought, Senapati. But we need to guard our backs as well."

The men nodded, their faces serious. They knew their Lord was talking about the Mughals.

"Niraji Punt, you will have to make another diplomatic move for us. Visit Bahadur Khan, the Mughal Subadar, and convince him to sign a treaty with us. It should not be too difficult since he already has too much on his hands. He has had to intervene in the Adilshahi power struggle on Aurangzeb's orders and now finds himself in a sticky situation. He should be relieved when we extend a hand of friendship. It would be in the interest of both parties if we agree not to molest each other."

Niraji Punt nodded his agreement. "I will begin preparations immediately, Sire."

"Do not forget to give him some expensive presents!"

"Certainly, Sire," Niraji Punt smiled dourly.

"Good! It does seem that our fortunes will take us south this year, far beyond the boundaries of our Swarajya. It will be a difficult campaign, fraught with risk. But the Goddess Bhavani shall see us through. Before we embark on this journey however, we must take some decisions about another matter. Bahirji has brought news that the Siddi has taken over as the Governor of Janjira and Commander of the Mughal Emperor's fleet. His activities along our coast have intensified and are doubtless causing great hardship to our people. We must launch a fresh campaign against him. And this time I want it to be a decisive campaign. I want Janjira!"

The Chhatrapati looked at his men keenly. Most just looked away or regarded the floor. A campaign against the Siddi of Janjira was bound to be a tough one. Janjira Fort had time and again proved to be unconquerable. Besides, their own naval force was not strong enough to defeat the Siddi's fleet. This campaign could spell doom for whoever agreed to lead it.

Moro Punt hesitated only for a moment before he stood up and bowed to his King. "Your Highness, I will lead this campaign."

The Chhatrapati had half expected Moro Punt to volunteer. "Punt, you have just returned from an exhausting tour of duty. You need to rest."

"I will rest once I have entered Janjira, Sire!"

The Chhatrapati laughed. "Janjira is as much your dream as it is mine, is it not, Punt?"

"Highness, I will not show you my face till I have taken Janjira."

The Chhatrapati had been restless all evening. He had refused food and ordered that he be left alone. He paced his chamber impatiently. Bahirji had sent an advance message that he would reach Raigad by evening. It wasn't like Bahirji to be late. Had something gone wrong? Had they been discovered?

Some time later, Mahadu entered and announced Bahirji Naik's arrival. Also, he had a visitor with him. Ah! They were here. The Chhatrapati could not hide his elation. "Send them in at once!" he said.

Bahirji entered and bowed. He was followed by a tall man whose face was covered by a cloth tied over it. His shoulders drooped as he stood with his hands folded in front of him.

"Show me your face," the Chhatrapati ordered.

The man slowly uncovered his face. His eyes were on the King's feet. The Chhatrapati gazed at him intently. Once a hefty and fierce warrior, the man seemed to have aged much more than the eleven years that separated this day from their last meeting. The face was heavily creased and he had lost plenty of weight. But what was most striking to the Chhatrapati was that he looked a completely broken man.

"Netoji..." The Chhatrapati's voice was heavy with emotion. Over a decade ago, in a fit of rage, he had fired Netoji Palkar, then his Commander-in-Chief, for an error that had cost a thousand Maratha lives. Netoji had lived these past years amongst the Mughals, as a servant of the Empire. He had been forcibly converted to Islam, and been given the new name of Muhammad Quli Khan. While in the Mughal camp, he had been constantly under watch. He had made several attempts to escape, but had failed. At long last, a few weeks earlier, one of Bahirji's men had made contact with him. When the Chhatrapati had been apprised of this development, he had immediately ordered Bahirji to do his utmost to extricate Netoji from the Mughal camp.

Netoji Palkar raised his eyes to look at the man he had worshipped next to his God in the past. How he had waited for this moment; for a chance to ask for his King's forgiveness. Netoji's eyes filled with tears. He threw himself at the Chhatrapati's feet, sobbing like a child. "Maharaj! Forgive me! I committed the cardinal sin of joining the Mughals. But I have suffered enough these past years. Please take me back into your fold, Maharaj. Do not send me away again."

The Chhatrapati's heart melted as he heard Netoji's pleas. He reached down and raised him to his feet. "Why would I have ordered Bahirji to rescue you if I had wanted to send you back into exile, Netoji?"

"Allow me to serve the Swarajya again, my King! I will do any job you deem fit."

The Chhatrapati smiled at his former comrade. "Welcome back, Netoji Palkar. Go, rest now. We shall meet again later. I shall personally arrange for you to be taken back into the Hindu fold."

Netoji bowed low. "How can I repay your kindness, Maharaj?"

"By service to the Swarajya, Netoji."

Netoji could not speak. He bowed and left the Chhatrapati's chamber. A few days later, he was re-converted to the Hindu faith and inducted into government service.

Raigad, September 1676

"We have successfully concluded a treaty with the Mughal, Your Highness. The terms have been sent to the Emperor for approval." Niraji Raoji had returned from a visit to the Mughal Subadar Bahadur Khan, having achieved the task his King had entrusted to him. "The Emperor will definitely accept the terms as he too must desire peace with us right now. He is preparing for a big political intervention in Deccan politics."

"Good work, Punt!" The Chhatrapati smiled at his Minister. With the Mughal front quiet, he could safely embark upon the campaign to Karnatak. "Anaji Punt," the Chhatrapati turned to his Sachiv, "we should begin preparations for the new campaign."

Anaji Datto bowed and said, "We shall begin at once, Sire."

"While I am away from the Swarajya, the administration must run smoothly. I have decided to appoint Provincial Heads, who will be responsible for the territory under them. Moro Punt shall be in charge of the Northern Province, Anaji Punt will head the Southern Province, and Dattaji Trimbak will be posted at Panhala, to take care of the Central Province."

"Sire, Moro Punt is away on the Janjira campaign," Anaji Punt reminded his King.

"The Janjira campaign has dragged on for longer than expected. I would have thought a Commander of Moro Punt's calibre would have wrapped things up sooner."

"His Highness places too much trust in his Ministers. Perhaps he forgets he has a capable son," Prince Sambhaji said, directly criticizing his father's over-reliance on his Punts.

The Chhatrapati turned to look at him. The Prince returned the gaze defiantly. Of late, thought the Chhatrapati, Shambhu had been demanding a larger role in administration and military campaigns. He was inexperienced but confident and eager to show his mettle. He had come of age. Perhaps he had been shielded long enough. "Shambhu, I will put you in charge of more campaigns in the future,' he said to his son. 'Right now, I think it is important for the future King to remain safe."

"It is his Highness who should remain safe in the capital while his son fulfils the duty of a Yuvraj," Sambhaji stated, looking away. "Given a chance I can prove I am better than the Punts in administration as well."

The other faces in the assembly showed dissension at the Prince's comments. Anaji Punt, measuring his words carefully, said, "No one doubts the Yuvraj's competence. But it takes years to gain maturity in politics and the Yuvraj is still very young."

"But not lacking in intelligence!" Sambhaji snapped at him. "It doesn't take much to see how our people are being squeezed to pay more taxes by the Ministers! I have received numerous complaints that the populace is forced to pay money they can ill afford. Is it fair then to call this Swarajya? How are we different from the imperialists?"

"My Prince, we cannot support our ever-expanding armed forces if we do not collect taxes from the people. Given a choice, no one would want to pay tax. But the government cannot function without money." Beads of sweat appeared on Anaji Punt's brow. The exchange of words with Sambhaji was clearly upsetting him.

"Shambhu," the Chhatrapati raised a hand and said calmly, "Anaji Punt is right. We take care not to over-burden the people with taxes. But this is not the time to bring up these issues. Let us focus on the Gingee campaign now."

"I will be going with you on this campaign, I suppose, Highness?" Sambhaji was certain he would be part of the all important mission.

"No Shambhu, you will stay back. I will be accompanied by Yesaji Kank, Sarjerao Jedhe, Suryaji Malusare, Anandrao, Manaji More and Senapati Hambirrao. The diplomats and office-bearers who will go with me are Raghunath Punt Hanmante, Nilo Prabhu, Shamji Nayak, Balaji Avji Chitnis and Gangadhar Punt."

"Why can I not go with you to Ginjee?" Sambhaji asked, exasperated by his father's decision.

"Shambhu, this campaign is likely to be risky. It would not be wise for both of us to risk our lives at the same time. If I get killed in battle, you must be alive and well to take over as King."

Sambhaji began to protest but the Chhatrapati raised a hand to silence him. "Finally, we must put someone in charge of Raigad itself. Raoji Somnath shall remain here, in charge of the capital while I am away. As for you, Shambhu Raje, I have decided to put you in charge as Governor of Shringarpur district for now. Your father-in-law is the administrator there. Learn the nuances of administration from him." The Chhatrapati concluded his arrangements for administration of the Swarajya during his absence.

Sambhaji's eyes blazed with anger. His father had added the final insult by banishing him from Raigad to a peripheral district, while the Ministers took up the plum central posts. But what stung him more than his father's decision was the fact that he was being humiliated in front of the assembly. Abruptly he rose from his seat and bowed to his father saying, "His Highness must excuse me. I have important business to attend to." Without waiting for his father's assent, he turned and stormed out of the audience chamber. The all-important meeting continued in the absence of the Crown Prince.

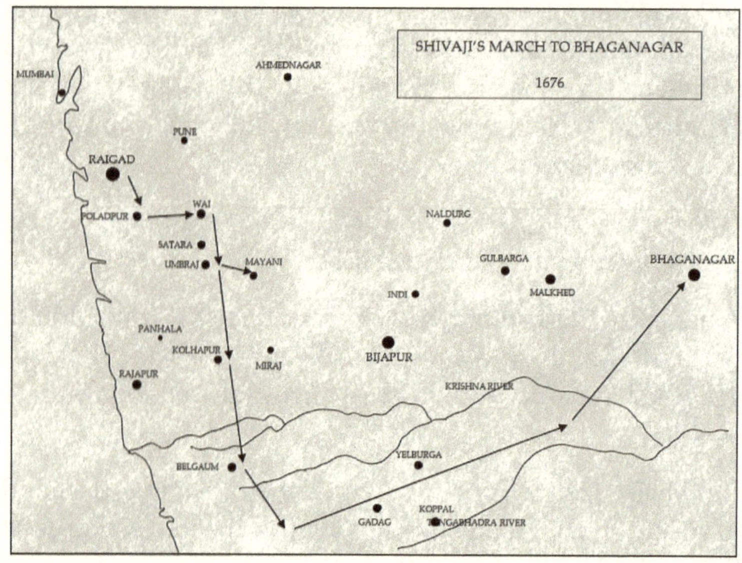

A massive Maratha army trudged its way out of the capital fort, embarking upon a campaign that would mark the Chhatrapati's definitive entry into Deccan politics. If this campaign succeeded, it would have far-reaching consequences on the future of the fledging Maratha state. Twenty-five thousand horsemen and forty thousand foot soldiers followed their King to achieve glory.

Preparations for the King's march had begun a month before, when advance units had moved south and raided the Adilshahi Balaghat district, primarily to create a diversion and secure the route. Senapati Hambirrao Mohite marched ahead of his King into Gadag district, south of Bijapur, where he engaged Qasim Khan Miana, Commander of Koppal Fort, and his brother Hussain Khan. The brothers were defeated by the Maratha Commander-in-Chief and Hussain Khan was captured alive. Qasim though, held on to his fort, which was besieged by the Marathas.

Chhatrapati Shivaji marched south from Raigad to Poladpur, and then turned east toward Wai. That small town was annexed and the Marathas moved south, first to Satara (which was already under Maratha control), and then to Umbraj. From this place, detachments were sent north-east and eastward to Khatav and Mayani, to annex those military stations. The main body of the army continued south, marching east of Kolhapur into Belgaum district. They crossed the Krishna River and then turned east into Gadag district, which had been secured by Hambirrao.

The Maratha army marched north-east, in a wide arc across the fertile doab between the Krishna and Tungabhadra rivers. The main body, with the Chhatrapati's units, was flanked to the north and south by detachments moving parallel to it. A vanguard and a rearguard completed the King's protection from any attacks by Adilshahi troops. Unlike the usual Maratha campaigns, the march was slow and no attempt was made to conceal the Chhatrapati's position. What was kept a complete secret, however, was the destination. Neither the Mughal nor the Adilshahi administration had any clue where Shivaji Raja was headed.

After nearly five months, the Marathas camped on the outskirts of Bhaganagar. The arrival of the massive army had initially created panic in the Qutubshah's capital city. However, their good behaviour soon dispelled doubts and roused the peoples' curiosity about the proud Maratha King, tales about whom they had been hearing for years.

Maratha camp outside Bhaganagar, end February 1676

"Your Highness, we have received a firmaan from the Qutubshah," Suryaji Malusare said, having made his obeisance. They were in the Chhatrapati's command tent in the centre of the Maratha military camp.

The Chhatrapati turned to the stocky pot-bellied administrator, who stood attentively to one side. "Krishnaji Punt, let us hear what the Sultan has to say."

Suryaji handed the scroll to Krishnaji, who began reading the Persian text effortlessly and translating it into Marathi for his master. "The Qutubshah says he is pleased by His Highness' visit to Bhaganagar and wishes to come forth a short distance to welcome you into the city."

Chhatrapati Shivaji thought for a moment, then said, "Punt, I think we could make a better impression on the Sultan if we go forth first. Write to him. Say, 'Your Excellency is my elder brother, I the younger. You should not have to come in person to greet me. Your Prime Minister can be sent as your deputy.' If he accepts, Madanna will come to meet me. That will give me a chance to speak with him, prior to meeting the Sultan."

The men were startled by a commotion outside the tent. Hiroji rushed out to see what the matter was. A while later he returned with a flushed face. "We have received a complaint from some residents of Bhaganagar," he said.

"What about?" The Chhatrapati was irritated by the distraction.

"Some of our men forcibly carried away supplies from the local market without paying, and..." Hiroji hesitated to say the rest, as he knew the hand of retribution of his King would fall heavily on the offenders.

"And?" The Chhatrapati's face was already contorting with anger.

"A couple of them tried to molest some women accompanying the traders."

"How dare they?" the Chhatrapati growled. "In the face of explicit orders from me, how dare they commit such crimes? Do we know who these men are?"

"Yes, Sire. Yesaji and Sarjerao have rounded them up. They are outside right now."

The Chhatrapati strode out of his tent, followed by Hiroji and Krishnaji. A crowd had gathered around some men kneeling on the ground, their heads lowered and hands tied behind their backs.

Yesaji and Sarjerao bowed, and Yesaji said, "We have identified these miscreants from testimony given by the Bhaganagar residents. They have confessed to their crimes."

The Chhatrapati's eyes blazed with anger. "How dare you disobey my orders?" he demanded.

The men were too scared to raise their heads. Yesaji grabbed the leader by his hair and jerked his face up. "Answer the King!" he shouted. The man was sweating profusely, as much from fear as from the heat. "Forgive us, your Highness!" he managed to say through trembling lips. "We have committed grave mistakes. Forgive us!"

"I issued clear orders that no Bhaganagar resident was to be harassed. We are not here for a raid. We are here to extend the hand of friendship. You men have been instructed to buy your provisions from the markets. How did you dare disregard my orders?" The Chhatrapati was furious. In his face, the accused men could see their own deaths. "And you went so far as to commit the cardinal sin for any soldier of the Swarajya. You insulted their women! Since when did we start molesting women? What then is the difference between us and the imperial armies?"

The men were openly weeping now, begging for forgiveness. "Sire, have mercy! We will never commit such acts again."

"No, you will not!" the Chhatrapati said coldly. "Behead these men at once; right here, in front of me!"

The assembly was stunned into silence as the King pronounced the sentence. Yesaji and Sarjerao stared at him wide-eyed.

"Do it! Right now! Let this be a warning to the rest, never to disobey their King's orders."

Yesaji gritted his teeth and raised his sword. He paused momentarily, asking forgiveness from his God, and then brought the sword down on the back of the first accused's neck. One by one the sobbing, screaming men were beheaded.

The Chhatrapati's command tent, 4 March 1676

Two Brahmans bowed obeisance and stood smiling before the Chhatrapati. "Welcome to Bhaganagar Chhatrapati Shivaji Raje. My Lord sends greetings," Madanna, the Qutubshah's Prime Minister, said.

The Chhatrapati accepted the polite words with a smile and a nod, continuing to regard the man before him intently. Madanna appeared to be well into his sixties and though slender of frame, stood ramrod straight. His face was creased with age but exuded wisdom and a kind of self-assurance that comes only with a high position in society.

He was dressed simply in a white dhoti and *angarkha*[47]. A simple cloth turban covered his undoubtedly bald head. His only adornment was a gold embroidered shawl draped around his torso. His brother Akanna, who stood quietly behind him, was nearly a mirror image.

"Your Highness, I have come to escort you into the city. Arrangements for your stay have been made in one of the Sultan's palaces. His Excellency has personally seen to your comforts."

"I thank His Excellency wholeheartedly," the Chhatrapati replied. "I too, am eager to meet him. But first, let us discuss a few important issues." He directed the two Brahmans to be seated near him. "You are well aware of the reasons for my visit, Madanna Punt. I will soon begin a campaign in the Adilshahi Karnatak. I am sure you have seen the vast army at my disposal. Our first target is the fort of Gingee, which we will take shortly, and then progress south as far as the border of Tanjavur. I understand that the Qutubshahi is willing to extend monetary and logistical help to us while we are in the South."

"Certainly, Your Highness," Madanna said with an inclination of his head. "I have convinced the Qutubshah to sign a treaty. You will receive all the help you need, and more. We couldn't be happier to gain an ally as powerful as Chhatrapati Shivaji."

"Good. I believe Niraji Raoji has, while he was here, explained what we need. Is the Qutubshah agreeable to everything?"

"His Excellency will not disappoint and I am sure the Chhatrapati will win many famous victories in the South."

---

[47] Knee-length, full-sleeved coat

The discussions continued for some time. When he was finally satisfied that Madanna was indeed favourably inclined to their cause, the Chhatrapati rose to leave for Bhaganagar, capital of the Qutubshahi Empire.

The Maratha King's massive entourage entered Bhaganagar to a rapturous welcome from the local populace. The entire city had been decorated with garlands of flowers. The road to the palace was sprinkled with saffron water and *kumkum*[48], flags fluttered on both sides. Scarlet awnings were hung overhead, tied between houses on either side of the road so that the procession passed under an endless red canopy. People had gathered in thousands, cheering the Maratha King and his officers, showering them with flowers, both real and those made of gold leaf. Women waved lighted lamps in the air as the great Maratha passed by. People thronged not only the road, but the windows and balconies of the houses to catch a glimpse of the legend.

Leading the procession was a large superbly caparisoned bull elephant, carrying on its back the saffron-coloured Maratha standard. Following the standard was the advance guard of heavy cavalry. The finest horses from Arabia, suitably arrayed in rich trappings, carried the office bearers of the Maratha Swarajya. Then came the cavalcade pf the military officers and diplomats. Senapati Hambirrao Mohite was in the lead, seated on a large, armoured black stallion. Madanna, Akanna and the rest of the Qutubshahi contingent rode with them.

---

[48] Vermillion powder, considered auspicious in Hindu rituals

The Chhatrapati was seated in the *howdah*[49] of his personal elephant, which followed his officers. The animal was bedecked with gold and silver trappings and embroidered velvet cloth. The Chhatrapati acknowledged the cheers of the crowd by raising his hand and waving. His aides stood behind him, intermittently showering the crowd with gold coins. The King's elephant was flanked and followed by his personal bodyguard, after which came the cavalry and infantry of the rearguard.

The massive procession of over six thousand men snaked its way through the city and finally halted outside the royal palace. The Daad Mahal was a massive structure, with numerous galleries adorned with fountains. Over the main entrance was a large portico, where some of the Qutubshah's royal musicians sat cross-legged, playing soft music.

"Welcome to the Qutubshah's palace, Your Highness," Madanna said as the Chhatrapati alighted from his elephant. "His Excellency will personally come out to welcome you."

"Madanna Punt, pray send word to His Excellency that he should not come out to receive me. I will meet him in the durbar hall."

The message was conveyed to the Sultan, who was suitably impressed by the Maratha King's humility. The Chhatrapati was conducted to the durbar hall through a private entrance. He looked resplendent, dressed in a peach silk angarkha and trousers, both richly embroidered in gold. His turban was adorned with gems and strings of pearls. Gold rings studded with gems and rubies adorned his fingers, and around his neck hung strings of pearls and the traditional

---

[49] A carrier tied to the backs of elephants, meant for seating people

string of cowries. His left hand supported the *uparna*[50], which was slung over his shoulder. His right hand rested on the diamond-studded hilt of the Bhavani, thrust through the saffron *dushela*[51]. An aide walked behind him, holding the Umbrella of State over his head. Behind the Chhatrapati came his chief diplomats and officers, amongst them Raghunath Punt Hanmante, Prahlad Punt and Hambirrao Mohite.

As he entered the palace, the quorchi announced his arrival: *Sinhasanadheeshwar, Kshatriya Kulawatouns, Maharajadhiraj, Raja Shiva Chhatrapati...*[52]

Abul Hasan Qutubshah entered the durbar at the same time through an entrance on the opposite side, and his quorchi announced: *Ba-adab, ba-mulahizah hoshiyaar! Shahenshah, Parwardigaar, Hazrat Abul Hasan Qutubshah Padishah!*[53]

The two Kings approached each other as the assembly of Qutubshahi and Maratha nobles and officers offered obeisance. The Qutubshah smiled broadly as soon as he set eyes on the Maratha King. He was a man of ample girth, in his mid-forties, and sported a well-trimmed beard and moustache. Dressed in a dark green full-length coat, beautifully embroidered with flowers in gold thread, and a heavy brocade border, he had a rich silk turban on his head. The Sultan looked every bit the rich monarch he was. The finest diamonds from the mines of Golconda adorned the

---

[50] A long folded cloth worn over the shoulder

[51] A waistband made from a long, narrow piece of cloth; weapons like swords and daggers were stuck into it

[52] Enthroned King, Kshatriya by caste, Head of the *kula* (race), King of Kings

[53] With respect; stand facing; alert; Emperor; Almighty; Hazrat is an Arabic honorific to convey respect; Padishah means Emperor

aigrette on his turban, as well as his thick fingers. Strings of pearls and emeralds hung around his neck.

The two rulers embraced warmly. "Welcome Chhatrapati Shivaji Raje! Welcome to the Golconda durbar." The Qutubshah held the Chhatrapati's hand and led him to a specially prepared seat next to his own. Apart from the two rulers, only Madanna was seated; the rest of the assembly remained standing. The durbar proceedings began with welcome addresses from the monarch and his nobles. An exchange of gifts followed, among them fine silks, jewels, ornate daggers, horses and elephants. The chief officers and diplomats were also presented with valuable gifts and robes of honour.

While these official exchanges were in progress in the palace, nearly six thousand Maratha troops silently moved in and surrounded the palace, placing themselves in key positions. Their aim was to safeguard against any double-cross by the Qutubshah. In such an event, they had to be well placed to rescue their King.

The meeting continued for over a prahar, most of the time being spent in the Qutubshah listening intently as the famous Maratha recounted stories of his many campaigns, daring attacks and victories. The Sultan heard with great fascination as Chhatrapati Shivaji narrated the assassination of Afzal Khan and the night raid on Shaista Khan. Never having ventured outside his plush and comfortable life and surroundings, or been on a single military campaign himself, the Qutubshah perceived these extraordinary tales as the stuff of myth and legend, and listened to them with the curiosity and excitement of a small boy. As time went by, his initial apprehensions about the Maratha fell away and he became increasingly confident that Shivaji genuinely wanted an alliance.

Chhatrapati Shivaji left no stone unturned to woo the rich monarch. He had come to the South with a definite military agenda. As he saw it, a treaty with the Qutubshah would not only safeguard his back as he turned toward the Gingee, but would also provide valuable finance for his campaign. The idea that the Deccan should remain with the Deccani rulers rather than passing to the Mughals, found great purchase with the Qutubshah and his nobles. An alliance of Deccani rulers was proposed with Chhatrapati Shivaji and the Qutubshah leading it.

Finally, much later, the Qutubshah gave leave to the assembled gentry. He anointed his royal guest's wrists with rose *attar*[54] and offered him *paan*[55], which he had prepared with his own hands. Chhatrapati Shivaji then retired to the Gosha Mahal, which was one of the royal palaces designated for his stay.

The next few weeks were spent in Bhaganagar, feasting and enjoying the pleasures offered so eagerly by the Qutubshah and his nobles. Madanna Punt organized a feast at his own house to honour the Chhatrapati, and his mother cooked the food with her own hands. The Chhatrapati was overwhelmed by this show of affection. Games and festivities were organized, where the Marathas got a taste of the luxurious lifestyle of the Qutubshahi gentry. The Chhatrapati met the Qutubshah on a few more occasions. The Lord of Golconda spared no expense and opportunity

---

[54] Concentrated essence

[55] Betel leaf with condiments

to impress his guest by presenting him and his men with expensive gifts, horses and elephants. If he could not match the Maratha with romantic tales of battles, he could and did outdo him with a show of riches.

One day, while the two rulers sat in the spacious balcony of the royal palace, the infantry and cavalry of both sides paraded in the courtyard below, presenting a guard of honour. The Qutubshah, in his typical flamboyant style, ordered his war elephants to be brought forward. When his lead charger, a massive bull elephant came forth, he beamed with pride and turned to the Chhatrapati to say, "Shivaji Raje, I bet you do not have any animal in your ranks to rival this beast!"

The Chhatrapati gave him a polite smile. "I do not need one, Your Excellency.' He replied. 'My Captain Yesaji Kank is more than a match for your elephant."

The Qutubshah was taken aback by this response. "Your Captain can match my charger?" he asked, eyebrows raised.

"Not just a match, but he can kill your elephant as well," The Chhatrapati said bluntly. "You see, the armies we fight have numerous such elephants. So we have trained our men to tackle them. Yesaji is one of my best fighters."

The Qutubshah looked at his guest for a long moment, unwilling to believe what he had just heard. How could a man, any man, combat a large bull elephant? He was much too intrigued to forgo such a contest. "Raje, I will gift your man one thousand gold coins if he kills my charger," he said.

The Chhatrapati sent word for Yesaji to come forward and take on the massive beast. The *mahout*[56] slid off the bull

---

[56] Elephant handler

elephant's back and stable hands incited the beast with an *ankush*[57]. Within moments the beast was trumpeting and stamping its legs in anger, focussing its energy on the lone man in front of him. Yesaji calmly drew his sword from its scabbard and stood his ground as the elephant charged, trumpeting ferociously. Yesaji waited till the last moment before leaping to one side, to avoid being crushed by the massive legs. The crowd roared as the beast reared up and turned his attention once again to his tormentor. Yesaji was up on his feet in a flash. He had by now gauged the elephant's speed and knew how fast he had to move to get the better of his foe. The elephant charged at him again. This time, Yesaji waited for just a moment longer and, as he slid to one side, struck with his sword. The blade went clean through the animal's trunk, severing it. The huge beast crashed to the ground shrieking in agony. Yesaji calmly sheathed his sword and returned to his position at the head of his ranks.

The Qutubshah was mesmerized by this show of bravado and skill. He gave Yesaji not just the promised thousand gold coins, but also a fine caparisoned stallion. "Raje," he said to the Chhatrapati, "I offer you a hundred of my men in exchange for this man of yours."

The Chhatrapati laughed. "Your Excellency, I have selected my men like a jeweller selects the choicest of gems. But why don't you try luring him into your service?"

Yesaji was summoned to the balcony. He made his obeisance and stood to attention as the Qutubshah regarded him almost with reverence. "I have never seen a man battle a war elephant like that before," he said. "I will offer you a large estate and untold riches if you agree to join my service."

---

[57] Pointed metal hooks used to train elephants

Yesaji knew this was another test his own Lord was subjecting him to. He bowed briefly and said, "I am but a humble servant of Chhatrapati Shivaji. I live and die at his feet. If you take me away from him, I cannot survive. What use then will I be to you, Your Excellency?"

In that moment the Qutubshah understood the true strength of the Maratha King. It was his men. While he himself had chosen to invest in creating more riches, Shivaji had chosen to invest in the loyalty of his men. Therein lay the difference between them.

While this show of wealth and valour was extant, diplomats from both sides worked furiously to ink out a treaty. At long last, the Chhatrapati's perseverance and Madanna Punt's influence with the Qutubshah bore fruit and a historic treaty was signed between the two rulers. According to the document, the Marathas were to get a subsistence of three thousand hons a day for as long as they were in the Karnatak, and a Qutubshahi contingent of four thousand horse and one thousand foot soldiers, under the command of Mirza Muhammad Amin, would accompany the Chhatrapati on the campaign. The Qutubshah also agreed to issue orders to all his officers and vassal chieftains to give all necessary assistance to the Marathas, including supplies, troops and munitions. In return for all this magnanimity, the Qutubshah was to receive a part of the territory annexed by the Chhatrapati, excluding Shahaji Raje's jagirs.

Nearly a month had passed and the Chhatrapati was getting restless. He was itching to get on with the campaign. As he relaxed on a plush baithak in the audience chamber, he said to his men, "We must begin preparations to leave for Gingee. Our diplomatic work here is almost done."

"I agree, Highness," Raghunath Punt said. "We should be able to leave Bhaganagar in a week."

The Chhatrapati nodded. "Excellent. Hambirrao, mobilize the advance guard to secure the ground ahead of us."

"At once, Sire." Hambirrao nodded. "I will order Hiroji to proceed with his units at the earliest."

"Designate the units which will stay back at Gingee to besiege the fort, while we move further south. Our timing seems to be perfect. While we begin our campaign, the Adilshah will be hard pressed to launch a retaliatory campaign in the Swarajya due to the rains."

The men nodded.

"The monsoon arrives later on the east coast. We should have wrapped up the campaign before the rains in Karnatak begin to bother us seriously," Raghunath Punt added.

"Punt, before proceeding to Gingee, I wish to visit the shrine at Srisailyam. Let us seek the blessings of Lord Mahadev before the campaign begins," the Chhatrapati said.

Raghunath Punt shifted uneasily. From the point of view of a military campaign, it would be an unnecessary diversion and a waste of valuable time. Each extra day on a campaign meant huge expenses. Yet the Chhatrapati was willing to suffer these to visit the shrine. "Sire," he said gently, "would it be wise to indulge in this visit and delay the march to Gingee? Would it not be more prudent to proceed directly to Gingee and begin the campaign?"

The Chhatrapati nodded, but said firmly, "The Lord calls out to me, Punt. I must go to him and place my head at his shrine."

4 April 1677

The massive Maratha army, reinforced by Qutubhshahi troops, left Bhaganagar at the stroke of dawn and marched southwest. The progress was stately, hence far slower than their usual forced marches. Yet they covered nearly seven to eight kos every day and on the ninth day reached a place called Nivrutti-Sangam at the confluence of the Krishna and Tungabhadra rivers. The Chhatrapati bathed in the holy waters and offered libations. The main Maratha army continued south-west towards Anantpur, while the Chhatrapati, accompanied by a few chosen officers and diplomats, with a bodyguard of a few hundred cavalry, turned east toward Srishailya.

The holy shrine of Srisailyam was some nineteen kos east of the sangam where the Chhatrapati had bathed. Embowered in hills and forests, the temple was a haven of peace and serenity. From the moment he set foot in the courtyard, the Chhatrapati was lost to the world. The Head *Pujari*[58] accompanied him around the temple complex, explaining its history and recounting the ancient lore connected to the place. The Chhatrapati heard nothing.

"This temple is most ancient, Highness," the pujari was saying. "Some say it is over one thousand five hundred years old. But most of the structures you see today were commissioned in the Vijaynagar era."

---

[58] Hindu priest

The Chhatrapati toured the complex oblivious to the others around him. He walked from structure to structure, mesmerized not just by the architecture and carvings but also the serenity of the place.

The huge temple complex faced east, covered nearly eight *bighas*[59] of land, and was enclosed by tall walls. It had four *gopurams*[60], numerous shrines, and halls. The most notable space, the *Mukha Mandapa*[61], had intricately sculpted pillars and led to the inner sanctum that housed the shrines of both Lord Shiva and his consort Parvati.

"These shrines are the oldest part of the temple, dating back over a thousand years," the pujari said. "The pillared hall we just crossed was built by the Vijaynagar Kings."

In the sanctum, the Chhatrapati performed abhishek to the *Shivling*[62], and offered his prayers. The voices of the pujaris reciting the holy mantras reverberated in his ears, shutting out all other sounds. He was in a trance, in a world of his own, meditating to the chanting of *Om Namah Shivay*[63].

Much later, he sat in the mandapa hall with his men. It was late afternoon and a gentle breeze diffused the summer heat. The hall was quiet and still.

"His Highness is fortunate to have reached such a state of bliss. Few can experience it in their lifetime," Raghunath Punt observed.

"I agree, Punt. I am indeed fortunate to have experienced this place. It is so peaceful and pleasant; almost like Kailas itself. One can feel the Lord's presence here."

---

[59] A measure of land, which varies slightly from place to place

[60] Towering, decorative gateways (delete rest)

[61] Main shrine

[62] Symbolic representation of Lord Shiva in stone.

[63] Sanskrit chant meaning 'I bow to Lord Shiva'

"Very true, Sire. We spend our lives on the battlefield. Most of us never experience such peace," Hambirrao said.

"At the end of Kingship, there is only hell, Hambirrao," the Chhatrapati said sardonically. Years of struggle, warfare and death were telling on him. "I can never atone for the wars I have waged, for the lives I have taken, for those lost on the battlefield. Each of us must one day answer for our actions in His durbar."

Hambirrao felt something was amiss. He had never seen his King in such a state, gazing into the distance, oblivious of the others around him. Never before had his King talked of salvation.

"Sire, you waged wars to drive out the barbarians from our lands. Even the Gods understand it was done for our people."

"Hambirrao, I do not think I can go any further. I think I have reached a place where I can attain salvation. I wish to offer my head at the shrine of my Lord Mahadev. Go back home. My son is capable of taking over as ruler. Place him on the throne. Do as you deem fit for our people."

The brief speech stunned the men. They gazed open-mouthed at each other. None knew what to make of it. The Chhatrapati merely rose and walked back into the sanctum to chant the name of Lord Mahadev.

For nine days, the Maratha King immersed himself in meditation and often repeated his desire to end his own life. He bathed in the holy waters of the *Neelganga*[64], and offered prayers, asking the Lord to pardon his sins. His men grew more worried by the day as they saw no sign of their King returning to the real world. Fearing that he would harm

---

[64] Name given to the Krishna River near the shrine

himself, Hambirrao had all weapons removed from the Chhatrapati's vicinity. Guards were placed to watch him at all times.

At last, on the tenth day, the Chhatrapati ordered his men to assemble before him and said, "Men, it is time we move on to Gingee. Order the advance guard to proceed."

His order was greeted by smiles of relief. With renewed vigour, preparations were made for the march ahead.

"You had us worried, Sire," Hambirrao said. "For a few days we thought we would lose you to the Lord."

The Chhatrapati laughed. "I will not say I had lost my way, Hambirrao; for the path to salvation seems to be the only true path. Yet I woke up to the knowledge that my work in this mortal world is not yet done. You must thank Goddess Bhavani for that."

"The Goddess, Sire?"

"Yes. She revealed herself to me in my dreams last night and said: *My son, you cannot attain salvation this way. I have many more deeds to accomplish through you yet.*

Hambirrao thanked the Goddess silently, bowed to his King, and proceeded to order his troops to mobilize.

❦

From Srishailya, Chhatrapati Shivaji's small entourage moved south-east. They were joined on the way by the main force stationed at Anantpur. After several days' march, the Marathas reached a place west of Chennai, and there turned south-west to Kanchipuram, on the north bank of the Palar River. They crossed the river and once again divided their force. The vanguard proceeded south-west to Gingee fort, while the main body of the army, with the Chhatrapati himself, marched in a more westerly direction to Vellore Fort.

The siege of Gingee was merely a show of Maratha power. The political grounds had been laid for the fort's surrender long ago. The fort's Abyssinian Commander, Nasir Mohammed, fed up of being harassed by Sher Khan, the Pathan chieftain of the southern Gingee district, had offered to surrender the fort to the Qutubshah. Now, following the recent treaty with the Marathas, the Qutubshah had ordered him to hand over the fort to Chhatrapati Shivaji's forces. A few days after the arrival of the Maratha vanguard, Nasir Mohammed negotiated a reward and a jagir for himself, and handed over the fort to the Maratha Captain.

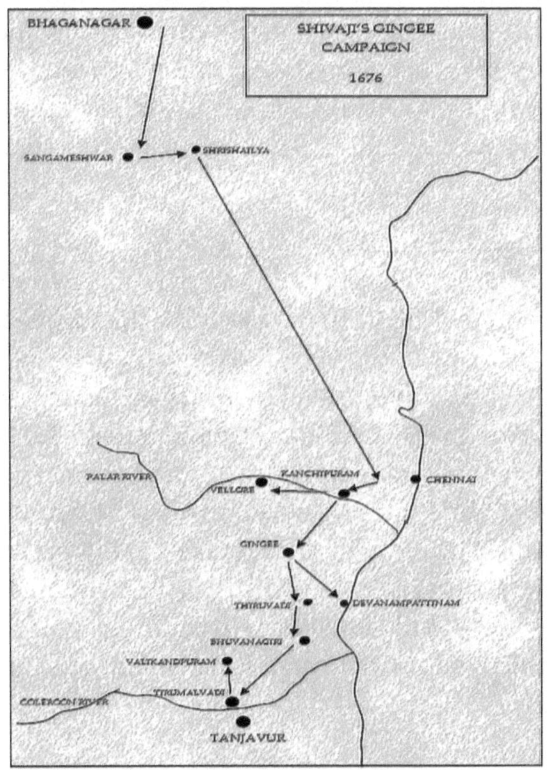

The story at Vellore, however, was quite different. The Vellore Fort, one of the strongest in the Karnatak, was commanded by another Abyssinian named Abdulla Khan. If the Chhatrapati had felt that he too, like Nasir Mohammed, would surrender without a fight, he was to be disappointed. Abdulla Khan prepared to defend the fort with his life, despite implorations from Nasir. The Marathas had no option but to besiege the fort and try to choke the Bijapuri garrison into surrender.

Meanwhile, the news of Shivaji Raja's presence in the Vellore camp spread like wildfire. One by one the polygar chieftains of the region visited his camp, offering their obeisance and gifts to protect their own fiefs from his wrath. They placed themselves in his service, throwing off the Adilshahi yoke. Particularly satisfying for the Chhatrapati was the arrival of the envoys from the Nayaks of Mysore and Madurai. As these two powerful Nayaks were now vassals, albeit nominally, further conquests in the Mysore region would be easier.

The envoys from the French East India Company settlement at Pondicherry also arrived to pay homage to the King. Chhatrapati Shivaji accused them of meddling in local politics and expressed his displeasure at their usurping of St. Thome and Veludavur, which they had handed over to the Adilshahi Commanders. He declared that their actions favoured Bijapur and went against the interests of the Qutubshah, who was now an ally of the Marathas. He ordered them to retake Veludavur from Sher Khan and return it to the Qutubshah. Further, he warned them that he would allow them to continue their factory at Pondicherry only if they chose to remain neutral in local politics.

The news of the surrender of Gingee arrived to gladden hearts in the midst of battle. Chhatrapati Shivaji secured the Vellore siege, named Commanders, and himself proceeded to Gingee. As soon as he set foot in the fort, he fell in love with it. Realizing its strategic importance, he ordered repairs and reinforcements. He knew that in the event of a decisive battle with the Mughal, this fort would offer a safe haven for the Maratha royals. From Gingee, they could fight the Mughal might for months, possibly even years.

Having secured Gingee, the Chhatrapati named Rayaji Nalge as the new Fort Commander and gave him a strong garrison to defend the fort. Vitthal Pildev was named Subadar of Gingee district. The Maratha force then marched south to Thiruvadi. The Pathans of south Gingee had to be dealt with if the Marathas were to claim rights over the entire region.

Sher Khan was a confidanté of Bahlol Khan, and was thus allied to the Pathani faction at the Bijapur court. He hated the Abyssinians as deeply as his mentor Bahlol, who was now Grand Vizier in Bijapur. For years he had tried to wrest Gingee Fort from Nasir Mohammed, without success. Now, with the fort lost to the Marathas, he faced a large enemy host on his northern border. But, being a Pathan, he allowed his ego to overrule wisdom and decided to face Shivaji Raja. Had he decided to surrender, he and his clan might have been saved from utter destruction.

Sher Khan advanced to Thiruvadi to face the Marathas, but no sooner did he set his eyes upon the vast Maratha force, he realized his mistake. He fled immediately, pursued by the Marathas, who succeeded in scattering most of his forces. With a handful of retainers, he and his son escaped into the forests to the south, hoping the enemy would not follow. But the Maratha Captains were under strict orders from their King not to let him go. They followed him into the wilderness and beyond. He was finally besieged at Bhuvanagiri, and was forced to surrender.

The Marathas had taken but a fortnight to subdue the Pathans. Sher Khan agreed to surrender all territory under his command and pay a handsome tribute as well. His son Ibrahim was left as hostage with the Maratha Captains till all dues were paid.

Seeing Sher Khan's ruin, the garrisons of the forts at Veludavur, Devanampattinam and others fled. The Marathas occupied these citadels without a fight. Sher Khan's father-in-law had been holding out in Thiruvadi; but he too, finally surrendered.

The Gingee district was now entirely under Maratha rule.

Second half of July 1677

From Thiruvadi, the Chhatrapati marched fifty-five kos south-west, to the Colleroon River and camped on its northern bank, at Thirumalvadi. South of the river was Tanjavur, the territory of his half-brother Vyankoji. The Chhatrapati sent an envoy to Vyankoji, inviting him to his camp for talks. After some deliberation, the younger Bhosale agreed and crossed the river with a guard of two thousand riders. Word was sent to the Chhatrapati that Vyankoji Raje had arrived near his camp. Setting aside royal protocol, the Maratha King rode out to receive his brother.

"You remind me of our great father Vyankoji Raje," the Chhatrapati said as the Bhosale brothers came face to face. "You look like what I remember of him from his younger days."

Vyankoji gave him a courteous smile and bent to touch his feet. The Chhatrapati raised him by his shoulders and embraced him. "Your place is close to my heart, Brother," he said.

Back in camp, the brothers settled down on comfortable baithaks prepared for the meeting in the Chhatrapati's command tent. Vyankoji was quite apprehensive. For one he had a fair idea of what to expect from his brother. He had been receiving news of his campaign in the Gingee district on a regular basis. The fact that he was now camped on the banks of the Colleroon could mean only one thing – Shivaji Raje planned to annex his entire fief. Vyankoji was wary of the Chhatrapati's military might and knew he could not counter him alone. His own purpose in visiting his brother was to try and pacify him and find a diplomatic solution.

The Chhatrapati regarded his brother intently. Vyankoji was a few years younger than himself. Fair like his father, he had the same fire in his eyes. A short, well-cropped beard, a curved moustache and healthy sideburns, gave his face a robust look, while long hair fell on his shoulders from under a heavily adorned turban.

"I am proud of your achievements in the South, Vyankoji Raje. You have kept the Maratha flame lit by our father, alive."

"With your blessings, Dada," said Vyankoji, bowing his head. "You, however, are nothing short of a Legend. The entire Maratha clan holds you in reverence."

"I have merely done the will of Goddess Bhavani. But Vyankoji, we must think ahead, into the future. The Mughal will surely descend to the South and try to swallow all southern kingdoms. We must build a combined opposition and keep the Mughal from usurping our lands. The Adilshahi is weak and ready to crumble. If Aurangzeb gets a foothold here, he will make it his mission to make our lives miserable."

"I agree with you, Dada. What would you have me do?"

"Vyankoji, I have established control over the Gingee district. South of the river, you are in control at Tanjavur. We must maintain our hold on these regions as best we can. And by the Goddess' grace, we shall. But what worries me is the Mysore region. Our father's estates are in that district. Since you have moved south, these fiefs have been neglected. It will not be long before either the Nayak of Mysore usurps them or the Adilshah annexes them. I simply cannot let that happen. I have to maintain continuity between my Swarajya in Maharashtra and my holdings in the Gingee by establishing a safe corridor across Dharwar and Mysore."

Vyankoji finally understood the purpose of the meeting. His brother wanted their father's estates! He took a moment to assimilate what he had just heard, then cleared his throat and asked, "What do you suggest, Dada?"

"Hand over half of our father's estates to me. I shall maintain Maratha influence in the Mysore region; something you do not seem inclined to do."

"If I am not mistaken, Dada, father's estates comprised of his holdings in Maharashtra and Mysore. He has already given you half, has he not?"

The Chhatrapati leaned forward and pinned Vyankoji with his piercing gaze. "What I hold in Maharashtra, we have won by our sweat and blood, make no mistake about that. My men and I have held three Sultanates at bay for three decades! You have merely annexed Tanjavur. And in the process, you are losing your hold over the Mysore region. Do not try to tell me that I received my Swarajya for free!"

"That was not what I wished to imply, Dada," Vyankoji hurriedly tried to correct himself. "I was merely trying to recollect the original division of estates made by our illustrious father."

"The past is long gone, Vyankoji. I have risked and lost much in life to reach where I am. I simply cannot let your indolence ruin the future of the Swarajya."

Vyankoji remained silent. The Chhatrapati allowed him some time to think. In the meanwhile, refreshments were served and the brothers avoided further discussion while servants were around. The Chhatrapati inquired about the health of Vyankoji's mother, Tukabai. Vyankoji in return offered condolences on Jijabai's demise.

Later, the Chhatrapati broached the subject again. "Well, little brother, what have you decided?"

"Dada, I will need time to discuss the matter with my Ministers and think this through." With that, Vyankoji stood up and bowed. "You must grant me leave now. I would like to rest."

The Chhatrapati nodded, raising a hand in acknowledgement. As Vyankoji turned to leave, he said, "Agree to my demands, Vyankoji, and hand me half of the Mysore estates. Else you may lose it all."

The Chhatrapati's parting remark chilled Vyankoji's blood. He was well aware how his brother had annexed Jawali, Shringarpur and other fiefs in Maharashtra, completely annihilating their original Lords. He had come here to gauge his brother's plans and was now convinced that Shivaji Raje would not stop short of imprisoning him if he did not agree to his demands.

Vyankoji retired to his designated tent for the night, worry writ large on his face. He ordered his bodyguard to surround the tent, fearing an attack by Shivaji Raje's men.

"The Chhatrapati has unsettled Vyankoji Raje. I am convinced he fears for his life now." Raghunath voiced this opinion as he sat in conference with his King.

"That was my aim, Punt," the Chhatrapati said with a half-smile. "I wanted him to know that I would give him no quarter even though he is my brother."

"I hear he has surrounded himself by his men. Does His Highness plan to rush him?" Hambirrao asked. He too, was in attendance.

"No, Senapati. I do not wish to harm my brother unless he is the first to pick up arms against me. There is no doubt we shall achieve our objective in Mysore, but I would prefer to do it without bloodshed in the family."

"If he tries to escape to Tanjavur under cover of darkness, do we stop him?"

"No, let him pass. Instruct our men that they are not to offend him or his escort. However, if he does go back without taking leave of me, I shall take it as a refusal to grant my demands, in which case we are free to annex all my father's estates in Mysore."

Late that night, when the camp was quiet, Vyankoji slipped out, crossed the river in darkness, and rode back to Tanjavur. He was not molested by Shivaji Raje's Marathas.

True to his word, Chhatrapati Shivaji's forces invaded Mysore and annexed his father's estates north of the Colleroon River, thus far held by Vyankoji. Jagdevgad, Chidambaram and Vriddhachalam were quickly taken. The Marathas then laid siege to Kolar Fort.

The Chhatrapati broke camp at Thirumalvadi and marched north to Valikandpuram, from where he made a detour north-east to offer homage at the Vriddhachalam Temple, while his main army marched north to Elavanasur Fort, which was still held by Vyankoji's men. Janardan Punt managed to negotiate the surrender of the fort with its Commander. Elavanasur was thus annexed without bloodshed and added to the Swarajya.

During his stay in the Colleroon camp, the Chhatrapati had concluded administrative arrangements for the newly conquered districts. An army of civil servants, mostly Brahmans and Kayasthas, had followed his army and systematically settled in the annexed lands, taking over administration from the previous government. In addition, the Chhatrapati had ordered several tactical changes and reinforcements. The military stations and ammunition dumps located on the plains were demolished and new fortresses built on higher ground and hills. Large boulders obstructing movements of troops were broken down. New tanks were built to supply water.

Slave trafficking was prohibited in these lands now that the Maratha government had taken over. The foreign settlements were warned against buying, selling or moving slaves. The local people were thus freed from the curse of slavery forever. The Chhatrapati's astute administrators checkmated the efforts of the English and French officers to dabble in local politics, warning them to stay away. The French were also warned to increase their trade and tax contribution under pain of eviction from Pondicherry. The Chhatrapati thus made efforts to make the new lands as profitable for the government as for the locals.

By this time, the Mughal-Bijapur war had changed complexion significantly. Smarting from his defeats at the hands of the Bijapuri Vizier Bahlol Khan, Subadar Bahadur Khan continued his efforts at Naldurg Fort. His men managed to corrupt the Bijapuri Fort Commander, who handed over the fort in return for a jagir. Following this success, the Mughals managed to conspire with the administrators of Gulbarga Fort. The Fort Commander was loyal to Bijapur, but was arrested nevertheless, due to betrayal by one of his men. Gulbarga too, fell to the Mughals. Bahadur Khan finally had something to write to the Emperor about. The south-eastern boundary of the Empire now touched the borders of the Qutubshahi Sultanate, close to Malkhed, the last Qutubshahi fort near the border, while the southern boundary was within striking distance of Bijapur.

But the Pathans had played their game as well. Bahlol Khan connived with Diler Khan, the Emperor's most trusted Pathani nobleman, and managed to turn Aurangzeb against Bahadur Khan. Aurangzeb, short-sighted and ever wary of conspiracy and rebellion, recalled Bahadur Khan to Agra, and stripped him of the Subadari of the Deccan. Diler Khan assumed charge in the Deccan Province temporarily.

Diler Khan was getting impatient to start a new campaign as he had to add to his achievements and boasts to the Emperor. Since an understanding had been reached with Bahlol Khan, the Mughal and Adilshahi forces now joined hands. Campaigning west against Shivaji's holdings would be difficult as both armies were exhausted, and the rains were still making life miserable in the Sahyadris. Besides, Bahlol was reluctant to lead his men into the mountains. Campaigning south against Shivaji Raje in Karnatak would be impractical as that would take them far south and expose their rear. Diler wracked his brains, and the more he thought the more his mind veered toward the east. He attempted to convince the Emperor to sanction a joint campaign with Bahlol Khan against the Qutubshah. Aurangzeb agreed, but being the tactician that he was, sent a large contingent of Rajputs under his Wazir, Asad Khan, to Ahmednagar, to safeguard against a Pathani dominance of the Deccan.

Masud, who headed the ousted Deccani faction of Bijapuri nobles, had been watching these developments closely. His onetime allies, the Mughals, had now become his foes; his arch-enemy Bahlol Khan, still held power in the capital, and he had insufficient men to launch an offensive himself. Yet he refused to give up on his ambition to usurp power in Bijapur. Bereft of other options, he offered to join the Qutubshah.

The combined Pathani forces of the Mughals under Diler, and the Bijapuris under Bahlol, marched east from Gulbarga toward Malkhed, some forty-two kos west of the capital, Bhaganagar. Diler wrote to the Qutubshah demanding both Shaikh Minhaj and Masud be handed over to him, along with a crore of rupees in ransom. Abul Hasan Qutubshah offered five hundred thousand. He simultaneously prepared for war and moved his troops toward Malkhed under his Commander-in-Chief, Muhammad Ibrahim.

The combined Mughal-Adilshahi forces took Malkhed Fort in a day and then pitched camp. From there, Bahlol moved east with five thousand Pathans to confront the Qutubshahi forces. But he had erred in his reconnaissance. Underestimating the enemy strength, he was gutted to be faced with some twenty-five thousand joint troops of the Qutubshah and the Deccanis, under Masud and Sharza Khan. A long and bloody battle ensued, in which Bahlol Khan was nearly routed. Seven hundred Pathans, among them several Captains, perished. Word was sent to the Malkhed camp, from where Diler rushed to rescue Bahlol from certain death.

The Qutubshah's forces retreated and pitched camp at Mangalgi, four kos north of Malkhed. From their respective camps, the rival armies engaged repeatedly over the next two months. The Qutubshah sent reinforcements under the command of Madanna's nephew, Yengana, and Shaikh Minhaj, the Deccani.

During one such engagement, the combined Mughal-Adilshahi forces pretended to retreat, permitting the Qutubshahi forces to pursue them, drawing them far from their camp. Then, through deceit, they outflanked the enemy and trapped them in an ambush, inflicting the worst defeat yet on the Qutubshah, who suffered heavy losses. It was only when succour reached them from Muhammad Ibrahim that they were rescued and could retreat to Mangalgi.

Following this reverse, Muhammad Ibrahim changed his tactics and outflanked the enemy camp at Malkhed, and penetrated deep into the Adilshahi. From there, he cut off the enemy supply lines, forcing the Mughal-Adilshahi army into serious hardship. But, in the process, the Qutubshahi camp at Mangalgi had been left unsecured. Diler Khan attacked the camp and looted it of all grain and provision, killing every man, woman and child.

Even after this disaster, the Qutubshahi forces regrouped and kept up the pressure on the combined forces, causing such a severe shortage of grain and provisions in the Mughal-Adilshahi camp that the soldiers began to starve. To make matters worse, Bahlol Khan was stricken with a mortal illness, and his retainers fled, abandoning him.

Diler Khan was at last forced to give up Malkhed, strike camp and begin the arduous journey back to Gulbarga. The enemy hemmed him on all sides, inflicting heavy losses, and looting his baggage. His men, starved and parched, were forced to stand guard night and day, surviving on seeds of toddy and date palms. For two days they were forced to seek shelter in a large ditch, devoid even of drinking water. The distance between Malkhed and Gulbarga, though merely twelve kos, took Diler's army twelve days to cover; the enemy disputing every step of the way. If Diler escaped alive, it was only because of the indomitable spirit of the Rajputs in the imperial army and their readiness to sacrifice life.

The war ceased temporarily, but Masud saw no end to his own problems. To get the Mughals out of the equation, he begged Abul Hasan Qutubshah to mediate between the three parties. The Qutubshah agreed, as he too was eager to end the war on his frontier. Diler, Bahlol, Masud and the Qutubshah finally met at Gulbarga and finalized a four-way peace treaty. According to the terms, a ceasefire was effected immediately. Bahlol Khan agreed to relinquish the

Vizier's post in favour of Masud, but retained the command of the Adilshah's army. Masud was to pay the Pathans six hundred thousand rupees as arrears of pay. As Masud himself did not have the money, he asked the Qutubshah to loan him the amount. Abul Hasan readily agreed.

The final point in the treaty was one which would hurt the Adilshahi royal family the most. Diler Khan made Masud agree to send Sikander's sister to the Mughal harem, as per the previous understanding with Bahadur Khan. In a war between the Regents, the Royal Princess turned out to be the biggest loser.

As the Chhatrapati resumed his journey north, moving away from Vyankoji's stronghold of Thanjavur, Vyankoji began conspiring with local chieftains of the Karnatak region. His aim was to form a united front against his brother and retake the territories he had lost. His plan did not succeed however, as most of the Chiefs, knowing Shivaji Maharaj's strength, preferred to remain aligned with the Maratha *Swarajya*. Vyankoji then assembled his own forces, mustering four thousand horse and ten thousand foot soldiers from his remaining holdings. With these, he marched to Valikandpuram, where, according to his sources, twelve thousand Marathas were stationed under the command of Hambirrao Mohite and Santaji Bhosale. Vyankoji's initial assault was brutal and Santaji was forced to retreat. But he regrouped with his Commander-in-Chief and returned at night to attack Vyankoji's camp. The Thanjavur forces were routed and scattered, their camp looted. Over a thousand fine horses and plenty of baggage fell to the Marathas.

The news of this attack was conveyed to the Chhatrapati, who was incensed by his half-brother's audacity. He wrote him a typically harsh letter, demanding submission: *Misguided by the Turks, you sent your army against my men, but were defeated. You should have realized that I am blessed by Lord Mahadev and Goddess Bhavani because I kill the wicked Turks. How could you hope to win against my men when you have Turks amongst your ranks? Now you must give up the remaining lands in your possession and instead, accept an estate granted by me. If you do not want that, I shall request the Qutubshah to grant you a suitable post and a jagir. Accept one of these options without being adamant!*

Vyankoji realized his mistake and hurriedly moved to conclude a treaty with the Chhatrapati. The treaty was duly inked and Santaji marched to Thanjavur to place the official seals. Vyankoji welcomed him with feasting. Vyankoji was allowed to retain Thanjavur and some other lands, in lieu of which he gladly paid three hundred thousand gold coins.

Following this treaty, Hambirrao withdrew his forces and joined the Chhatrapati in the long march back to Raigad. Raghunath Punt was left behind as Governor of the newly acquired territory in Karnatak. He soon raised a local force of ten thousand for the defence of the region. The Maratha forces spread out to campaign in the Hubli-Gadag-Bankapur region, levying contribution and annexing territory. The Hubli and Bankapur forts held out, however. But the Chhatrapati did not deem it wise to linger in the region any longer.

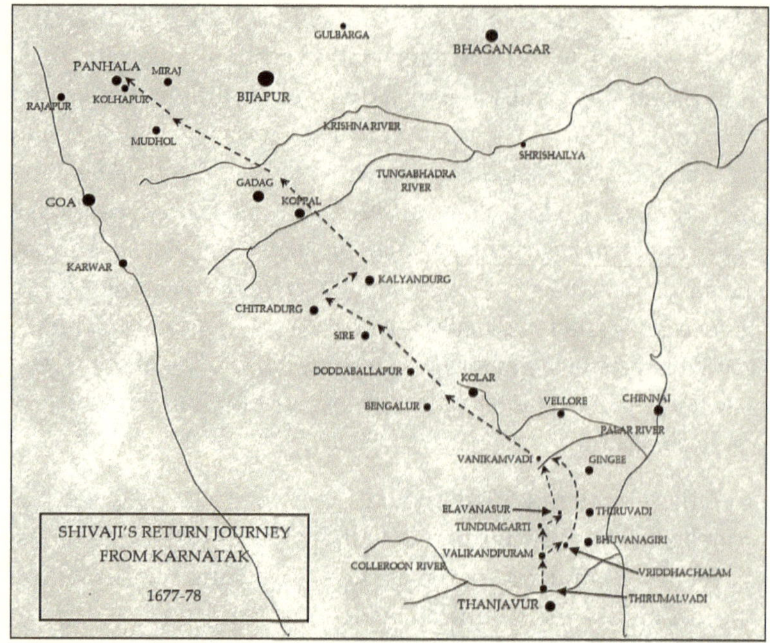

Meanwhile, Diler Khan withdrew to the north and Bahlol prepared to march back to Bijapur. However, he suffered a relapse of his illness and he died while still at Gulbarga. His deputy, Jamshed Khan, who held Bijapur in his absence, was uncertain what he should do and initially resisted Masud.

4

Plots and Counterplots

Jamshed Khan paced the chamber of his residence inside Bijapur's *Arkillah*[65], deep in thought. The recent developments were disturbing. His master, the Vizier Bahlol Khan, had failed in the campaign against the Deccanis, and died at Gulbarga. The news had reached him just a few days ago, followed by emissaries from Siddi Masud, who demanded that Jamshed hand over the command of Bijapur palace. Jamshed had a deep distrust of the Abyssinians and was reluctant to allow Masud into Bijapur. Though a large portion of the Pathan army was away with the ex-Vizier, he still had enough to defend the palace against Masud.

Jamshed turned to his Captain, Basheer Khan. "Masud desires to enter Bijapur and take over as Vizier. I do not trust him. He must first fulfil the terms of the treaty and pay our troops as agreed. Send him this message: *Pay up the money agreed in the treaty with Bahlol Khan before taking over the administration.*"

"Yes, my Lord!" Basheer left to organize the embassy.

Jamshed felt most uneasy. Above all, he was worried about his own future in Bijapur. Now, with Bahlol Khan dead and Masud's appointment as Vizier ratified by the Mughal

---

[65] The King's citadel within the main fortifications of the city or fort

Emperor and the Qutubshah, there was not much he could do. But he resolved to delay the inevitable till his own prospects were secured.

Some time later, a thought cropped up in his mind and he sent for his spy, Ahmed. The man entered the chamber silently and stood at attention, waiting for his instructions. Jamshed handed him a sealed scroll and said, "The Maratha King Seevaji is somewhere in Gadag district. Find him and deliver this to him personally. See that it reaches his hands."

"Yes, my Lord!" Ahmed took the scroll, bowed, and left.

Outskirts of Belavadi, February 1678

The Maratha force was camped half a kos from a small mud fort at a place called Belavadi, which lay on the way from Gadag to Panhala, where the Chhatrapati was headed. In his command tent, the Maratha King held a brief council with his officers.

"The fort is held by a woman called Mallawa, who is the widow of the local *Desai*[66]," Bahirji Naik informed his King. "We have sent her feelers, but she refuses to surrender the fort. It was her men that attacked our supply carts and looted them two days ago."

"Order her to return the goods her men seized from our supply line, along with a hefty compensation," the Chhatrapati said. "If she agrees to do so, we shall leave her in peace."

"My man did ask her to return our goods, but she flatly refused."

---

[66] Local Chieftain

The Chhatrapati clenched his fists in frustration. Taking the mud fort would be a matter of a prahar or two for his men, but he was loathe to storm a fort held by a woman. Besides, once the attack was launched, all or most of the defenders would be killed, which he was not ready for. The fort was relatively unimportant but he could not leave it unconquered. Above all, he could not allow the men who had looted his carts go unpunished. He hoped the Desai's widow would submit without a fight. He wished her no harm. "Allow her two days to think it over," he said to his Captains. "Send another embassy to warn her of the consequences."

Bahirji stayed put in the tent, looking intently at his Lord. The Chhatrapati realized his chief spy had something for his ears only. He excused his Captains, who bowed and left. When they were alone, Bahirji walked up close to his master and whispered, "We have received a communication from Bijapur." He retrieved the pouch he had concealed beneath his angarkha all this while, and handed it to the Chhatrapati.

The Chhatrapati read the letter and a faint smile appeared on his tired face. "It is from Jamshed Khan," he said. "He holds Bijapur citadel after Bahlol Khan's death and refuses to hand over command to Siddi Masud. He has offered us a chance to take over Bijapur if we pay him a handsome ransom and grant him a jagir."

Bahirji was stunned. "The Adilshahi Sultanate on a platter," he murmured.

The Chhatrapati laughed. "It is quite unlikely that we will be able to lay our hands on Bijapur that easily. Siddi Masud will doubtless march to Bijapur, and if he gets a whiff of this conspiracy, he will not concede without a battle. It will be a three-way mess between us, the Pathans and the Abyssinians!"

"Do we let it pass, then?"

"No. Let us ride to Bijapur immediately, with five thousand horse. We will have to be quick to reach the city before Masud hears anything. Let us see what happens then."

Masud was exasperated. He had just received the news that the Maratha King Seevaji had arrived near Bijapur with a large force.

"How did Seevaji get involved in this?" he demanded of his spy.

"My Lord, I have heard Jamshed Khan communicated with him," the man told him.

"May Allah curse the man!" Masud spat. "It is one thing to contest power within the Sultan's court, but how could he be so naïve as to invite the Marathas into this? Is he out of his mind?"

"My Lord, we must move fast. Our embassy has to reach Bijapur before Seevaji gets there." The man who spoke this was Masud's Brahman administrator, Vyankatadri.

"Vyankatadri, you are my best man for this mission," said Masud. "Make haste and ride to Bijapur. Drill some sense into Jamshed Khan's head. Offer him money, a jagir…anything! But make him agree to let me into the citadel."

"I shall do my best, my Lord." Vyankatadri pondered a while, then elaborated a bold plan to his master.

Vyankatadri left for Bijapur the next morning. After his departure, the news of Siddi Masud's ill-health arrived. The Abyssinian Commander was confined to his tent and was visited by his *hakims*[67]. Every day brought worrisome news that his condition was worsening. Finally, on the fourth day, a pall of gloom consumed the camp as Masud's quorchi announced his death. Sharza Khan, Masud's Lieutenant, took charge of Masud's force. He decided to send Masud's body, with a small escort, to Adoni for burial. Once the cortege was on its way, Sharza Khan left for Bijapur with the rest of the troops.

Bijapur citadel, a few days later

"I have received the sad news that Commander Siddi Masud is dead," Vyankatadri informed Jamshed Khan, acting Regent in Bijapur.

Jamshed Khan faked a look of surprise while he closely observed Vyankatadri's face. "Is that true? It is sad indeed." Jamshed had received the news from Ahmed, his spy, the previous night. Though disinclined to believe it initially, Ahmed had assured him it was true.

Vyankatadri made a bow. "Jamshed Khansahib, that makes you the Regent of the Adilshahi."

"It does, does it not?" Jamshed gently stroked his beard, deep in thought. The past few weeks had seen rapid political developments. His master, Regent Bahlol Khan, had died while campaigning in Gulbarga. Siddi Masud had successfully placed his claim to the Regentship, but had not paid the dues to the Pathani troops. And now he too, was dead. Though the road for Jamshed to take over as Vizier

---

[67] Physicians practising traditional medicine

was now wide open, the question of the soldiers' pending salary remained unanswered. He had no means to pay his troops.

Jamshed's quorchi entered the chamber to announce, "The Captain of the Guard is here."

The Captain entered, bowed and said, "My Lord, Sharza Khan has arrived at the eastern gate to the city."

"Does he come alone?" Jamshed asked.

"No, my Lord. He has over four thousand Abyssinian troops with him. He has requested to be let into the city."

Jamshed sat bolt upright. What was Sharza Khan up to? "Do not let him in, you hear me?" Jamshed said roughly. "What does he want anyway?"

"He says he wants to offer his services to Bijapur, since his own master is now dead."

"Tell him to go look for a job elsewhere. Does he think I am a fool to allow thousands of those black-skinned pigs into the city?"

Vyankatadri seized the moment to intervene. "Khansahib, it would do no harm to hear what he has to say. Soldiers are always useful to a Sultanate."

Jamshed considered this. Vyankatadri was right. He could at least hear out the Abyssinian. It was indeed true that he was seriously short of man-strength in the city. Besides, his own Pathani troops were disgruntled over non-payment of wages. Were they to revolt against him, he would have no other forces to fall back on. If the Abyssinians were willing to serve the Sultan honestly, they could help to balance power.

"Alright. Let only Sharza Khan inside. He should come alone, do you understand?"

"Yes, My Lord," The Captain bowed and left.

"Speak!" Jamshed ordered, when Sharza Khan stood before him.

Sharza bowed. "Khansahib, our master Commander Masud is dead and we, his soldiers and Captains, do not have employment. Two years ago, we were evicted from the city by the former Vizier, Bahlol Khan. Now we have come to ask the new Vizier to take us back."

"What assurance do I have of your loyalty?"

"My Lord, we have always served the Sultan loyally. It was only due to the differences between Bahlol Khan, Khawas Khan and Siddi Masud that we were distanced from Bijapur."

"Is Masud really dead?"

"I closed the casket containing his body with my own hands, and sent it to Adoni for burial."

Jamshed threw a glance at Vyankatadri to try and gauge what was on his mind. The Brahman, who had been staring at Sharza, now turned to Jamshed. "Khansahib, these are but Bijapur's own troops. Why should there be any doubts over their loyalty?"

"If I may be allowed to speak, my Lord?" the Captain of the Guard interjected. Jamshed nodded. "We are seriously short of men for guard duty on the ramparts. The men are already doing double shifts. With the Abyssinian troops added to our force, it will add to our strength while lifting the load from our men."

Jamshed gave the matter some more consideration. Finally convinced that the addition of Sharza Khan's contingent would strengthen his own position, he agreed. Following his approval, four thousand Abyssinians entered the city and a fourth of these were then let into the citadel.

The new moon night was dark and still. Every man, woman and child was asleep by the second *prahar*. The streets were abandoned. Not a soul stirred… or so it seemed. A few hundred dark-skinned men crept unseen and unheard, toward Jamshed Khan's residence. The man in the lead gave silent instructions and his men split into groups that went in different directions, surrounding the mansion.

Sharza Khan led the assault force toward the main gates to the mansion. Once they were within firing range, they could see in the dim glow of the torches, the guards on night duty on the ramparts. Sharza Khan instructed his archers to take position. The men did so, and at Sharza's signal, released their arrows. Two Pathani guards dropped dead, clutching their throats. A minor commotion could be heard inside the walls. Several Pathans rushed up the ramparts with torches to try and see who had attacked, but were greeted with more shafts. As more Pathans fell, guards from the other ramparts rushed to the gate. In the confusion, no one noticed a group of Abyssinians place ladders against the rampart walls and rapidly climb up. Meanwhile, Sharza Khan's group kept up the firing on the gate. In short order, over fifty Abyssinians had scaled the rampart, entered the courtyard and launched an attack on the gate from within.

Inside the mansion, all hell had broken loose as the rest of the garrison was alerted and word sent to Jamshed Khan's chamber. Jamshed peered out and quickly assessed the situation. In the light of the torches he could see his Pathans skirmishing with the Abyssinians. For a brief moment, he could not believe his eyes. Had that scum Sharza Khan betrayed him?

Jamshed wasted no time in arming himself and rushing out. He rallied his guards, gave rapid instructions and then hurled himself into the fight. The Pathans put up a stiff resistance, but were short of numbers. The Abyssinians overwhelmed them. The gate was opened and Sharza Khan's entire force entered the mansion. Before the other Pathani units in the citadel could be alerted, the guards had been overcome and Jamshed himself arrested.

Jamshed stood with his hands shackled behind his back. Four Abyssinians stood guard over him with naked blades. He saw a man approach. In the darkness he could not see the man's face. "The stupid game you were playing with the Marathas is over, Jamshed!" the man said in harsh tones. "Now hand over command of the citadel to me."

One of the guards brought forth a torch and held it up so the men could see each other. Jamshed was shocked to see who had addressed him in such a high-handed fashion. "Masud? I was told you were dead!"

"And you believed it?" Masud asked spitefully. "How can an idiot like you be Regent of the Adilshahi? Jamshed, do not be a fool. The Gulbarga treaty was signed by your master Bahlol Khan, who agreed to relinquish the Vizier's post to me. Abide by Bahlol's word and I shall spare your life. If you do not, you will be dead before you see another sunrise."

Jamshed remained silent, his head hung in defeat. He knew he had been done in.

The night passed without further event and the trio of Siddi Masud, Jamshed Khan and Vyankatadri sat down for discussions the next morning. As it turned out, things worked out in Masud's favour. With his great diplomatic skills, Vyankatadri made Jamshed see the folly of inviting the Maratha King to Bijapur. Masud offered to pay the Pathans part of their pending dues. Jamshed finally agreed to disband his troops garrisoning the citadel and hand over command to Masud's officers.

Masud wasted no time in installing himself as the new Vizier. Realizing the pitiful condition of the royal family, he removed the Pathan guards from the palaces and gave the boy Sultan and his mother some space to breathe.

When he was informed of this development, the Chhatrapati returned to Belavadi with his men.

Over three weeks had been wasted in this drama. The Belavadi Fort was still unconquered since the Chhatrapati had left no instructions to attack in his absence. Frustrated that the ploy with Jamshed had failed, the Chhatrapati ordered his forces to attack. "Do not kill the woman if you can avoid it," he told his Captains Hiroji and Sakhuji as they left to organize the charge.

The Marathas stormed the small fort. The Chhatrapati had expected results in a short time, but was surprised when the fort remained unconquered for almost a day after the attack commenced. The widow led her men into battle and held her ground. Ultimately though, the superior Maratha force won through and the lady and her family were taken captive.

Hiroji returned to the King's tent the next day. "The fort is our's, Your Highness. The Desai woman has been arrested." But even as he said this, Hiroji stood with his head hung.

"Why is there no smile on your face when you come with news of victory?"

"Sire, one of our men has transgressed." Hiroji hesitated. This was the second time during the campaign that he had been required to inform his King about misbehaviour by one of their men.

"What is it, Hiroji?"

"Sire, Sakhuji misbehaved with the Desai woman after her arrest."

The Chhatrapati's face became grim. Controlling a large military force on a campaign was no mean task. Yet his discipline was so strict that rarely did any of his men molest women.

"Sakhuji was always prone to such acts. He must be punished. Bring him here."

Within moments, Sakhuji was escorted into the Chhatrapati's tent. "Why Sakhuji?" The Chhatrapati's tone was almost pleading. He was always deeply disturbed when he received such news.

Sakhuji stared at the ground, saying nothing. He had thought that being a Captain, he would be let off with only a warning. Suddenly he burst forth, "That bitch caused us so much trouble!" Sakhuji glared back angrily at his Lord. "She should have been publicly..."

"Sakhuji!" The Chhatrapati's voice sent a shiver down every spine. He rose and walked up to his Captain, locking his blazing eyes upon him. "How dare you utter such words in front of your King! Do you think you are serving one of the Sultans? You stand in front of Shivaji, the Maratha Chhatrapati. If any of my men misbehave with women, I shall have to answer to my mother Jijabai in heaven!"

Cowed now, Sakhuji began to tremble. "Forgive me, Sire…" he managed to mutter.

"Forgive you? If I forgive you today, I shall have to deal with ten other Captains like you tomorrow." The Chhatrapati turned his back and ordered, "Take him away and put out his eyes with red hot irons. He will never set eyes upon a woman again."

Sakhuji screamed for mercy as he was dragged away to his fate.

Masud took over the Bijapur administration as Vizier and Regent. His first job was to force Jamshed to remove all Pathan regiments from the Bijapur fort to the suburbs. Once the fort, and more importantly, the Arkillah, was secured by Masud's Abyssinian troops, he systematically removed important government officers, diplomats and clerks loyal to the Pathans and replaced them with his own men.

By now, the Pathan troops in the suburbs were getting restless. They demanded their full arrears which Masud had been unable to pay, as the Qutubshah had defaulted on the promise made at Gulbarga. This angered the Pathans so much that they broke out in a full-scale mutiny. They harassed the common people of the Bijapur suburbs and raided the houses of Bahlol Khan and Jamshed's relatives, carrying away whatever they could. Hurling abuse at Bahlol's widow and sons, they even tore ornaments from the persons of the ladies of the harem. The Bijapur suburbs were bathed in blood as a free fight ensued. Masud utterly failed to control the rioting. He remained helplessly inside his house, behind locked doors. Finally, in desperation, he appealed to Shivaji Raje, exhorting him as a former subject of the Adilshahi, to help Bijapur. The Chhatrapati agreed to send a force to control the mutiny.

But Diler Khan had other designs. Though he had gone north, he was constantly in touch with Malik Barkhurdar, who had stayed back in Bijapur as the Emperor's official agent. Malik informed him of the latest developments. Diler declared that communication with Seevaji was a breach of the Gulbarga treaty by Masud. He wrote to the Emperor about this and asked for permission to invade Bijapur. The Emperor was inclined to agree since he too, had received news that with the Pathani troops disbanded and the Deccanis divided, Bijapur was vulnerable.

Diler began actively corrupting Bijapuri officers through Malik Barkhurdar. A large number of the disbanded Pathani troops thus enlisted in Mughal ranks. This accomplished, Diler moved his camp from Pedgaon to Akluj, some fifty kos north-west of Bijapur.

Panhala Fort, May 1678

The Chhatrapati had returned to his dominions and called his first Council after returning to the Swarajya. He had been away for over a year and wanted updates from his Ministers regarding the state of affairs in his kingdom. The Sachiv, Anaji Punt, was present, as was Dattaji Trimbak,

Governor of the Panhala region, and Raoji Somnath, who had served as Governor of Raigad in the King's absence. To the Chhatrapati's left, Moro Punt and Hambirrao occupied their customary positions as Mukhya Pradhan and Senapati. To his right, in a pensive mood, sat Yuvraj Sambhaji.

"Your Highness, we congratulate you on the success of the southern campaign," Moro Punt began. "Our Swarajya has extended so far south as was unimaginable a few years ago."

"Every man on campaign with me deserves to be congratulated, Punt. The Chhatrapati alone cannot accomplish much. He is fortunate to have so many good men serve him. Tell me, how has our Swarajya been while I was away?"

"Sire, the boundaries of our Swarajya have remained secure this past year and a half that you have been away on campaign. The government has been functioning smoothly. Our Commanders and Ministers have done a commendable job."

The Chhatrapati nodded in satisfaction. "Has the crop been up to expectations?"

"Much more, Sire!" Moro Punt beamed happily. "These past few years our lands have seen peace, like never before. The populace works hard and cultivates gold!"

"Tax collections, Sachiv?" The Chhatrapati turned to Anaji Punt.

"Collection has been good Sire, barring a few provinces." Anaji Punt threw a sideways glance at the Yuvraj.

The Chhatrapati noticed this and enquired, "Which provinces have performed below par?"

"Well, Shringarpur, for one," Anaji Punt said matter-of-factly.

Sambhaji glared at him. "Perhaps the Sachiv might tell the Chhatrapati how he and other Ministers harass the people for money!"

The Ministers shifted uneasily. Another confrontation with the Yuvraj seemed imminent. Perhaps it would be better for them all if he stayed away from council meetings, they thought.

"If we do not collect taxes, how do we pay the government employees and our vast army? The Yuvraj perhaps has an alternative means?" The irony of Anaji Punt's words was lost on no one. The verbals duels between the Punt and the Yuvraj were legendary.

"We campaign long enough in Mughal and Adilshahi lands, Sachiv! The booty collected should suffice to pay the army." Sambhaji's voice rose. "Maybe the Ministers should reconsider some of their extravagant expenses."

"The returns from our annual campaigns are not enough, Yuvraj!" Anaji Punt was determined to take this argument to conclusion once and for all. "Besides, a prosperous kingdom generates its own revenues from its own lands. We should not have to rely upon campaigning for revenue."

"Enough, you two!" The Chhatrapati raised his hand, silencing them. "We must all try to understand each other's view point. While it is true that we need money to run the kingdom and support our armed forces, it is also true that if our methods are making people pay taxes beyond their means, there must be something fundamentally wrong with our calculations."

"Calculations!" Sambhaji scoffed. "If only our Ministers and officers would do their jobs!"

"The Yuvraj might want to discuss his recent failures on campaign." Moro Punt now joined the war of words. "He did suffer defeat at the hands of the Portuguese near Goa, did he not? Far from bringing in booty, it was a drain on our resources."

"And what about your colossal failure at Janjira?" Sambhaji fired back. "How many months did you spend there? How much money did you waste and how much did you bring back, Mukhya Pradhan?"

Moro Punt was not used to receiving such flak in front of the Council. His lined face turned to stone. "If criticism is the only thing the Yuvraj brings to the Council meeting, it makes no sense for us to be here," he said.

"Yuvraj Sambhaji is a good soldier," Hambirrao spoke for the first time. "He is young and inexperienced, but he will learn with the years." The Commander-in-Chief thus supported the Crown Prince. Sambhaji looked at him with a fleeting expression of gratitude, while the Ministers were only exasperated.

The Chhatrapati realized that relations between Sambhaji and the Ministers were going from bad to worse. This did not bode well for the future of the Swarajya. He knew his son well. Sambhaji was a fierce soldier, utterly devoted to God and country; but he was also short-tempered and impulsive. There was no telling what he would do in a fit of rage. People who behaved thus, could harm themselves at times. Prataprao Gujar had been the most glaring example of late. Sambhaji needed calm, wise and level-headed administrators around him at all times; but if he could not get along with them, it would not help him much. As for himself, he had practically built this Council from scratch, selecting each man on merit. Every Council Member had their shortcomings, but it was for the King to guide and bind them into one superbly functioning government unit. He had done that, but could Shambhu?

The council meeting ended with the Chhatrapati failing to make peace between the Ministers and the Yuvraj.

Later that evening, the Chhatrapati sat alone in his chamber, awaiting his son, whom he had sent for earlier. Shambhu's behaviour was becoming a cause of deep worry for him. At this stage of his life, he needed the comfort of knowing he had a wise and capable son to rule the kingdom after him. His recent spiritual experience at Shrishailya had made him feel that his end was near. He could hear his Lord calling out to him, and felt an indescribable urge to offer his life to him. But how could he if the future of his Swarajya was not secure?

The door opened and Sambhaji entered. He quietly walked up to his father, knelt before him and placed his head on the Chhatrapati's feet.

"Bless me, Father, so I may prove worthy of you."

"Get up Shambhu." Shivaji Raje raised his son by the shoulders. "Come, sit beside me." He nodded to Mahadu, his quorchi, to leave the chamber. Father and son were left alone. "How have you been these past eighteen months? How was your stay at Shringarpur?" he asked.

"It was a good experience Father, though I can't say I was happy."

"And why is that?"

"I could not help but feel that you had ignored me while planning the Gingee campaign. Neither was I allowed to accompany you to the South, nor was I given a post of responsibility in the Swarajya while you were away."

"You were Governor of a district. You do not feel that is a responsible job?"

"It is, but the Crown Prince deserves more. I was expecting to be made Master of Raigad in your absence. Father, how will I ever prove myself if you won't trust me? Unless…"

The Chhatrapati looked at him questioningly. "Unless what?"

"Unless, you plan to offer the throne to Rajaram instead of me."

"Shambhu, *you* are the Crown Prince. Rajaram is but a child. Why would I want to give the throne to him?"

"How can I say? Maybe the Queen wants to sideline me in favour of her son?"

The Chhatrapati fell silent. Ever rising discord between Sambhaji and Soyarabai was another cause for worry. What he feared the most was bloodletting between brothers for the throne. It was no secret that Soyarabai would favour Rajaram over Shambhu. But the final decision about his successor lay with him, not the Queen.

"Shambhu, believe me, you are my choice as successor. But even a legal heir must prove himself worthy of the throne before his people, his nobles and his Ministers. If you cannot prove yourself as a capable King, how will they ever accept you?"

"The Ministers are a joke! If I had my way I would throw all of them from the fort ramparts!"

"Shambhu, be sensible. You cannot run a government without Staff, Officers and Ministers. The King's job is to safeguard the kingdom and add to its territory."

"Yes, but we need more capable people in office."

"Like who? Like that Kannauji poet you hang out with? You think he is more capable than my Ministers?"

"Kalash is like a brother to me. Sometimes I feel he is my only support."

"I hear that you have been interacting with *tantriks*[68] from Shringarpur. I was told you have participated in gory rituals with them. What is this new craziness?"

Sambhaji remained silent.

"Remember Shambhu, choosing the right people to surround you will always be the most difficult and most important decision you will ever make. If you chose the wrong people, expect only your own ruin."

"Father, I just want to know who you plan to name as the next Chhatrapati. Will it be Rajaram or me?"

"The more worthy son shall take the throne, Shambhu. But if that is not agreeable to all, I may also propose a division of the Swarajya into two parts. The part in Maharashtra shall go to Rajaram, and the newly captured territory in the South shall go to you. Though it would grieve me to divide what we have created with our blood, I can accept this division as long as my sons rule in both places."

---

[68] Followers of Tantra, works teaching magical and mystical formularies

Shambhu looked up, his eyes glittering. "The settled estates in Maharashtra go to Rajaram, and the unsettled, potentially strife-torn new territory to me? Father, why this injustice?"

The Chhatrapati felt exasperated. Sambhaji simply could not see his point. "Rajaram is not capable yet of handling a newly captured territory and creating a stable government there. To place him in the Gingee province would be to rely upon a Regent, and to accept the associated risks. Here in Maharashtra, we have a stable government and Rajaram will have enough time to take over himself."

The Chhatrapati's words jolted Sambhaji. "Why do you say this, Father?" he asked, his heart pounding as he realized the significance of his father's words. "Why will Rajaram need a Regent to rule? You will live long and rule as King till you are old. Rajaram will be a grown man when it is time for you to go. I do not want anything. I will be happy to eat rice and milk and be your servant! Please do not talk about leaving us so soon!" Tears filled Shambhu's eyes.

"My life draws to its end every day, Shambhu. If you want to see me go in peace, mend your ways. Keep those tantriks away from yourself. Learn as much as you can about administration from our Council. Learn about military campaigns from Hambirrao. Make our people your allies, not your foes. You cannot fight the Council and win."

Sambhaji was silent.

"I have decided that you shall go to Parali Fort. Try to imbibe some wisdom from His Holiness, Shri Samarth Ramdas Swami, who lives there." Ramdas Swami, an ascetic, was the Chhatrapati's *guru*[69]. In all his life the Chhatrapati had not known a more realized man. He felt his son would benefit from spending some time with the guru. Besides, it would distance him from his irresponsible advisors at Shringarpur.

Shambhu, however, was flustered by this new order. *What more needs be done to distance me from Raigad,* he thought. He was now convinced that his step-mother Soyarabai had connived with the Ministers, to influence his father into giving the throne to his half-brother Rajaram. He lingered for some time but could not think of anything else to say to his father. Finally, he bowed and left.

As the Chhatrapati watched him close the door, he thought of Saee. She would have known how to handle their son. *What am I going to do with him, Saee?*

Late July 1678

For over a year the Vellore Fort had been besieged by Maratha forces. The Adilshahi Fort Commander, Abdullah Khan, stoically defended the fort with the garrison at his disposal, hoping against hope that he would receive succour from Bijapur. The help did come, but alas too late. Disease struck the fort garrison and men died by the hundreds, reducing their number from two thousand three hundred to a mere three hundred men.

The relieving force from the Adilshah was chased away by the Marathas under the ever reliable Captain, Santaji. At last, with no hope of survival, Abdullah Khan decided to negotiate for peace. He agreed to hand over the fort for a sum of thirty thousand hons and the grant of a small estate

---

[69] Knowledge and spiritual guide

for subsistence. The Maratha Commander agreed, and Vellore Fort with its attached territory was annexed to the Maratha Swarajya.

Meanwhile, Masud's troubles in Bijapur continued unabated. With the Mughals drawing the Pathans away, the mutiny had died down, but a large Maratha force had meanwhile landed in the suburbs around the capital city. Masud watched helplessly as one danger was replaced by another, the latest being his own doing. The Maratha Commander demanded control of one of the city gates, which Masud naturally declined. A few days later, the Marathas tried to smuggle men and arms into the city, but the attempt was thwarted by the alert city guard. Masud could never really trust the Marathas, especially after the attempt by the Maratha King to buy out Jamshed Khan and take control of the city. Now, after this latest failed attempt to enter the city by deceit, Masud was convinced Seevaji Raja planned to take the city from him. There was thus an open rupture between Masud and the Marathas.

The Maratha Commander ordered the plunder of Bijapuri territory and his men ravaged Daulatpur, Khusraupur and Zuhrapur suburbs. Once again, Masud watched mutely from inside the city walls while his people suffered. Finally, he wrote to Diler Khan, requesting him to send a Mughal force to drive away the Marathas.

Diler Khan promptly sent a force which was duly welcomed by Masud, who despatched Vyankatadri and some other officers to the Mughal camp. The two forces joined hands to oust the Marathas. Plenty of firing ensued between the joint forces and the Marathas. In one such bombardment, the Maratha Commander was killed and the Maratha army was forced to retreat. However, the Chhatrapati himself soon arrived in Sangole with eight thousand troopers, some fifty kos north-west of Bijapur. The bear had been replaced by the lion.

To add to Masud's woes, there was a rift between him and Sharza Khan, one of his Lieutnants. Hearing of Seevaji's arrival at Sangole, Masud ordered Sharza to march forth with Diler Khan and Vyankatadri, but Sharza refused to comply. Instead, he combined forces with Abdullah Khan, the ex-Commander of Vellore Fort, to cause more trouble for the beleaguered Bijapuri Vizier. Abdullah, under Sharza's influence, refused to hand over to Masud the money he had received from the Marathas.

Masud was now in an impossible situation. Both Diler Khan and Seevaji were at his doorstep, threatening to strike at the city, while his own Captains schemed against him. Within the ramparts, he was left with only eight thousand men to defend the citadel. Even these were harassing him for wages, which he could not pay. All his efforts to re-establish Abyssinian supremacy at the Bijapur court had come to nought. Disorder and anarchy prevailed within and outside the city walls. Masud endlessly threatened Sharza Khan's faction with dire consequences, while Sharza and his men, in turn, sat armed and ready for battle.

Through Vyankatadri's diplomacy, Masud convinced Diler Khan to join with his men to subdue Sharza Khan. He sent his son with five thousand men to the Mughal camp. But Sharza remained one step ahead of the Vizier. He offered to join Mughal service and enlist his entire force under Diler's command. The result was that some ten thousand Bijapuri soldiers, including Sharza and other Captains, joined Diler Khan. Masud was thus left in deeper waters, with hardly three thousand men at his command in the city, and his son in the Mughal camp.

To diffuse the tension between himself and the Mughals, Masud decided to honour the Gulbarga treaty and send Sikander's sister to the Mughal camp.

5

The Scion Falters

The Vizier's Mansion, Bijapur Citadel

The middle-aged nurse stood in front of Vizier Siddi Masud, with head lowered in abject servitude. He looked at her closely and realized she was his only hope to patch up a peace with Diler Khan. She was the only person who could convince Princess Shahr Banu to depart for the Mughal harem. He could of course send her using force, but that would have gone down badly, both with the palace servants and the Bijapuri people. And if the latter revolted in anger, he would not be able to control them with the paltry, disgruntled forces at his disposal. He needed the Princess to go willingly.

Shahr Banu was a mere girl of sixteen, but had displayed a wisdom and maturity far beyond her years in understanding political matters and managing palace affairs. Not only did the palace staff love and obey her, but the old servants of the State too, stood by her side. The people of Bijapur also held her in reverence as a beloved idol from the royal family. Masud feared this public favour. He knew he could never really be in control within the citadel as long as Shahr Banu was around as she held too much control over the hearts of the people. He would much prefer her to be away in the Mughal harem in Agra.

Masud chose his words carefully. "Taush-Ma, I am relying upon you to help me. If you convince the Princess to go to Agra, I shall reward you handsomely,"

"I will try Grand Vizier, but know this, the Princess has been quite distressed since she heard the terms of the treaty. She has repeatedly said she will not leave her brother alone in the hands of a Regent."

Masud cursed, clenching his fists. "Then you must convince her to," he stated coldly.

Taush-Ma raised her eyes from the ground to look at Masud. The Vizier's blazing eyes were fixed on hers. In his hands, he held a naked blade and slowly ran his thumb over its edge as he spoke. Taush-Ma realized she would die unless she did the Viziers' will. "Certainly, my Lord," she said, bowing.

Exiting the Vizier's house, she walked straight to the royal palace and headed up the stairs to the zenana.

Royal Palace, Bijapur Citadel

Once she reached the zenana, Taush-Ma sought out the Princess, who was immersed in reading a Persian manuscript. "Your Highness has been reading for some time," she said.

Shahr Banu raised her beautiful face from the book. Taush-Ma felt a pang of guilt and sadness at the thought of this delicate girl alone in the Mughal harems, thousands of kos from home. Tears welled in her eyes, but she forced them back firmly.

"And where have you been?" the Princess asked. "I haven't seen you in a while."

"I…I was just outside, my Lady," Taush-Ma stammered. She did not want her to know of her meeting with the Vizier. "I met that soldier friend of mine…" she said, smiling coyly.

"No wonder you were nowhere to be seen!" It was no secret that the harem attendants had male visitors late at night. The Princess was irritated that her nurse had been spending time with her male friend during the day.

"He told me something that Her Highness must hear," Taush-Ma continued.

"I have no wish to listen to your silly talk with your lovers!" Shahr Banu snapped.

"It is important, my Lady. My friend told me that many thousands of our troops have joined the Mughals and plan to attack the city soon. The Vizier has very few men in the citadel. My friend says they will not be able to withstand the attack. I fear what may happen if the Mughals enter the palace!" Her face displayed horror as she slapped her hands to her ample bosom for effect.

Shahr Banu was quiet for a while, her face lined with worry. "Is that true?" she asked. "I never thought it would come to this. I must have a word with the Vizier."

"I am told the Vizier's political moves have failed. Now only one thing can save Bijapur."

"And what is that?"

"Her Highness must agree to go to the Mughal harem as per the treaty between Bijapur and the Emperor."

"No! Never! I will never leave my brother at the mercy of these Abyssinians!"

Taush-Ma sighed. "Alas! Then the days of the Adilshahi royal family are numbered. Diler Khan's Pathani hordes will enter the city, looting, pillaging and raping their way to the royal palace, and then kill every member of the royal household, including us maids. Poor Sikander Padishah! He will not last a moment before their swords…"

"Enough, woman!" Shahr Banu's voice rose. "Do not utter such inauspicious words. I will never allow anything to harm my brother as long as I live."

Taush-Ma walked up to the Princess, whose eyes glittered with tears. "Then, my Lady, you must agree to abide by the Gulbarga treaty and prepare to go to the Mughal harem. That is the only way to stop the Mughals from attacking us."

A few days later, the staff of the royal palace watched teary-eyed as Shahr Banu, Princess of Bijapur, seated herself in a fabulously caparisoned palanquin. Before she drew the curtain, she threw one last forlorn look at the palace that had been her home for sixteen years. Swallowing her grief, she lifted her chin and gave the order to move. The palanquins were raised to the noise of wailing from the ladies of the zenana. The royal procession moved out of the palace grounds, never to return.

Shahr Banu was wary about the treatment she would receive in the Mughal harem. The Sunni Mughals looked down upon the Shia Muslims of the Deccani Sultanates, calling them heretics. Thus, she expected a hostile reception. But what she was more worried about was the fate of her brother, the little Sultan Sikander, whom she had supported ever since their father's death. The Queen Mother was a weakling and could not stand up for the royal family. With Shahr Banu gone, Sikander was practically at the mercy of the Regent.

As the procession moved slowly towards the north gate of the city, the people of Bijapur lined the streets to have one last look at their beloved Princess. There was much wailing among the people too, as they watched her entourage disappear beyond the city walls forever.

Raigad, 14 December 1678

Bahirji Naik strode rapidly toward the Raigad palace. Following him were Hiroji Farzand and Suryaji Malusare. The three men wore tense looks, in keeping with the grim nature of the news they had to give their King. It was late evening and the Chhatrapati had just retired to his chamber after a busy day. They reached the King's chamber, only to be accosted by his quorchi.

"The Lord is resting, Captains. I beg you not to disturb him at this hour," Mahadu said.

"This is urgent, Mahadu!" Bahirji hissed at him. "Wake his Highness now!"

"But Captain…" Mahadu protested, as he always did when people came at odd hours, insisting on disturbing the King.

"Not this time, Mahadu!" Bahirji was in no mood to be stopped outside the chamber. "This is most urgent. Wake the King!"

Mahadu deliberately took his time to size up Bahirji, then he entered the King's chamber to announce the visitors. The Chhatrapati was not asleep yet and opened his eyes as soon as Mahadu walked up to his bed. "What is it, Mahadu?" he asked.

"Bahirji Naik and the other Captains wish to see you. I tried to stop them, but they say it is urgent." Mahadu fervently hoped the King would order the Captains to go away.

The Chhatrapati laughed. "Let them in, Mahadu. They would not disturb me at this hour unless it really was urgent."

Reluctantly, Mahadu retraced his steps to let the Captains in. Bahirji and the others hurried up to the Chhatrapati, bowed and stood before him, worry writ large on their faces.

"Apologies Sire, but this could not wait," said Bahirji.

"What is it, Bahirji?"

"Sire, the Prince…"

The Chhatrapati sat bolt upright. What had happened now? A thousand worries raised their heads at once. "Is Shambhu alright?"

Bahirji looked at Hiroji for courage. The news he had would certainly shatter the King.

"Bahirji, speak up! What has happened?" the Chhatrapati's voice rose.

"The Prince left Parali Fort yesterday with a few of his close aides and rode to Diler Khan's camp at Pedgaon."

The Chhatrapati was on his feet. "He did…*what*?"

"He has entered Diler Khan's camp, Sire. I am afraid the Prince has joined the Mughals!"

"Impossible! Shambhu may be guilty of a thousand indiscretions, but he would never join our enemy!"

"I am sorry, Highness, but he has," Bahirji said gently, his usually impassive face lined and grave.

"Is this news reliable?" The Chhatrapati knew the answer. Bahirji would never feed him unreliable intelligence.

"It is, Sire."

The Chhatrapati flopped down on a divan and cradled his head between his hands. "What have you done, Shambhu?" he wailed. "How could you join the Mughals when your own father sheds his blood to fight them?"

His men were upset to see their King in such despair. Hiroji moved forward and knelt before him. "Do not worry, Sire. We will bring him back."

"What have I done to deserve this, Hiroji?" The Chhatrapati lamented. "My son…a traitor!"

Bahirji spoke up. "Sire, Shambhu Raje is misguided. That Kannauji poet and those tantriks around him constantly fill his ears with nonsense."

Maharaj looked up, tears in his eyes. His pained expression tore at the hearts of his men. The only time they had seen him weep was when his wife, and then his mother Jijabai, died.

"Make contact with Shambhu, Bahirji. Bring him back, even if you have to bind him like a prisoner to do so."

"I will put my best men on the job, Sire. I vow to you I will bring him back."

Sambhaji's defection to the Mughals hit the Chhatrapati harder than anything else he had endured in his entire life.

The King berated himself endlessly for his own failures as a father. His long absences from home, away on campaigns, meant that Shambhu had practically grown up without a parent. Following the demise of his grandmother, there had been no authoritative influence during Shambhu's crucial growing years. Soyara had been obsessed with Rajaram ever since his birth, and had defaulted in her duties as step-mother. In any case, Soyara had never been enamoured of Shambhu. Putala had played her part and cared for Shambhu, but she could never assert herself over Shambhu's overpowering personality.

Initial anger at his son's betrayal soon dissipated as fears for his life took over. The Mughals were untrustworthy and Aurangzeb a despot. With the Maratha Prince in his custody, there was no telling what he would do with him. Besides, with Shambhu in the Mughal camp and Rajaram still a little boy, the Maratha Swarajya had no able heir. Should he die under such circumstances, the Swarajya itself would be in peril.

The Chhatrapati knew he had to shake himself out of this gloom. He had to bring Shambhu back.

Mughal military camp, Pedgaon

Diler Khan looked at Sambhaji's pensive face as the two sat in his command tent. The Maratha Prince had spoken little since joining the Mughal camp and seemed unsure of his own motives. Diler did not trust him one bit. He had to keep a close watch on Sambhaji to make sure he would not escape. The Emperor would reward him handsomely for Seeva's son.

A few days ago, a messenger had arrived from Sambhaji. "The Prince is riding hard toward your camp," the man had said. "He is being pursued by his father's men. He wishes to join Mughal service and requests your help."

Diler Khan had been astonished, and initially doubted the authenticity of the message. Suspecting a trap, he had sent Ikhlas Khan with an advance guard of three thousand troopers and himself followed with five thousand more at a distance. They had intercepted Sambhaji's party a few kos from camp and successfully chased away the Maratha troopers pursuing him. Ikhlas Khan had then escorted Sambhaji back to the Mughal camp.

Diler silently congratulated himself for having successfully enticed Sambhaji into Mughal service. With the Prince gone, Seeva would, for sure, be crippled, he thought.

"What does the Prince ponder?" he asked.

Sambhaji, who had been lost in his own thoughts, suddenly jerked to attention. "I was wondering if the Emperor will accept my plea for service."

"He will, Prince. Your capability as a soldier is well known to him. Besides, I have recommended you. The ever so merciful Alamgir will accept you into his fold with a suitable rank."

Sambhaji was restless. He rose from his seat and began pacing inside the tent.

"What bothers you?" Diler asked at last.

"It has been a few days since I came here and all I have done is attend meetings with you and your Captains. I am eager for action. My hands are itching to wield my sword."

"And you shall Prince, very soon. We will begin planning our next campaign."

Sambhaji was glad he would be doing something worthwhile for a change. "What is to be our target? I think we should move against Siddi Masud. I hear he is seriously compromised at the moment. Let us storm Bijapur and capture the city!"

"The campaign against Bijapur can wait for the moment," Diler said. Then, gently stroking his beard and watching Sambhaji's face closely, he added, "We march on Fort Bhupalgad."

Sambhaji was startled by that. Fort Bhupalgad was in his father's dominions, some sixty-five kos south of their current position. He realized immediately that Diler Khan wanted to test his integrity by taking him into battle against his own father. He had known of course, that if he was to be in Mughal service, he would have to eventually pick up arms against his father. He could not avoid it. The thought burned a hole in his heart and he began questioning his own decision to defect.

Diler Khan rose and walked up to him. "Are you up to fighting your father, Prince?"

Sambhaji gritted his teeth. "When do we leave for Bhupalgad?"

Bhupalgad Fort, 3 April 1679

The fort of Bhupalgad was one of the easternmost outposts of the Maratha Swarajya. Diler Khan's choice of Bhupalgad was not random by any means. Besides pitching Sambhaji against his own father to test his resolve, Diler Khan was after the large hoard of grain, provisions and money stored in the fort. Bhupalgad was a crucial link in the supply chain for the armies of the Swarajya and by taking the fort, Diler

Khan planned to strengthen his own supplies and weaken the Marathas.

The fort was located on a broad spur extending south from the hills, with a practically unscalable, precipitous drop into the valley on the north, east and south-east. On the west and south-west however, the rise to the fort was easier to climb. Besides this part of the fort was commanded by hills to the west that were a mere quarter kos away. Diler Khan had ordered his troops to invest the fort, and chosen the south-western side to launch a concentrated offensive. He had some large cannon hauled to the top of a hill and began bombarding the western rampart. Meanwhile, his men cut off supply lines from the plains to the south.

The fort's Maratha Commander was Firangoji Narsala, the tough stubborn soldier who had, two decades before, defended the fort of Chakan against Shaista Khan's massive forces for over two months. Diler Khan knew the story and realized it would be tough to take the fort from Firangoji. The siege and attack had been on for two weeks now and Firangoji showed no sign of blinking. Then at last the Mughals had had some luck. Their shelling demolished a tower on the south-western side and the time was ripe for a final assault. Diler decided to put the Maratha Fort Commander in a spot by placing Sambhaji at the head of the Maratha assault.

Sambhaji prepared to lead a crack force of two thousand men towards the demolished tower. However, before doing so, he sent an envoy to Firangoji, ordering him to surrender.

Firangoji Narsala looked over the south-western rampart of his fort at the Mughal camp half a kos away on the plain. Early that morning, the Mughal guns had managed to destroy a tower, creating a breach which was certain to be assaulted soon. It was not a wide breach and Firangoji knew he could defend it till the reinforcements he had sent for, arrived. He had positioned his musketeers and archers on the ramparts to sweep the approach to the breach. His entire force was armed and battle-ready.

Firangoji's greying moustache quivered on seeing the assault force approach the base of the hill. He recognized the Mughal standards easily, but was startled to see a saffron flag amongst the troops. His Captain, standing beside him, spotted it at the same time. "That is one of our's, Commander!" the Captain said incredulously. "Some Maratha Captain has joined the Mughals!"

Firangoji gritted his teeth and said, "That is no ordinary Captain. That is the Yuvraj's standard."

The Captain was aghast. "The Yuvraj?"

"I do not know what is going on," Firangoji said, "but send word to the guard immediately that they are not to open the gates without my direct order."

"Yes Sir!" The Captain rushed off to relay the message.

Firangoji continued to watch the enemy advance. They stopped at some distance and a small party began climbing up the hill towards the ramparts, carrying a white flag. It was undoubtedly an embassy. Firangoji wondered what message they brought. He descended from the ramparts and walked toward the demolished tower. A while later, the Mughal messenger arrived with a letter.

Firangoji glared at the man as he took the scroll and began reading: *Surrender the fort on the orders of the Maratha Prince Sambhaji Raje...* Firangoji checked the seal at the bottom. It was the Prince's seal alright. So the Yuvraj has joined the Mughals! It seemed unbelievable to him. The messenger was dismissed and Firangoji returned to his residence, to consult with his Captains.

"Sir, if we decide to fight and the Prince charges in person, what should we do?" one of Firangoji's Captains asked the question uppermost in all their minds.

Firangoji stroked his beard in deep thought. He too, was baffled. He would much rather have had the Mughals charge the fort so he could throw caution to the winds and fight them. But with his King's son in the lead, what was he supposed to do? If the Prince died in the battle, how would he face his King?

"We cannot fight Sambhaji Raje. It is too risky," Firangoji said.

"Sir, the only option is to surrender," the Captain reminded him.

Firangoji closed his eyes and prayed: *Forgive me, my King! I must choose between the pot and the fire. Either way I will get burned. But I feel it is prudent to surrender the fort and spare the Prince's life.*

"Prepare to hand over the fort," he finally said to his Captains. "The King will never forgive me for this, but if we decide to fight the Prince, his life will be at stake."

Yuvraj Sambhaji watched as the Commander of Bhupalgad Fort was produced before him, his hands tied in a white cloth, the sign of surrender. Sambhaji knew the veteran soldier well. He had heard the story of his battle with Shaista Khan at Chakan from his father and knew Firangoji Narsala was not just a fierce soldier but also a man of honour. Ever since he had landed at Bhupalgad, he had been pained at the thought of attacking the fort and killing the Maratha garrison. They were, after all, his people. He had hoped fervently that Firangoji would surrender the fort on seeing him in the enemy ranks, and was glad he had.

Firangoji's face showed pain as he stood before his Lord's son, now an enemy. "Why, Yuvraj?" he asked quietly. "Why do I see you in the enemy camp?"

"Times have changed Firangoji, and one must change with them." Sambhaji turned his back on the Commander. "I am glad you decided to surrender."

"I surrendered to my King's son because I did not wish to take his life. I did not surrender to the Mughals!" Firangoji snapped.

"Your King's son does not wear bangles on his wrists, Firangoji! You need not have worried about hurting him. Your surrender, however, did save the lives of your men." Sambhaji turned to his men. "Take him away and set him and the other prisoners free to go back to their King."

"Not so fast, Prince!" The words startled Sambhaji. It was Diler Khan. He had arrived with his Captains in tow. "We shall release the prisoners, of course, but after they have been punished for picking up arms against the Emperor."

"These men have surrendered, Diler Khan. We must set them free. That was what I promised them in my *nishan*[70]."

"*You* promised them, Prince. I did not. The Mughal army does not let prisoners off just like that." Diler Khan pushed Sambhaji away and stood in front of Firangoji, staring at him with such malice, that a lesser soldier would have cowered. "Ikhlas Khan," Diler called to his Captain. Ikhlas stepped forward, eager to carry out his Commander's orders.

"Round up all the prisoners and cut off the left hand of each man. Let the Marathas know what lies in store for them if they rebel against the Emperor."

"Diler Khan!" Sambhaji screamed at the Mughal General. "How dare you issue such an order? These men have surrendered. We cannot mutilate them. Release them at once!"

"How *dare* I?" Diler Khan was clearly upset at being confronted. "Prince, in case you have forgotten, I am still in command here. You are but a refugee in my camp. The Emperor has yet to approve your plea for service in his army. You are in no position to order me."

The short-tempered Maratha Prince flew into a rage and physically pulled Diler Khan away from Firangoji. "You cannot commit such a dastardly act!" Sambhaji yelled. "I will not let you! Release these men at once!"

Ikhlas Khan and the other Captains around Diler drew their swords. More Mughal soldiers rushed forward and held Sambhaji. "How dare you insult the General?" Ikhlas Khan growled. "Do you want to lose a limb too?"

---

[70] Official communication from a Prince, literally meaning sign or seal

Sambhaji's quorchi Ganpat, who had fled from Parali with his master, hurried forward and took the Prince aside. "A thousand apologies, Diler Khansaheb,' he said, "I will take the Prince away. He is a little upset today."

"Leave me Ganpat!" Sambhaji shrugged off his servant's hands.

"Your Highness, please understand," Ganpat pleaded under his breath. "We are in the Mughal camp. Our lives are in danger. Pray come away with me and leave Firangoji to his fate." Saying this, he nearly dragged a remonstrating Sambhaji from the scene.

Diler Khan stared angrily after the retreating figure and said, "Ikhlas, my orders to be carried out right away."

"My Lord." Ikhlas bowed and left.

"Do not do this Diler Khan, I plead with you!" Firangoji begged the Mughal General. "My men are innocent. They fight for their King and they have surrendered because I asked them to. Kill me if you want, but let my men go free."

Diler Khan merely flashed him a toothy smile and walked away.

"Diler Khan, I beg you, do not do this! Let my men go! Kill me instead," Firangoji kept screaming as he was dragged away. "Yuvraj, stop them! Stop them! Save my men, Yuvraj!"

All his pleading was to no avail. Diler Khan's orders were carried out by his delighted men. Seven hundred loyal Marathas lost an arm each. The screaming continued well into the night, tearing Sambhaji's heart as he sat helplessly shedding tears in his tent.

"I will not ask His Highness for forgiveness, for I have lost a fort and I deserve to die." Firangoji Narsala was a picture of defeat as he stood before his King, hands clasped before him.

"Why did you surrender, Firangoji? Why did you not fight?" The Chhatrapati was furious. Not only had Firangoji lost a fort, but also seven hundred able men, who would never fight again.

"Sire, I would have fought Diler Khan to my last breath. But it was the Yuvraj who stood before me. How could I draw my sword against him?"

"The Yuvraj was marching under the Mughal banner was he not?" The Chhatrapati's blazing eyes made Firangoji shudder. "Anyone fighting for the Mughal is our enemy! And it is your duty to defend the forts against such men."

Firangoji was silent. Days ago, when he had made the decision to surrender to Prince Sambhaji, he had known that one way or another his own neck would be on the line.

"You should have known that you would never be forgiven for this. If you do not understand your King by now, you never will. Get out of my sight, Firangoji! You will be stripped of your rank and punished for this lapse." The King turned his face and waved him away.

The disgraced Commander was led out. The assembly, comprising Moro Punt, Anaji Punt, Hambirrao, Bahirji Naik and Hiroji Farzand, sat in silence. Diler Khan had landed a telling blow on the Swarajya. First, he had corrupted the Maratha Prince; then he had taken a key fort on the boundary of the Swarajya. With the loss of the fort, the Marathas had lost valuable supplies and ammunition stores, not to mention seven hundred men and a Commander of Firangoji's calibre.

"If a senior Commander like Firangoji could err thus, others will too, for sure," the Chhatrapati said to his men. "We must send urgent messages to our other forts in the east and south-east. The Commanders must defend their keep even if faced by the Yuvraj. No gates should open to him. Moro Punt, send letters to this effect with my seal immediately."

"It shall be done Highness," Moro Punt assured him.

The Chhatrapati was quiet for some time, trying to calm the turmoil in his mind. *Jagdamb! Jagdamb!* Clutching the string of cowries around his neck, he closed his eyes and chanted the Goddess' name.

Bahirji Naik moved restlessly. The news he had was certain to upset the King further. To his misfortune, the Council meeting had begun on a sour note already. He knew the Chhatrapati was anguished by the Yuvraj's actions. Added to that was news of the fall of Bhupalgad and the mutilation of their men. Bahirji hesitated to speak. He stole a glance at the Chhatrapati and was startled to find the King looking straight at him. Bahirji read the question in the King's eyes: *Any news of the Yuvraj? Any news of my son?* Bahirji shook his head almost imperceptibly, just enough for the King to know.

"What news do you bring, Bahirji? I was told you have something of utmost importance to say in Council," the Chhatrapati said.

Bahirji stood up and addressed the assembly. "Your Highness, Aurangzeb has re-imposed the *jizya*[71] tax on

---

[71] A tax paid by non-Muslims to their Muslim rulers

all non-Muslims in the Empire." His announcement was greeted by an uproar as the Ministers and administrators of the Swarajya voiced their disapproval. "The announcement was made in the Imperial durbar a few days ago."

"Aurangzeb has sounded the death-knell of the Mughal Empire," said the Chhatrapati, fuming. "This act will result in a rebellion by Hindus across this ancient land. His own Hindu nobles will be disaffected."

"Emperor Akbar had abolished the discriminatory tax. The Emperors Jahangir and Shah Jahan too, did not impose it. Aurangzeb's decision promises a return to the dark ages for the Hindus," Moro Punt said solemnly.

"Akbar was a far-sighted ruler. Unfortunately, Aurangzeb is both short-sighted and narrow-minded," said the Chhatrapati.

"My informant tells me the Emperor ordered that all infidels in the capital and the provinces pay jizya with heads bowed in humility," Bahirji continued.

The Chhatrapati gave a sardonic laugh. "What's left to humiliate? I would like to see Aurangzeb demand jizya from the Rana of Mewar! This act of the Mughal Emperor only strengthens our resolve to fight such oppressive regimes to the end of our days."

Imperial Court, Delhi, 25 May 1679

"Khan Jahan Bahadur Khan Kokaltash!" The quorchi announced as a beaming Bahadur Khan stepped forward, knelt before the Emperor's throne and touched his lips to the ground. Rising, he bowed his head and stood with his eyes fixed on the ground, never once looking at his sovereign.

"Welcome back to court, Bahadur Khan." Aurangzeb's sharp voice pierced the silence of the court. "You are deserving of your Emperor's praise for your work in Jodhpur."

Speak only when spoken to… Bahadur Khan bowed again and slowly looked up at Aurangzeb. He was well aware of Mughal court etiquette. "I am but a servant of the Alamgir," he said.

Aurangzeb regarded Bahadur Khan with his searching eyes. After recalling him from the Deccan, Aurangzeb had sent Bahadur Khan to Rajputana, to seize the property of Maharaja Jaswant Singh, who had died recently without leaving an heir. But, besides this political agenda, Bahadur Khan had also had another task; one which the Emperor was more interested in hearing about. "Tell me how you spread the law of Islam in Rajputana," he said.

"I would rather show His Majesty, if he so permits."

Aurangzeb raised a hand to signal permission. Bahadur Khan gestured to the quorchis, who hurried off and returned a few moments later with two large jute sacks.

"Empty the sacks so His Majesty may see the contents," Bahadur Khan ordered.

No sooner did the quorchis cut open the sacks, than there tumbled out hundreds of fragments of broken idols of Hindu gods and goddesses. Aurangzeb's face remained calm and composed, though he was exultant. Bahadur Khan had fulfilled his heart's utmost desire – to overthrow the practices of the *kafirs*[72].

---

[72] Infidels/ Non-believers

"Bahadur Khan, you are a true follower of the faith," he said in measured tones. "You have done Allah's will. But tell me, are these the only idols you found in the whole of Jodhpur?"

"Your Majesty, I have brought back many cartloads of broken idols," Bahadur Khan proudly declared.

"*Bahut Khoob*[73]!" Aurangzeb said in a rare display of pleasure. "These broken idols shall be cast into the steps of the Jama Masjid, to be trodden upon daily by the faithful."

"*Subhan Allah!*" Bahadur Khan exclaimed, raising upturned palms to the heavens. "It is a most pious act, Your Majesty."

Aurangzeb nodded in satisfaction. Raising his hand, he said "*Takhliya*[74]!"

The durbar bowed low and saluted as the Emperor rose from his throne and retired to the harem. Aurangzeb had declared war on the Hindu faith with little regard to the fact that many of his courtiers were Hindus. His actions may have raised his esteem in his own eyes, but alienated his Hindu subjects and nobles forever.

Meanwhile, the stand-off between Bijapur and the Mughals had reached a point of no return. Mughal forces spread out in the Adilshahi territory, looting, pillaging and laying waste. Sambhaji was one of the Captains in the field, and had a few skirmishes with the Adilshahi troops.

Diler Khan and Malik Barkhurdar continued their scheming and corrupting of Bijapuri Captains, further compromising

---

[73] Excellent/ well done

[74] Solitude; used as a command by Sovereigns when they desired to be left alone

Masud's already meagre force. In despair, Masud turned once again to the Marathas for help. When Diler heard this, he tried to woo him with false promises, but Masud refused to toe his line. Diler had by now corrupted Vyankatadri, who was still in his camp. With his connivance, Diler crafted a new treaty, offering peace if Masud stepped down and made Hakim Shamshuddin the Vizier and Regent, with a permanent Mughal force deployed in Bijapur city. Vyankatadri went back personally to Bijapur to convince Masud to accept. Masud realized this would be virtual annexation of Bijapur, as Hakim, who had earlier defected from Bijapur, was Diler Khan's puppet. He refused and arrested Vyankatadri and his associates, attaching their properties. Finally, he asked Chhatrapati Shivaji to send Maratha troops to help him.

6

Battle For The Seas

Rajgad Palace, July 1679

A slightly-built, middle-aged man stood before the King with folded hands, ready to do his Lord's will. He was simply dressed in a white *sadara*[75] with a checked cloth tied around his waist, falling to his knees. Another cloth was tied around his head. His face with its ready smile would have qualified as almost pleasant, except for the robust handle-bar moustache he sported. The man who stood beside him, though similarly dressed, was a contrast in appearances: tall, hefty, and sporting a full beard that reached to his chest. Both men were Naval Commanders, who served the Maratha Chhatrapati. The smaller man was Maynak Bhandari, the taller was Daulat Khan.

"Welcome to Raigad, Commanders!" the Chhatrapati addressed them affably. "What news do you bring from the Konkan coast?"

"The Abyssinians continue to be a nuisance to our coastal lands, my Lord," Maynak Bhandari spoke up. "The Siddi docks his fleet at Mumbai, gets supplies, and then sails along the coast looting and pillaging coastal towns and villages."

"And what has our naval force done to stop him?" The Chhatrapati was well aware of what was going on

---

[75] Cotton, sleeveless top garment

but demanded an explanation from his Commanders nevertheless.

"We have done all we can, my King, but countering the Siddi menace from the sea proves challenging still. His naval force is far stronger than ours."

"If I may, my King," Daulat Khan added, "our land forces need to do more to protect our coastal holdings from these Abyssinians."

"It is almost impossible to stop the Siddi's depredation from the land, Daulat Khan. The area is simply too vast to be patrolled. Besides, most of our forces are busy elsewhere. How then do we stop these trouble-makers?"

The assembly was silent. No one had a viable plan in mind for the Abyssinian problem. The Chhatrapati had thus far ordered several missions to take Fort Janjira, the Siddi stronghold, but they had all failed. Three years ago, Moro Punt had led the most ambitious campaign to take the fort, but he too, had been unsuccessful. Taking Janjira from the mainland had proved far more difficult than the Chhatrapati had imagined; and the Maratha Navy was not yet strong enough to take Janjira with a sea battle.

"The mainland opposite Janjira is in our control," the Chhatrapati mused, "which means we should have been able to choke the Siddi's supplies. Yet he prospers."

"Ever since the Siddi accepted Mughal overlordship, Your Highness, his troubles seem to have waned." Bahirji Naik spoke up. "The Siddi's position had become quite precarious when he could no longer get supplies from the mainland. The English and Portuguese too, refused to help him. But now the Mughal Governor of Surat pressurizes the English President to help the Siddi. The Surat Council in turn orders the English Council at Mumbai to allow the Siddi's fleet to winter at the island. Albeit unwillingly, the Mumbai Council has complied with this order. The Abyssinians thus continue to get supplies from Mumbai and our efforts at Danda Rajpuri come to naught."

"The Siddi calls himself 'General of the Emperor's Armada'," Maynak added, nodding in agreement with Bahirji's assessment.

"We need a strong naval base off the coast near Mumbai, both to hamper the movement of Siddi's fleet, as also to check English maritime traffic and trade," the Chhatrapati said.

"Is His Highness thinking of Khanderi?" Maynak asked.

"Yes, Maynak. Over seven years ago, we attempted to fortify Khanderi, but failed. Now, with a much improved naval force, we should make another attempt at converting the abandoned island into a fortified naval base. If we succeed this time, our ships will have a safe haven to dock and we can also patrol the Western Seas more effectively. We could even stop the Siddi from plying his fleet between Janjira and Mumbai."

The island of Khanderi was ideal for such a base. It was located almost six kos south of Mumbai and one and a quarter kos off the mainland at Thal. The island was surrounded by rocks, except on the north-eastern side, where there was a cove deep enough for anchoring small vessels. Between Khanderi and the mainland was another smaller island – Underi. The mainland at Thal, opposite these islands, was in Maratha control.

"Maynak, Daulat Khan, I am entrusting this new responsibility to you," the Chhatrapati ordered. "Start work on the fortification of Khanderi within a month. Detail a special force of at least a thousand sailors, and four or five hundred workers, for the job. I will immediately grant a hundred thousand hons from our Kalyan and Chaul treasuries for this mission."

"It will be done, my King!" Maynak said, bowing. "The English ships are safely docked at Mumbai for the monsoon. They do not ply in the rains. With any luck, our activity on Khanderi should go unnoticed for some time."

The Chhatrapati nodded. "But what about the Siddi? Where is his fleet at the moment?"

"The Siddi has docked his ships at Surat, Your Highness," Bahirji Naik replied.

"Splendid!" The Chhatrapati held up a clenched fist. "He will not bother us either. Get to work Maynak, Daulat Khan!"

Maynak Bhandari and Daulat Khan began work on the new campaign in earnest. Maynak landed on Khanderi Island with a hundred and fifty men and began fortifying the eastern front of the island. It was not till a month later that the English at Mumbai received definite news of their activity, and by then mud and stone works had been erected at various places. Maynak had even succeeded in planting four guns for the defence of the island. Meanwhile, Daulat Khan's men busied themselves in ferrying materials and provisions from the mainland to Khanderi.

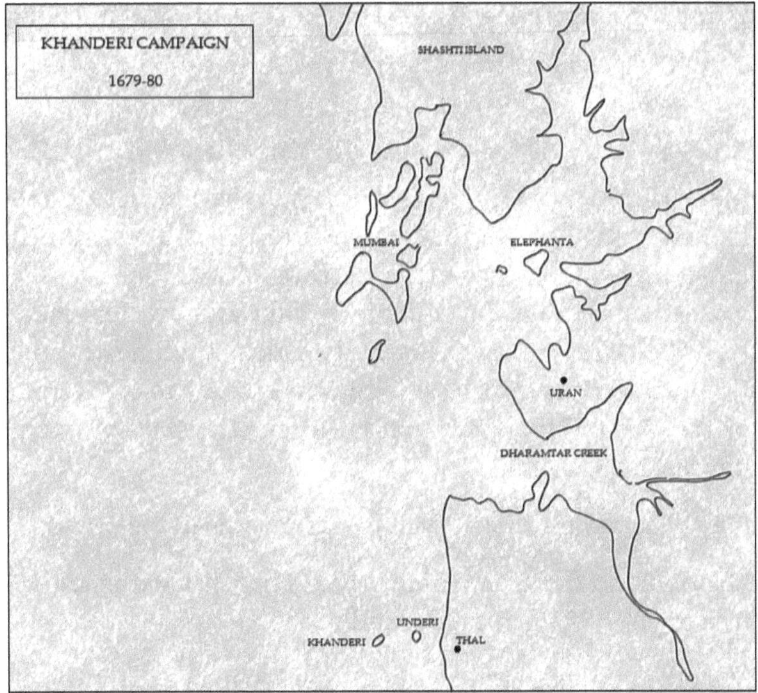

Once the English realized what the Marathas were up to, they decided to oppose them with all their might. An armed squadron of three *shibaads*[76] was stationed off the east coast of Khanderi to try and stop the movement of Maratha boats between the island and the mainland. This small squadron was later reinforced by the frigate *Revenge*, while another frigate, *Hunter*, was ordered to ply up and down the west coast.

Despite these measures, the Marathas continued their work. More men were deployed on Khanderi, their number increasing to four hundred. The English found it difficult to curtail their activity and the Mumbai Council repeatedly

---

[76] A medium-sized ship used mainly for trading

wrote to the English President at Surat for clear instructions on how to deal with the situation.

Maynak Bhandari stepped carefully over the rocks and looked across the sea to the mainland. The waters seemed quiet. He could not see the English vessels stationed off the west coast of Khanderi Island in the darkness. His man, who was carrying a mashaal, struggled to illuminate the Commander's path as he continued across the rough terrain of the island. The night guards stiffened as they saw him approach.

"How is it going, Hari?" Maynak asked one of the guards.

"Nothing so far, Commander. The English have made no moves yet," the man called Hari replied.

"Good! Let's keep it that way." Maynak climbed to the top of a small cliff and looked across the cove off the north-eastern face of the island. Something did not seem right to him.

"Get me some torches," he yelled. Two guards rushed over with lighted torches and the men craned their necks to try and spot moving forms in the water. "You!" Maynak barked at one of the men. "Go over to that rock and shine the torch over the water."

The man hurried off. With torches shining from both sides of the cove, visibility was better. The men waited and watched. A while later, one of them spotted movement on the far side of the cove. "There!" he hissed, pointing. Sure enough, a large dark form was moving toward the island. Within moments it was clear that it was a large boat.

"English!" Maynak shouted. "Get your guns!" There was a scramble as the men jostled each other to get into position for firing. "Fire!" Maynak screamed again. "Give those bastards hell!"

Maratha guns went off from the island. Their fire was returned by the English vessel.

"Alert the artillerymen," Maynak ordered. "Fire the cannon!"

One of the four cannons installed on the island was on the north-eastern side. That gun was now turned further north and began booming in the direction of the cove. The English continued to fire. One of Maynak's torch bearers was hit.

"They are shooting at the torches!" Maynak said. "Plant the torches on some shrubs and move away."

His men complied with the order. The exchange of hostilities continued for some time before the English guns fell silent.

"Looks like they have retreated," Maynak said. "Keep a strict vigil all night. They might return."

On board an English shibaad, stationed off the west coast of Khanderi, morning of 19 September, 1679

Captain William Minchin stepped into the Master's cabin of the shibaad and was at once assailed by the stench of liquor. "Jesus Christ, man! Is this the time of day to drink?" Minchin asked in an irritated voice of the man sprawled in a chair with a half-full glass in his hand.

"Welcome aboard, Captain!" Lieutenant Francis Thorpe, the Master of the squadron of three shibaads, offered him a chair.

Minchin looked around distastefully at the filthy stateroom and preferred to remain standing. "I hear you had a bit of a misadventure last night."

"Tried to land my men on the island," Thorpe said, his tongue feeling furred and thick in his mouth. "The bastards discovered my boat by a light match!"

"I also hear you have been drinking without rest since you anchored here two days ago!"

Thorpe smirked and took another gulp from his glass in reply.

"I would advise you against doing anything rash, Lieutenant Thorpe. Do not try to land on the island again, or engage with the *Murhattas*[77]! As soon as the sea breeze picks up, I will try to get my frigate into the bay. Till then, simply follow the orders you have received from the Deputy Governor, I implore you."

Thorpe said nothing, but nodded imperceptibly. Then he took another sip from his glass.

"And for Christ's sake put that stuff away."

Minchin left and went back to the *Revenge*, the frigate he was in charge of, anchored some distance away towards the mainland. "I do not expect much of that buffoon Thorpe," he said to his Second Officer. "He will bring shame on His Majesty's navy, mark my words."

No sooner had Minchin sat down to eat, he heard heavy firing in the distance. It took him only a moment to realize Thorpe had engaged with the Murhattas on Khanderi, against his advice. "Thorpe, you imbecile!" Minchin cursed and rushed to the deck.

---

[77] English corruption of the term 'Marathas'

From the stern, Minchin could see the three English shibaads engaged in an altercation with the island. Big and small guns were being fired from both sides. "Thorpe is trying to land on the island again!" Minchin observed to his Second Officer. "Man our boat at once. Send as many men as we can spare to help that idiot."

The officer rushed off. Minchin saw his men speeding off in one of the boats towards the action. One of his men fetched him a telescope. Through it, Minchin could see that one of Thorpe's shibaads had approached very close to the island, while the other two remained at some distance. Seeing Minchin's boat, those shibaads turned and rowed towards it. All three vessels then returned to the *Revenge*.

Sergeant Nash boarded the *Revenge* with his men, some of whom were injured. "We lost one *shibarr*[78], Sir. The Murhattas got hold of it. Three of our men, including Lieutenant Thorpe, were killed."

Minchin blew out his cheeks in frustration. "That drunk finally did what I was afraid of. You should have stayed put in position."

"The Lieutenant ordered us, Sir! We could not but obey."

"You would have done well to simply jump off than follow his orders!" Minchin turned to his Second. "Send all injured men to Mumbai for treatment. And the damaged shibarrs as well."

At about the same time, Maynak Bhandari stood grinning as the Europeans captured with Thorpe's shibaad were paraded before him. "That will teach you Europeans a lesson to keep your hands off my island!" he spat. He ordered the

---

[78] English corruption of *shibaad* by the English

mast of the captured shibaad removed and the guns from the boat installed on the island. The English thus had their own guns turned against them.

Over two months had passed since the Marathas had begun fortifying Khanderi. During this period, the English Council at Mumbai tried unsuccessfully to stop the Marathas from plying their small vessels between the mainland and the island. Their larger vessels could not ply in shallow waters close to shore, while the Marathas, who knew this weakness of the English Navy, always remained out of reach, in the shallows. A few days earlier, Daulat Khan had arrived on the scene with a large fleet of over thirty-five *gurabs*[79] and *galiots*[80]. When the English squadron spotted them, they immediately pulled up anchor and took fighting positions. Daulat Khan, who had no intention of a confrontation just then, directed the entire fleet into the Nagaon Creek, south of Thal. From there, the Marathas made sorties with small groups of vessels, carrying provisions to Khanderi, using various diversionary tactics to get past the English vessels.

Early on this particular morning, Daulat Khan led a fleet of forty vessels out of Nagaon Creek. Sailing north, close to the shore, he reached Thal, opposite Khanderi. From his position, he could see the English squadron lined up west of Khanderi, just out of reach of the Maratha guns. At Thal, Daulat Khan ordered his fleet to turn to sea and advanced toward the English squadron, with all guns blazing. Using both the tide and the seaward winds to perfection, Daulat Khan approached the English at such great speed that it

---

[79] A small ship with two or three sails, driven entirely by wind

[80] Single-masted cargo or fishing boats / small fast galleys

left them with little time to react. The English had anchored with their bows towards the mainland and sterns towards the island, most of their guns pointed at Khanderi. They had only small guns planted on the bow side, thus making their firepower inferior to Daulat Khan's. To make matters worse, Daulat Khan's rapid progress left them with no time to turn their vessels around to have their big guns firing at the Maratha fleet. Panicked, they simply cut the anchor ropes, hauled up their masts, and sailed south, with Daulat Khan in hot pursuit.

The frigate *Revenge* and a gurab named the *Dove*, were the last to turn south and as a result came under heavy fire from Daulat Khan. The Maratha fleet advanced in a semi-circle on these vessels. The English sterns now being in the correct direction, a heavy exchange of fire ensued, but the *Dove* took the brunt of the Maratha onslaught and was finally overwhelmed. As a sign of surrender, the Captain of the vessel lowered the flags and mast. Daulat Khan's men took possession of the *Dove* and took it to Khanderi.

In the meantime, the *Revenge* was still being pursued. Captain Minchin decided to pull a fast one on the Marathas and suddenly went silent, lowering the flags. Daulat Khan took this as a sign of surrender and approached the frigate. But once his vessels were within range of the guns, Minchin suddenly gave the order to fire. The unsuspecting Marathas now found themselves at the receiving end and in the ensuing carnage, lost three gurabs and three hundred men. Several more vessels were damaged and over a hundred men injured. Daulat Khan was forced to flee to shelter in the Nagaon Creek, where the *Revenge* could not pursue them.

Despite this reverse, Daulat Khan knew he had made a point with the English, and a night later, he once again used the same tactics to launch another attack. This time, the English wasted no time in weighing anchor and sailing south, out of reach of the Maratha fleet's fire. In the process, they left Khanderi unguarded. No sooner had the English squadron sailed away, than Daulat Khan abandoned the pursuit and turned to ferry supplies to the island. The fledging Maratha Navy thus outsmarted the far more powerful and experienced English.

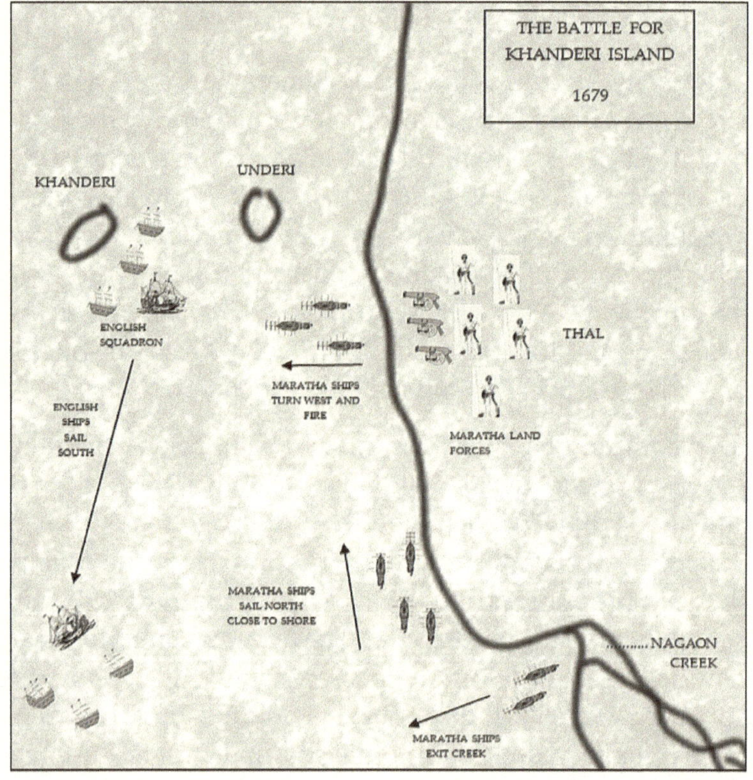

LAST QUARTER, 1679

Though the stand-off between the Maratha and English navies continued, work on the fortification of Khanderi

Island proceeded unabated through all the warfare. Every day, Daulat Khan and his men found new ways to outsmart the English and supply Khanderi with provisions, ammunition and men. Try as they might, the English could not stop them. The Marathas plied their small vessels in the shallow waters near the coast, where the larger English ships could not pursue them. The English tried diplomatic channels to convince the Maratha King to stop work on the island, but the Chhatrapati flatly refused to vacate the island. The English then tried to reach an understanding with him by working out a favourable treaty. But while these diplomatic moves were being worked upon, the English officers commanding the squadron off Khanderi, had a tough time controlling Daulat Khan's activities.

The Marathas pressurized the English by amassing troops on the mainland opposite Mumbai, and threatening an invasion of the islands. This caused temporary panic in the English factory. But the Marathas could not find access to Mumbai from the mainland. They requested the Portuguese to grant them access through their territory, north of the English, but the Portuguese refused. Daulat Khan then threatened an invasion of Mumbai from the sea, though he did not have the means to actually do it.

A few weeks later, a third party joined the battle at sea. The Siddi of Janjira, who presently sailed under the Mughal banner, arrived at Khanderi with a large flotilla of thirty-three small and large ships and seven hundred men. The Siddi's arrival with this powerful naval force changed the situation entirely, because the focus now shifted from a Maratha-English struggle to a full scale Maratha-Siddi naval battle. With the Abyssinians now taking a keen interest

in the Maratha activities on Khanderi, the English quietly
decided to back out and work only on pushing a treaty with
the Maratha King.

7

A Prince Returns Home

Rajgad 1779

Diler was furious when he realized all his intrigues had failed. In a fit of rage, he moved from diplomatic pressure to war. He had his men destroy Bhupalgad Fort and then advanced south, crossed the Bhima and camped at Dulkhed, some twenty-two kos north of Bijapur city. He needed supplies, money, artillery and ammunition, but hit a road block because Prince Muazzam, who had been appointed in place of Bahadur Khan as Subadar of the Deccan, was his sworn enemy. The Prince refused to grant his requirements, accusing him of wasting time and resources of the Empire. He agreed to pay Diler only if Bijapur was captured and annexed. Diler's campaign thus came to a grinding halt even before it had begun.

Prince Muazzam repeatedly wrote to the Emperor, complaining about the Mughal Commander: *Diler Khan has spent a vast amount of money and accomplished nothing. The capture of Bijapur is impossible. Siddi Masud is likely to hand over the city to Seevaji, in which case the Empire will be left stranded.*

Diler Khan and his associates Hakim Shamshuddin and Malik Barkhurdar, in turn send despatches to the opposite effect: *Bijapur is utterly defenceless Your Majesty, and can be easily captured. We must strike at once!*

Aurangzeb was infuriated at this war of words between his Subadar and Commander. He wanted results, against both Bijapur and the infidel Seeva. Instead, his men wasted time and resources quarrelling with one another. How was he to then subdue the Deccan? This Mughal mess also gave the Chhatrapati valuable time to intervene in the matter. Taking heed of Masud's recent plea for help, he decided to enter the fray.

The Chhatrapati first sent an advance force under Anandrao to prepare the ground, and then himself marched with ten thousand men. The forces rendezvoused at Selgur, sixty-three kos west of Bijapur. A Maratha envoy was sent to Bijapur with robes of honour for Sikander Adilshah and Masud. The Chhatrapati arranged to send two thousand cartloads of supplies to the Adilshahi capital. He also encouraged his people to send grain to Bijapur for sale.

At Selgur, the Maratha force divided. The Chhatrapati marched with half the force in a north-eastern direction, while Anandrao marched north-west. Both forces entered the Mughal Deccan province north of the Bhima River and began plundering and burning; carrying the devastation to the very banks of the Narmada. The aim was to divert Diler Khan's attention from Bijapur and force him to march north in pursuit. The Chhatrapati's forces gathered loot worth crores of rupees, in addition to valuable goods and over twelve thousand fine horses. Such was the impact of this campaign that the Mughal jagirdars were ruined and complained to the Emperor.

Diler Khan completely ignored this Maratha campaign, choosing instead to continue his focus on Bijapur. He thought that if he could only annex Bijapur, it would be his crowning glory, earning him not just a pardon from the Emperor, but honours as well. He banked on the fact that he had Sambhaji in his grasp, hoping to incite a civil war in the

Maratha ranks, and thus capture the Maratha hill forts. But the Chhatrapati had turned the tables on him by launching this scathing campaign.

His actions infuriated the Emperor, who recalled Hakim and Malik to court. These two worthies, on receiving the firmaan, fell out with Diler Khan. The three began accusing each other of supplying false information about Bijapur.

In a final attempt at peace with Diler, Masud sent Abd-ur-Razzaq and Sayyid Alam to the Mughal camp for negotiations. Diler Khan demanded that Bijapur break their alliance with the Marathas and pay the pending dues to the Empire. He also demanded that Masud's son be sent to his camp as a hostage. On the sly, he corrupted Abd-ur-Razzaq, who defected to the Mughals and offered to go back to Bijapur to convince Masud.

Sayyid Alam however, remained true to Bijapur, and having learnt of Razzaq's intrigues, informed Masud that he could not be trusted. Masud naturally refused to agree to Diler's demands.

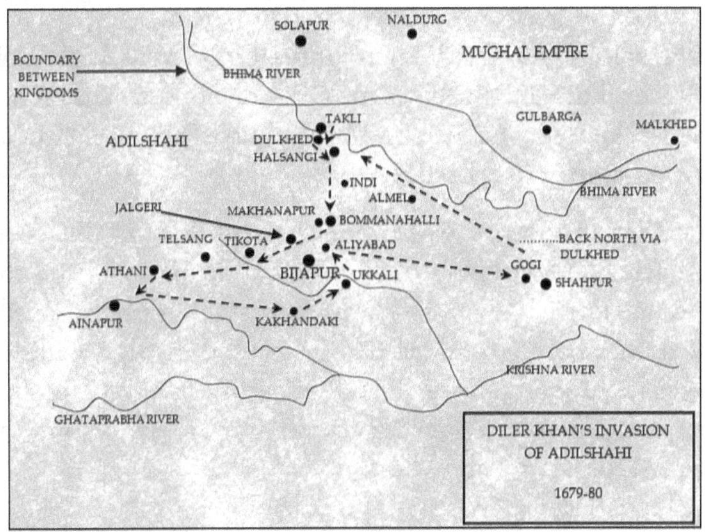

Seeing that his *coup de main* had failed, Diler in frustration marched south to Bommanahalli, within two kos of Bijapur. Wary of besieging Bijapur from the north, lest the Marathas attack his rear, he turned west towards the Miraj-Panhala region. A campaign in this region, besides diverting the Marathas from the Deccan province, would also be profitable, as the petty chieftains in this region had already been won over by Mughal agents. From Bommanahalli, Diler marched south-west to Tikota, burning, pillaging and plundering.

Tikota, Mid-November, 1679

Tikota was a rich and populous village seven kos west of Bijapur. Diler Khan knew he could get plenty of booty here. Besides, he had news that many wealthy merchants from surrounding areas had taken refuge there after hearing of the Mughal raids.

The sudden arrival of the Mughal vanguard under Ikhlas Khan into Tikota was unexpected and threw the village into chaos. Hundreds were killed and thousands imprisoned to be sold as slaves. Women jumped into wells with their children, killing themselves to escape dishonour. The village was sacked and burned to the ground. This was Mughal depredation at its worst.

The Maratha Prince was a mute spectator to it all. As he watched women being dragged away to be raped by the Mughal soldiers, Sambhaji was disgusted and repulsed by the scenes before him. He had been on campaign with his father before, but never had their army behaved in such an inhuman way. When it became unbearable for him, he headed for Diler Khan's tent.

"Khansaheb, the behaviour of your men is deplorable. Why do you commit such ghastly atrocities on innocent civilians?" Sambhaji said to the Mughal General.

Diler walked up to Sambhaji and placed a hand on his shoulder. "You too, are now a part of the Mughal army, Sambhaji Raje. You are the Emperor's mansabdar. Get used to it, because this is how we Mughals campaign in enemy territory. We believe in completely destroying the people. Once they are broken, those who rule them have no source of income."

Sambhaji was aware of these Mughal tactics. He had experienced such depredations a decade ago when Diler Khan had descended on the Swarajya with Jai Singh. How could he forget those days? "At least spare the women and children,' he pleaded. 'Why kill them? Why molest the women?"

Diler laughed. "My men are entitled to some entertainment, Raje. I cannot deprive them of that. If I restrict them, they will simply refuse to march."

"That is disgusting! I implore you not to enslave so many people. Release them after you have taken what you want from them."

"We get a good price in the slave market for these kafirs. Their lives are a waste in any case. I will not release them."

"Khansaheb…"

Diler raised a hand "Enough, Prince! If you have nothing better to discuss, I suggest you return to your post. I have work to do."

"I cannot be a part of this insanity!" Sambhaji said and left the tent fuming. For the first time since leaving Parali Fort, he cursed himself for having been so naïve as to desert his father.

The Maratha camp of some nine thousand troopers was spread out in a plain a few kos west of Jalna, in the Mughal Deccan Province. The Marathas had recently looted Jalna and gathered immense booty in cash, jewels, expensive materials, horses and elephants. The Chhatrapati, personally leading this force, sat relaxed in his command tent in the centre of the camp. Hambirrao Mohite, the Maratha Senapati, and Sidhoji Nimbalkar, a trusted Captain, were the others present.

"Our campaigns in Mughal territory have been very successful, Sire. The booty collected is immense," Hambirrao declared proudly. "We have also received news from Anandrao; his force too, has raked up plenty."

The Chhatrapati nodded in satisfaction. "That is true, but our prime objective of diverting Diler Khan from Bijapur seems to have remained unfulfilled," he said.

"Diler Khan seems hell bent on taking Bijapur. Does His Highness think he will succeed?"

"I doubt it," Shivaji Raje opined. "The stand-off between Diler Khan and the Mughal Prince means that Diler will be short of money and supplies, without which he will be unable to launch a decisive attack on Bijapur. Besides, news of our raids here will have reached the Emperor. I believe Aurangzeb will order Diler Khan to turn back from Bijapur."

"He will, Sire," Hambirrao agreed. "But where does that leave us with Bijapur?"

"Having helped Siddi Masud, we can expect a favourable treaty with him soon. But we will have to wait for the Mughals to retreat before we decide on a future course of action."

The tent awning parted and Bahirji Naik entered, looking unusually tense. At once the Chhatrapati roused himself and sat up from his reclining posture.

"I have bad news, Sire," Bahirji began. "Ranmast Khan, the Commander of Jalna, has set off from his fort in pursuit. He should be upon us by mid-day tomorrow."

Shivaji Raje's brow furrowed. "We can take him on, but that will endanger the booty we have with us," he said.

"That is not all, Sire," Bahirji said grimly. "A large reinforcement has left from Aurangabad to aid Ranmast Khan. We may not be able to take on both forces at once."

The Chhatrapati caressed his beard, deep in thought. If they lingered here and the two Mughal forces merged, they would indeed find themselves in a tight situation.

"We should move right away, my Lord," Bahirji suggested.

"Prepare to strike camp immediately. We march through the night. But leave a force here for rearguard action," the Chhatrapati instructed.

"I will stay back," Hambirrao offered. "His Highness can go to Fort Pattagad with the booty."

"No." Sidhoji Nimbalkar stood up. "The Senapati should go with the King, to safeguard His Highness. I will remain with five thousand men to stop the Mughals. I will not let the enemy pass."

"Sidhoji…" The Chhatrapati was reminded of a similar scene twenty years earlier, when another brave Captain, Baji Prabhu Deshpande, had offered to stay back to fight a rearguard action. Baji had perished in the terrible bloodbath at Ghodkhind.

"Make haste, Sire," Sidhoji urged. "I will keep my promise. Your Highness shall reach the fort safely."

And so it was, that Sidhoji Nimbalkar entrenched himself in Ranmast Khan's path, while the Chhatrapati marched east with Hambirrao and Bahirji Naik. Ranmast Khan fell upon Sidhoji and his men, but the Marathas held him at bay. The battle raged for three days, Sidhoji giving the Mughals no quarter. Alas, Sidhoji was slain by a musket shot. Ranmast Khan then managed to scatter the Marathas and resumed his pursuit. Soon, the reinforcements from Aurangabad, under Sardar Khan's command, joined him. Together, they pressed on, determined to accost the fleeing Maratha King.

Hills east of Fort Pattagad, 22 November 1679

Bahirji Naik's face lost some of its colour as he listened to what the man with him had to say. Having heard, he headed straight for the King's tent, with the man in tow.

Bahirji entered the Chhatrapati's tent, signalling the man to follow him inside. The Chhatrapati, who was conversing with Hambirrao, stopped and threw a questioning look at his chief spy.

"This man has come from the Mughal camp, Sire," Bahirji explained. "He is a Rajput, from the contingent of Kesari Singh, who has been sent from Aurangabad under Sardar Khan's command." Bahirji turned to the man. "Tell the King what you have come here for."

"Glory to the Maratha King!" the Rajput began, bowing low. "My Master, Kesari Singh, has sent me to inform you that the Mughal force is three kos from your position. We will cover the distance by tomorrow. My Master urges you to make haste and flee."

"And why does Kesari Singh want to help me with this information?"

"My Master does not wish to fight a fellow Hindu King," the Rajput said. "He admires and respects you."

"How many men do Sardar Khan and Kesari Singh have?"

"Twenty thousand, Your Highness."

Those in the tent shifted uneasily on hearing the number. They had perhaps four thousand in their own camp. The Rajput messenger was dismissed.

"We are gravely compromised Sire," Hambirrao observed.

"My Lord, the Rajput informed me of their route," Bahirji said. "I will lead our men to Pattagad by a secret path through the hills. The Mughals will not be able to pursue us."

The Chhatrapati looked intently at Bahirji, never doubting him. "Lead then, Bahirji. I trust you with my life."

"Do not concern yourself, my King. I will take you to safety."

The Marathas struck camp that very night and fled by the difficult and little travelled path chosen by Bahirji. They marched ceaselessly for three days and nights, but finally reached the safety of Fort Pattagad, exhausted and minus some of the baggage and loot they had abandoned to lighten their load.

A few days after the carnage at Tikota, the Mughal force marched to Athani, twenty-two kos west of Bijapur. The third prahar of the day was almost over, and being the onset of winter, the weather was pleasant. The palanquin bearers kept up a hectic pace carrying their royal passenger, the Maratha Prince, while his personal bodyguard marched alongside. They were preceded and followed by Mughal contingents.

Along the way, a straggler quietly joined the Prince's entourage and tagged along. He spoke to Ganpat, the Prince's quorchi, offering to help as a porter. The Mughal soldiers keeping a watch on the Prince, suspected nothing. Such stragglers were common in large armies, doing odd jobs.

That evening, the army camped close to Athani. The straggler settled in the shadows with the Prince's servants. As the second prahar of the night began, he got up, silently crept into the Prince's tent and tapped Ganpat. Sambhaji's quorchi was awake, waiting for him. A single lamp burned in the corner, illuminating the tent. Together, they woke the Prince.

"Wha…?" Sambhaji awoke and Ganpat gently placed his hand over his Master's mouth.

"Quiet, Your Highness. We have a visitor."

"A visitor? At this hour?"

The straggler came forth and Ganpat brought the lamp closer. Sambhaji got up from his bed when he saw the straggler's face. "Ganoji!" he exclaimed.

Ganoji Shirke smiled and placed his hands on Sambhaji's shoulders. The next moment they embraced. Sambhaji was overjoyed to see his brother-in-law. "Yuvraj," Ganoji said, "we must get out of this camp right now. I have horses ready a kos east of here."

"What if we are seen?" Sambhaji asked.

Ganoji's face was grim. "If we are caught, Ganpat and I will die for sure. They may spare you. But we cannot think about that now. Let us just get out of here!"

"Where are we headed?"

"To Bijapur. The Chhatrapati and Siddi Masud are in alliance right now. Masud has been informed and he will help us. Besides, one of our contingents is stationed at Bijapur."

Sambhaji nodded. Under the circumstances, this was their best option. Sambhaji knew he had to get back to Swarajya, to his father. His future lay there, not here with the Mughals. A year ago he had made the worst decision of his life and he was desperate to undo the damage. He yearned to return and place his head on his father's feet.

Ganoji left the tent as silently as he had entered it and rounded up the Prince's bodyguards. Together, they crept back and surprised the Mughal soldiers on guard around the Prince's tent, cutting them down. It was all done so deftly and quickly that the Mughals hardly made a sound before falling. There was no time to lose now. Ganoji entered the tent and signalled to Sambhaji, who was ready to leave with his own weapons.

The small party left the camp in darkness and headed east to Bijapur.

Diler Khan was furious at the Captain of the Guard responsible for keeping an eye on the Maratha Prince. Despite all his precautions, Sambhaji had escaped. He had lost his trump card. Now the Emperor would be even more displeased. "What were your guards doing Aslam Khan?" Diler Khan demanded. "You were supposed to watch Sambhaji!"

"Pardon the lapse, General. The infidels made short work of our soldiers. None of the guards on night duty are alive to question."

"Get out of my sight!" Diler waved him away.

"Ikhlas," he turned to his deputy, "summon Khwaja Abd-ur-Razzaq and send him to Bijapur at once. I have a feeling Sambhaji will go there and Masud will let him into the citadel. Instruct Razzaq that he must convince Masud to hand over Sambhaji to us. Bribe him if required. Razzaq must leave at once."

"It will be done, my Lord!" Ikhlas left to find Razzaq.

By the time Razzaq had covered half the distance to Bijapur, Sambhaji had been welcomed into the citadel by Siddi Masud. Grateful for the help he was getting from the Chhatrapati in dealing with the Mughals, Masud considered this an adequate way to repay the Maratha King. If he helped the Maratha Prince get back safely to his kingdom, the Chhatrapati would doubtless be pleased.

Meanwhile, sensing the Mughal threat to Panhala, the Chhatrapati had relayed instructions to ready the fort for war. Thirty large guns were moved from Ankola, Karwar,

Someshwar and Phonda forts to Panhala. However, incensed by the turn of events, Diler Khan abandoned his plan to attack Panhala and turned east. Marching due south of Bijapur city, he destroyed the fertile lands known as the city's granary, thus compromising food supplies to the city.

Abd-ur-Razzaq reached Bijapur, met Siddi Masud and tried his utmost to convince him to hand over the Maratha Prince to the Mughals. Masud, however, was unwilling to trust a man who had just defected to the enemy. Besides, he knew that without the help of the Marathas, he had no hope of stopping the Mughals. Hence he quietly informed Sambhaji of Razzaq's motives and let him slip out of Bijapur. Sambhaji, Ganoji and the others left Bijapur and fell in with a Maratha escort that took them safely to Panhala.

A year after he had taken the drastic step to defect to the Mughals, the Maratha Prince at last returned home.

ROYAL PALACE, FORT PANHALA, 13 JANUARY 1680

The father stared at the errant son, more in sorrow than in anger. They were in the Chhatrapati private chamber, alone. The Chhatrapati sat on a divan, dressed simply in a dhoti and sadara; the ornaments, embellishments and bejewelled turban were missing. Sambhaji stood before him in formal attire, sword by his side, his hands folded, his head bowed, and his confidence shaken. The Chhatrapati did not smile. The Yuvraj stood bereft of his usual arrogance.

The Chhatrapati broke the silence. "Where did I go wrong, Shambhu? Where did I err in your upbringing?"

Shambhu stood in silence. He had committed the unpardonable sin of defecting to the enemy, and now he stood before his King for justice.

"Did you not think even once of your father, your King, before going to Diler Khan's camp? Your father has fought against these enslaving imperial powers for over three decades, and you went and joined them?"

"I do not deserve your forgiveness, Father," Shambhu said simply.

The Chhatrapati rose and walked to his son. "Have you considered what would have happened to me if that monster Aurangzeb had killed you? I promised your mother on her death bed that I would look after you. What was I to say to her?"

"Father, I …"

"You want to raise a sword against your own father, Shambhu? Is that what you want?" The Chhatrapati pulled Shambhu's sword from its scabbard and presented it to him.

For the first time Shambhu raised his head and looked at his father. He expected to see pure rage and hatred in those eyes, but he saw only pain. His father was in tears.

"Here, take your sword," the Chhatrapati shoved the hilt into Shambhu's hand. "Cut off my head. Then you will be King. That is Mughal culture…the son murders the father to ascend the throne. Since you embraced the Mughals, why not practice their customs? That will put an end to all the problems, won't it?"

Shambhu broke down. The sword slipped from his hand and he fell at his father's feet, embracing them tightly. "I am sorry, Father. Forgive me. I hate the Mughals with every breath of my being. It is not our culture to shed blood between father and son. I could never raise a weapon against you. I do not want anything. Just let me remain at your feet!"

The two remained as they were, shedding tears. Even as he wept, the Chhatrapati stood erect, hands folded behind his back, refusing to place a forgiving hand on his son's head while Shambhu drenched his feet with his tears.

"Get up, Shambhu!" the King said firmly and walked away. "The punishment for treason in the Swarayjya is death. You have been pardoned from death only because you are my son. But that does not mean I have forgiven you. You will have to earn that. From this moment you will be watched constantly by my men. You do not have permission to go anywhere without your King's consent. For now, you retain your title of Yuvraj. My proposal to divide the kingdom between you and Rajaram is still valid. I will concede to your demand and let you have the territory in Maharashtra, while Rajaram can have the newly conquered southern lands. But one wrong move from you and you will lose it all. I will then be forced to declare Rajaram as my sole heir. Do you understand?"

Shambhu nodded in silence.

"You are my elder son, so behave like it. You need to be wiser in your choices and decisions. I will soon be returning to Raigad for Rajaram's wedding. Under the circumstances, it is best you remain here. After the wedding is over, I shall return to Panhala. We shall then take stock of our holdings, man-strength, forts and possessions."

Shambhu bowed, and left the chamber. The Chhatrapati let out a long sigh, but the creases on his forehead remained.

8

The Legend

The tall and hefty dark-skinned Commander stood on a rocky outcrop on the western side of Underi Island. His officer handed him a telescope, which he held to his right eye and pointed at the mainland to the east. He looked hard at the long line of boats plying close to the shore.

"It's the Marathas," he said to his man. "Khairiyat, order every man on the island to battle stations!"

"Yes, my Lord!" Khairiyat hurried off, leaving Siddi Sambul alone on the rock. "If it is battle they want, I will give it to them, by Allah!" he growled.

Three weeks earlier, he had landed three thousand men and a few guns on Underi Island and begun fortification, with a view to countering the Maratha occupation of Khanderi. Almost immediately the Marathas had positioned big guns on the mainland at Thal. Shelling between Underi and the mainland had continued unabated till this day. His ships were simultaneously firing at Khanderi. Four days earlier, the Marathas had made an attempt to attack his island, but he had fought them off.

Now, Sambul watched impatiently as the thirty odd Maratha vessels divided into three groups. One group proceeded to the north-east of Underi, another group turned south, and yet another circled the island and sailed to the west.

Sambul hurried away and joined his officers. "They are attacking us from three sides," he said. "Divide our men into four platoons. Three platoons should be stationed on the west, south and north-eastern sides. The fourth remains as a reserve force. Position our musketeers at key positions behind rocks and see that there are enough big guns on all sides."

The Abyssinian officers quickly relayed his orders. Underi was well prepared for the Maratha assault and Sambul was confident he would be able to beat them off again.

A prahar after the Maratha vessels had been spotted, the firing began. The Marathas rained cannon and musket fire on Underi and the Abyssinians replied spiritedly. Daulat Khan rallied his men well, but he had committed the error of dividing his force, which left too few vessels and men on each side. Sambul, on the other hand, had enough men to counter the Marathas wherever they attacked. As the day progressed, Maratha losses mounted and the Abyssinians gained the upper hand.

Sambul himself was on the north-western side, commanding operations. The Maratha fleet on this side was the largest of the three and Sambul recognized the banner of their Commander on one of the vessels. Sambul ordered his gunners to focus their fire in the direction of the Maratha Commander. His guns boomed tirelessly. As he watched, one of the shots hit a Maratha gurab, blowing it apart. Sambul smacked his fist into his palm and cheered loudly, encouraging his men.

By late afternoon the Marathas had lost several vessels, sunk by Abyssinian fire, and over two hundred men. Daulat

Khan, smarting from these losses, was forced to withdraw. He ordered his remaining ships back to Nagaon Creek.

Having devastated much of the Adilshahi lands and grain fields south of Bijapur, Diler Khan reached Aliyabad, a suburb north-east of the city. There, he stationed his twenty thousand strong force and launched attacks on the city's ramparts and gates. Daily, Diler marched with his guns, firing wildly at the impregnable city walls, exhausting his men and horses and wasting ammunition. Try as he might, he could not breach the fort walls, while the Bijapuri garrison fired at the Mughals from the ramparts and killed many. Diler's force was woefully insufficient to besiege the entire city and hence he was unable to prevent all provisions from reaching Bijapur, though he did cut off the city's water supply. In his own camp, however, the shortage of grain and supplies kept mounting to critical levels. Diler's frustration knew no bounds and what he had failed to achieve militarily, he made up for by destroying the gardens, cultivations and houses around Bijapur.

By this time Bijapur had lost most of its old Captains and was left with a meagre force of a few thousands. Masud was powerless to stop the Mughals, but the Almighty willed that the city would not fall to Diler Khan.

News of Diler Khan's failure reached the Emperor, who censured him and ordered him to turn back: *Your first duty was to guard the imperial dominions. What folly is this, which you have practised? You have neither protected the Empire nor gained your objective against Bijapur. Withdraw immediately from Bijapur and turn to the defence of the Empire.*

In the face of the Emperor's firmaan, Diler was compelled to break camp and withdraw. But he was not finished with Bijapur. Instead of going north, he marched south, giving vent to his worst passions, roaming like a rabid animal, looting, slaying and inflicting unspeakable misery upon the peasantry; turning the entire region south of Bijapur into a barren wasteland. His men carried away thousands to be sold into slavery, and exacted large sums as ransom. Diler finally pitched camp at Gogi, four kos north of the fort of Sagar. It was here that his worst misfortune struck him, for this was the land of the Berads, reputed to be the bravest soldiers in the South.

The Berad chieftain, Pam Nayak, offered to make peace with Diler, offering him a ransom of thirty thousand *hon*[81]. Diler refused the offer and demanded ten times more. When Pam Nayak refused to pay, Diler Khan advanced from Gogi to Shahpur, a walled village at the foothills of Fort Sagar. There, he split his army into three divisions, exchanging fire with the Berads through the day. By evening, the Berads conducted a sortie and scattered one of Diler's divisions, thus forcing him to retreat to Gogi. The next day, he returned with his entire force and breached the gate of Shahpur, looting it before once again entrenching himself near the fort. A heavy exchange of fire ensued between the Mughals and the Berads and continued till noon, by which time the Berads, safe within the fort walls, had inflicted heavy losses on the enemy. Pam Nayak also managed to sneak out his infantry and stationed them around the Mughal positions. When Diler ordered a retreat to Gogi, this hidden Berad infantry came out of hiding and attacked the hapless Mughals from all sides, turning the battleground into a killing field. Diler lost seventeen hundred men in the

---

[81] Gold coin

battle. He and his son barely managed to escape with their lives to Gogi.

This terrible encounter broke the spirit of the Mughal army and when Diler Khan once again ordered his men to launch an attack on the Berads, they flatly refused to move. The Emperor's agents, who had joined Diler's camp with orders to force Diler to turn back, openly rebuked and berated the Mughal General, humiliating him before his own men. Finally, defeated, disgraced and abandoned by his men, Diler Khan ordered a retreat northward. Yet again, as was his wont, Diler's march was marked by burning, plunder, and the enslavement of peasants.

Raigad, third week of March 1680

The Chhatrapati entered his bed-chamber with heavy steps and sank down upon his bed. His breathing was heavy and beads of perspiration covered his forehead. Mahadu rushed forward to help him. He gently removed the King's footwear, covered him with a shawl and hurried off to fetch water.

Shivaji Raje felt restless, though he did not know why. Outwardly, all seemed well. His Swarajya was healthy and peaceful, with a robust administration governing it. His armed forces were more powerful than ever before and feared across the lands, even by the Mughals. His navy had blossomed into a strong arm of his forces, ready to take on the powerful European and Abyssinian navies. He had hundreds of forts under his command. Above all, his wayward son had returned home. Any other King would have slept soundly. Yet the Chhatrapati's mind remained troubled.

Mahadu returned and his Master sat up and drank the water before flopping down again. "Mahadu, massage my legs," the Chhatrapati said. Mahadu sat down cross-legged on the floor and began a gentle massage.

What worries me? the Chhatrapati mused, trying to analyse his troubled mind. *My life draws to an end. My Lord summons me and I must go to him…soon. But what becomes of my beloved Swarajya after me? Who will care for it, nurture and protect it? Shambhu? He is far too immature, impulsive and hot headed to be a wise ruler. The Ministers cannot see eye to eye with him. What if they clash with him? Without their support, Shambhu cannot rule. The period after the death of a King is always stormy for any kingdom. Will Shambhu be able to brave the storm and come out unscathed to ascend the throne?*

Rajaram is far too young to hold his own right now. He has the support of his mother, but will Shambhu let power go to him without a fight? Will there be bloodletting between the brothers? Will my family see bloody fights of succession like the Mughals?

Aurangzeb is sure to descend into the Deccan. When he does, will my Swarajya have a firm ruler to stop him? The Chhatrapati's worried mind found no answers. He rubbed his aching head.

"His Highness works too hard. He needs rest," Mahadu, who had been watching his master"s tired face, said.

"It is not work that bothers me, Mahadu. It is worry that eats me from inside."

"The Prince has returned. Isn't that a reason for rejoicing? Why does the master worry?"

"I worry for our Swarajya, Mahadu. Who will care for it after me?"

Mahadu was disturbed. "His Highness will remain healthy and rule for many years."

"That is not what my heart tells me. My time draws near."

"My Lord, please do not speak such inauspicious words. The Goddess will grant you good health and happiness."

"I do not care for my own happiness Mahadu, as long as my people are happy and safe."

"His Highness has two able sons to carry on his legacy. He has a devoted family and so many who love and serve him."

"A King is the loneliest person in the world, Mahadu. He has no friends. He cannot trust anyone fully. He must face life alone."

Mahadu began to say something, but the Chhatrapati raised a hand to silence him. "Go now and leave me alone," he said.

The Chhatrapati did not sleep. He lay awake, alone and in pain, his mind riddled by fears for the future.

The second prahar of the day was drawing to an end. Queen Soyarabai entered the Chhatrapati's chamber to find him on his bed. At once, her forehead creased with concern. The King never lay in his bed at this time of the day. She sat down on the bed by his side and gently touched his hands. The *Chhatrapati* opened his eyes and looked at her. It was obvious to Soyara that his face looked drawn out and tired.

"His Highness looks unwell," Soyara said. "What is the matter?"

"Oh, it's nothing; just some indigestion." The Chhatrapati closed his eyes again.

"His Highness has not been eating well these days, of which, I am aware, though he has not visited my chamber of late." Soyara could not help but throw a barb at her husband for refusing to see her these past few weeks. "Is he angry because I suggested that Prince Shambhu *Raje* should not be the Crown Prince anymore?"

"I am not upset with you, Soyara. You are correct in your own right to suggest so. But I am the King. I have to think about the well-being of my Kingdom and my people."

"And Prince Shambhu, His Highness believes, is a capable heir?"

"Shambhu is an adult, authoritative and commands the respect and obeisance of the Commanders and Ministers. Rajaram is a child. The army may not rally to him."

"Shambhu is impulsive, short tempered and ill mannered. He also lacks foresight. Even if the Commanders rally to him at first, he will not be able to preserve their adherence to him. And speaking of the Ministers, they have made it amply clear to me that they would much prefer Rajaram as a Crown Prince now."

That comment startled the Chhatrapati. He gave his Queen a long hard look, till she turned her face away in discomfort. Had she already hatched a plot with the Ministers to remove Shambhu from the line of succession?

"They are both my sons Soyara, and it makes no difference to me who ascends the throne after me. But it could make a difference to the state and I must choose the more able son to succeed me."

"So is the son who abandoned his father and joined hands with the enemy more capable as a ruler?"

Soyara's face showed resentment. For a few brief moments she forgot that her husband, the King was unwell. Her mind was racing with thoughts on how to convince him to declare Rajaram as the Crown Prince.

"I do not think you will have to wait too long to find out." The Chhatrapati waved his hand, indicating the Queen to leave.

Soyara was much distressed on hearing this. "Why does His Highness say so? You will live long and rule till we are both old."

The Chhatrapati was quiet. Soyara was moved to tears as she got up to leave. "I shall send the Vaidya to see His Highness."

RAIGAD PALACE, 23 MARCH 1680

The Chhatrapati woke early, a griping pain in his abdomen. He called out to Mahadu to fetch some water. Mahadu rushed over with the water. The Chhatrapati drank but a couple of sips before the pain intensified and he dropped the *lota*[82], bending over in agony. Mahadu was alarmed and called out to the guards outside. "Send for the Vaidya immediately. And summon the Mukhya Pradhan, and the Sachiv as well."

Soon, the Vaidya appeared by the King's bedside and administered a potion of his own making. The cramps, however, did not ease and the Chhatrapati lay in distress,

---

[82] Copper/brass pot

tossing in his bed. His Ministers stood by, faces lined with worry.

The Vaidya indicated with a glance for Moro Punt to come aside. "The pain has not lessened despite the medicines," the Vaidya said seriously. "His Highness is also running a high fever."

"So what is your opinion?" Moro Punt asked him a formal question in his capacity of Mukhya Pradhan.

"It is difficult to say right now," the Vaidya said, careful with his words. "It seems to be a *navjwar*[83], for it does not respond to our medicines. I will try all means at my disposal, but it is my duty to tell you the outlook does not look good at the moment."

Moro Punt looked grimly across at Anaji Punt. The two left the chamber, summoning Mahadu to follow them. "Mahadu, seal the King's chamber. No one enters or leaves the chamber without my or Anaji Punt's consent. Only the Vaidyas and Queen Soyarabai are to be allowed in. No one else, do you hear?"

Mahadu nodded and left, tears trickling down his weathered face. He had gauged the reason for all the secrecy and was beside himself with grief for his Master, whom he worshipped next only to his God.

"We must see the Queen without delay," Anaji Punt suggested.

The two hurried towards the Queen's chamber.

The Chhatrapati's illness plunged the royal palace into gloom. While the other Queens and the royal servants

---

[83] A new type of fever or illness

were aware that the King was unwell, the seriousness of his condition was kept a well-guarded secret. Only the Ministers and Queen Soyarabai knew the truth. They took every precaution to keep the unfavourable news from leaking out, both in the interests of State, as well as to keep Prince Sambhaji in the dark. Messages were relayed to Vitthal Mahadkar, the Killedar of Fort Panhala, and to Hiroji Farzand, Suryaji Kank, Somaji Naik Banki and Babaji Dhamdhere, the Chief Officers at Panhala, to keep a strict watch over the Prince. These officers were placed under command of Janardan Punt Hanmante, who was charged with the responsibility of keeping the news of the King's illness from reaching the Prince's ears.

Meanwhile, the King's condition deteriorated. The fever showed no sign of ebbing, his abdomen cramped in pain, and a bloody flux left him ever weaker. He ate nothing and his slender frame shriveled to skin and bone.

3 April 1680

The twelfth day of the Chhatrapati's illness dawned with no good news. The King was now delirious, with only brief periods of lucidity. Mahadu sat by his bedside, sponging his forehead to bring down the fever and applying hot foments to his abdomen to lessen the pain. Neither helped the suffering King.

"Mahadu…" the Chhatrapati's lips moved.

"My Lord?" Mahadu bent close to the King's face.

"Summon the Ministers…"

Mahadu did as he was told, and the Ministers arrived soon after. Moro Punt Pingale, Anaji Punt, Pralhad Punt, Niraji

Raoji, Raoji Somnath, Balaji Avji Chitnis and the others stood around the King's bed with folded hands and heads hung. Most could not bear to look at him. The brave and powerful ruler looked a mere shadow of himself. The eyes that had shone like the sun were now sunken and bereft of their fire, the smile that had drawn so many to him, was gone. But what hit the men most was the melancholy that showed on his face.

"Your Highness, the Punts have arrived," Mahadu said to him gently, then withdrew.

The Chhatrapati opened his eyes with great difficulty and looked around to see the familiar faces who had stood by him for decades to achieve the impossible. He raised a hand and motioned the men to come nearer. They knelt by his bedside. Moro Punt held the King's hand. "Sire, you must rest. We can discuss things when you are better."

The Chhatrapati shook his head. "My time is over. I will soon leave this world. My Lord summons me…"

"Please do not say that, Your Highness. What will we do if you leave us?" Anaji Punt had tears in his eyes.

"The Lord has given me only so much time, Punt. Who can disobey his command?" The King's words came in mere whispers and his men strained to hear. "I created this Swarajya out of nothing, keeping the imperialists at bay. So much land, hundreds of forts, a hundred thousand strong army, horses, a full treasury…" He paused and winced as a wave of pain swept through his body. "But now, as the time to depart draws near, I do not see anyone capable enough of being King after me. My elder son, Shambhu is of age, but unfit by nature to be King. Rajaram, is still immature. Who will care for my kingdom, my people?"

The Ministers looked at one another, none daring to tell the King they had intentionally kept Sambhaji away from him.

"I suggested partitioning the kingdom into two, so that both Shambhu and Rajaram get half, but Shambhu was not pleased. After me, the army will most likely support the elder Prince. Shambhu may take the throne. If he does, he may not spare the Ministers and Officers who oppose him. Who knows how he will treat his brother?"

The King's words sounded ominous to the men as most were in favour of placing Rajaram on the throne.

The King continued, "Shambhu may well spend the treasury and waste the kingdom by his irresponsible behaviour. Aurangzeb will descend upon him and capture him by deceit. Later, if Rajaram survives, he may resurrect the kingdom and restore it to glory. You are all wise men. Do as you deem right and place one of my sons on the throne. I depart soon…"

The Chhatrapati was quiet now. He had uttered his last wishes and left it to his administrators to decide whom to crown as the next King. He had neither summoned the Queen, nor expressed a desire to meet Sambhaji. Had he asked for the Prince, none of his men could have denied him that wish in his last moments. Then the ministers' plans would have failed. But having said what he had to, the Chhatrapati waved his hand and muttered, "Leave me now to chant the Lord's name…"

For the last time, the Council of Ministers offered their obeisance to their Lord and Master. Then they left him alone to meet his Creator. The Chhatrapati soon became stuporous, muttering incoherently, "I must go now… see a bright light... mother awaits me... Why did you leave, Saee? Lord Mahadev..."

In the final moments, only Mahadu remained with him, desperately clutching his feet and weeping. The Chhatrapati's wives were in their chambers, his sons away.

At mid-day, the extraordinary man who had inspired millions to rebel against bigoted foreign rulers and, against all odds, established a free State for his people, the first Maratha Chhatrapati, breathed his last and passed into Legend.

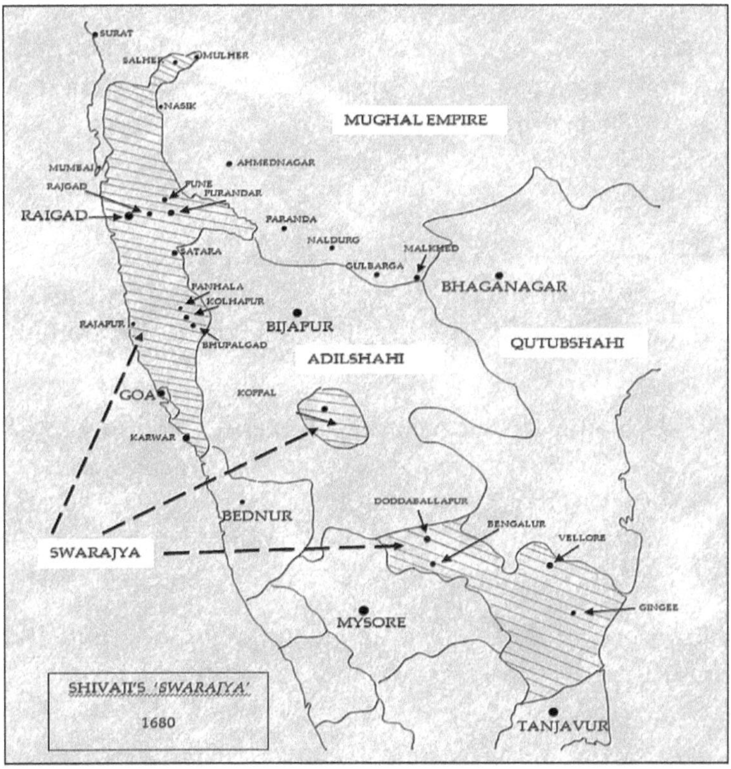

RAJGAD, 4 APRIL, 1680

The Ministers had gathered in the Queen's chamber. Moro Punt, Anaji Punt, Niraji Raoji, Raoji Somnath and Balaji Avji stood with sombre faces before the Queen. Soyarabai was dressed in a simple white saree, the traditional garb of a widow, the usual ornaments and embellishments missing. Her eyes were red and swollen; it was obvious she had been crying. Outwardly, however, she was composed and sat erect, facing the Administrators. "News of the Chhatrapati's demise must not reach Prince Shambhu's ears," she said sternly. "Place our most trusted men at all gates and exits. Every person going in and out must be stopped and questioned."

The men nodded mutely. They knew this was the key to the success of their plan to prevent Sambhaji from ascending the throne. If they failed, they could all face death, even the Queen.

"Send our spies to Vitthal Mahadkar and Hiroji Farzand at Panhala. The Prince must be kept under watch at all times and his men kept away from him. Balaji Avji, compose a letter addressed to the Killedar of Panhala, instructing him to restrain Prince Sambhaji within his chambers."

Balaji Avji Chitnis jerked to attention on hearing that. "Pardon me from writing such a letter, Your Highness. If anything goes wrong, it shall be incriminating evidence against me!"

Soyarabai was exasperated. "Chitnis, be sensible. If we all abdicate, how will our plan succeed? We must convey our orders to our people at Panhala."

Balaji firmly shook his head. "I will not write it. I will ask my son to write it. He is well trained in official matters."

Soyarabai agreed reluctantly. "Compose an official letter addressed to the Prince, informing him of the Chhatrapati's demise, and send it to Mahadkar with instructions to hand it over to the Prince only after Rajaram's ascension."

Balaji Avji nodded. Soyarabai scanned the faces of the men before her. They looked grim, scared even. If Sambhaji managed to get out of Panhala, there was no telling what he would do.

"What about the Senapati, Your Highness?" Anaji Punt raised a question that had been haunting him since they had hatched the plan. "He is one person who could upset our plans. If he decides to go over to the Yuvraj, it will be the end for us."

"Anaji Punt is quite right," Moro Punt said. "Hambirrao is fond of the elder Prince and is likely to aid him. He has sided with the Prince openly in the past, even in the Chhatrapati's presence."

The Queen quietly pondered the matter. She too, was aware of the danger posed by the Senapati. In a power struggle like this, the Commander's support could tilt the scales.

"Perhaps the Queen could try and convince Hambirrao?" Anaji Punt suggested carefully. "After all, he is the Queen's brother."

Soyarabai nodded briefly. "I will send him a personal letter. But someone has to visit him personally and convince him to side with Rajaram. I think the Mukhya Pradhan and the Sachiv should carry out this responsibility. But first we must prepare for Rajaram's ascension."

Anaji Punt swallowed on hearing this. He was most uncomfortable about leaving Raigad in these circumstances. "Your Highness...I?" he muttered.

"Yes, Anaji Punt. You and Moro Punt are the two people he is most likely to heed. He may not be inclined to listen to my command in this matter."

"Her Highness is right," Moro Punt said. "We will leave for Karhad as soon as the ascension ceremony is over."

Fort Panhala, a few days later

Sambhaji paced about his chamber impatiently. He had sent for Hiroji Farzand a prahar ago, but the officer had not arrived yet. Repeated messages to the Killedar too, went unanswered. For days now, he had been locked in his chambers, not permitted to meet anyone. Even his personal staff had been kept away. Had his father ordered this, he wondered? Or was this the doing of his scheming step-mother and her cronies in the ministry? He needed answers and needed them fast.

There was a muffled knock on the door. Hiroji Farzand entered and bowed. "You sent for me, my Prince?"

"I sent for you a prahar ago!" Sambhaji snapped.

"My apologies, my Lord. I had to descend from the fort for some urgent work. I have only just returned."

"On whose order have I been placed under arrest, Hiroji?" Sambhaji looked the Officer squarely in the eyes.

"The order has come directly from Raigad, my Prince."

"Who signed it?" Sambhaji asked pointedly.

"I have not seen the letter, Your Highness. It was addressed to the Killedar, who in turn issued orders to us."

"I sent for Mahadkar but he has not shown his face."

"I will find out what delays him. Any other orders for me, my Prince?" Hiroji was as non-committal as he could be.

"Be careful, Hiroji. You are speaking to the Crown Prince. Do not forget that."

Hiroji flinched, lowering his gaze. Then he bowed and left.

Sambhaji lay awake on his bed till late that night. For days now he had been waiting for some word from his trusted men, who had been kept away. Without their help, he could never get out.

His quorchi Ganpat gently touched his shoulder. "Ganoji is here, my Lord."

Sambhaji hastily sat up, happy to see the man he had been eagerly waiting for. "Ganoji! I have been praying you would find some way to come."

"My Lord, something big is being planned, though I am not sure what. All our men have been ordered to stay away from the palace and are watched day and night. None of us are allowed out of our barracks. I managed to slip out with great difficulty."

"Any news from Raigad?"

"None, my Lord. But I fear something terrible has happened. Both Hiroji and Mahadkar seemed very upset when I saw them."

"I have to get out of here, Ganoji! I must get to Raigad to find out what is going on."

"That is impossible right now, Your Highness. We do not have sufficient men to take control of the fort." After a pause he added, "There is one other thing…"

Sambhaji looked at him expectantly.

"There are some murmurs about some spies who have been held at the gates trying to slip in. They were taken to Mahadkar, and then they disappeared."

Sambhaji considered this. Spies? Could they be from Raigad, from his father? Or were they from his step-mother? "Find out more about them, Ganoji. They could have the answers for us."

Ganoji bowed and prepared to leave. Sambhaji stopped him. "Be careful, Ganoji. You are my only hope. Rally our men somehow and get a message to Hambirrao, asking him to send men to help us. Don't get caught!"

Sambhaji watched Ganoji leave. He knew he could trust the man. After all, Ganoji Shirke was his wife Yesubai's brother.

Ganoji Shirke disappeared into the night and returned to the barracks. He rallied the Prince's men, who had been restrained there, and exhorted them to stay faithful to the Prince. A man was secretly sent to Karhad to meet the Senapati and relay the Prince's plight to him. At Panhala, Ganoji busied himself trying to discover more about the spies who had been held at the gates. In a couple of days, he managed to get hold of one of the spies and, having threatened him with a knife to the throat, the man told him what he knew. Ganoji waited for a message from Hambirrao, before taking decisive action.

⁂

A force of two thousand mounted soldiers arrived at the gates of Fort Panhala the very next day. The man in the lead, Mahadji Nimbalkar, kin to the Prince Sambhaji, carried Senapati Hambirrao Mohite's banner. A grim-faced Mahadkar arrived at the gates and addressed Mahadji Nimbalkar. "On whose order do you demand entry into the fort?"

"By order of the Senapati, Hambirrao Mohite," Mahadji replied, handing him a scroll. "I have a message for the Prince."

"What message?" Mahadkar asked.

"That is for the Prince's eyes and ears only!" Mahadji snapped. "Let me through, Killedar. You do not have authority over the Senapati."

Mahadkar carefully read the scroll for him, an order from the Commander, and pondered briefly. He would have to let Mahadji Nimbalkar in. But he decided he did not have to let the entire platoon in. "Very well," he said, "you may enter, but with no more than twenty-five people. The rest can stay outside for now."

Nimbalkar scowled. "Fine! Have it your way. Just remember you will have to answer to the Senapati for this!"

Mahadji entered the fort with twenty-five of his best men and headed straight for the barracks to rendezvous with Ganoji and his men. Ganoji welcomed him and apprised him of the situation in the fort. Once they had joined hands, they had some fifty-odd men willing to die for the Prince.

Before the Killedar could summon Hiroji Farzand and take action, Ganoji, Mahadji and their men had reached the palace. There, a brawl broke out between Sambhaji's men and the Killedar's guards. Mahadkar and Hiroji arrived at the tense scene and tried to apprehend the Prince's men, but failed. As fate would have it, Ganoji and Mahadji finally entered the Prince's chamber.

Sambhaji stood confidently across from Killedar Mahadkar, surrounded by his most trusted men. Ganoji Shirke, Mahadji Nimbalkar, Tukoji Palkar, Trimbak Deshpande, Hiroji Mahadik and Achloji Mahadik flanked the Prince with unsheathed swords. The spy apprehended earlier by Ganoji was produced.

Ganoji placed a blade across the man's neck. "Speak up! Who sent you here and why? Tell the Prince what you told me earlier."

The man gave the Killedar a resigned look and said, "I was sent here by the Sachiv, with an order for the Killedar."

"What was the order?" Ganoji asked him roughly.

"To restrain the Prince."

Sambhaji walked up to the man and gave him a long hard stare. "Who gave you this order?" he asked.

The man hesitated to speak.

"Who gave this order?" Sambhaji asked again, more sternly. Ganoji pressed his blade into the man's neck and drew blood.

"Do not kill me!" the man begged. "The order came from the Queen."

"And is the Chhatrapati aware of this?" Sambhaji asked.

The man broke down, sobbing like a child.

"Answer the Prince!" Ganoji shook him.

"The King is dead!" the man sobbed. "The Chhatrapati has left us. He was ailing for twelve days and died a week ago."

The words hit Sambhaji like a hammer. He staggered back, unsteady, unwilling to believe his ears. Mahadji steadied him by the shoulders and made him sit down. *Father…dead?* Sambhaji was too stunned to react.

Everyone was shocked by the spy's news. "You knew about this?" Ganoji asked the Killedar.

Mahadkar knew the situation was out of his control now. He had to save himself. "I knew," he said, "but I was instructed to keep this news from the Prince. Forgive me, Your Highness, I was only following the Queen's orders."

"Arrest him!" Sambhaji ordered. "Arrest Hiroji Farzand, as well."

His men apprehended Mahadkar immediately. Hiroji, however, was nowhere to be found. When Sambhaji's men had entered the palace, Hiroji had quietly slipped out and left the fort.

Orders were soon relayed to the gates and Mahadji's entire unit of two thousand men was allowed into the fort. Panhala was now firmly in Sambhaji's control.

Hambirrao Mohite sat in a pensive mood in his command tent in the Maratha military camp, quietly analysing the political situation he found himself in. The King was dead, and the Administrators, as well as the royal household, had been torn into two groups, each supporting one of the Princes. He had received a letter from Queen Soyarabai, exhorting him to stand behind her son, the younger Prince, Rajaram. He had also received word that the Mukhya Pradhan and the Sachiv were on their way to meet him. He had no doubt they would simply echo the Queen's sentiment. It was no secret the duo did not see eye to eye with the elder Prince and would try everything in their power to keep him from the throne. Sambhaji's list of allies was short.

In this scenario, Hambirrao's support would prove decisive; he was acutely aware of this. Even if the Ministers managed to keep most of the forces away from him, Hambirrao commanded over ten thousand horse in his camp and could definitely tilt the balance of power in favour of one of the Princes. Hambirrao thought long and hard about the pros and cons of each Prince taking the throne. Though Soyarabai was his sister and Rajaram his nephew, he knew he had to do what was best for the kingdom. It was true that Sambhaji's temperament and character were far removed from that of his father; he was not ideally suited to be King. Yet he was the elder, more capable of commanding the loyalty of nobles and officers and leading their armed forces in battle. Rajaram as ruler meant the real power would be in the hands of the Queen and the Ministers. Sambhaji was his own man and his rule would be decisive. Besides, if Aurangzeb descended on the Deccan in person, Sambhaji was the only person who could stop him. Hambirrao made his decision.

The Commander's quorchi entered and bowed. "The Punt Pradhan and the Sachiv have arrived," he announced. Moro Punt and Anaji Punt entered the tent. The trio exchanged somber greetings. Hambirrao seated his high-profile visitors respectfully.

"These are difficult times Hambirrao," Anaji Punt said, approaching the delicate topic. "We must place an able heir on the throne; else how long will it take for anarchy to take over the kingdom?"

"I agree, Anaji Punt." Hambirrao looked straight into his eyes. "The question is, who decides which Prince is more capable?"

Anaji Punt looked at Moro Punt for support. Both knew this was a crucial moment. "The consensus of the Council is…"

"What is *your* opinion?" Hambirrao leaned forward, interrupting the Sachiv.

"Hambirrao, most of the Ministers are of the opinion that Yuvraj Sambhaji will not make a good King. Hence, we have decided to place Prince Rajaram on the throne," Moro Punt said with more confidence than his companion.

"Well, at least you had the courtesy of calling him the Yuvraj," Hambirrao said. "Because, truth be told, he *is* the Yuvraj. And that means he is also the late Chhatrapati's choice as successor."

"Only because he is the elder," Moro Punt argued. "Prior to his death, the Chhatrapati himself told us why Yuvraj Sambhaji was an inappropriate choice for King."

"Well, I wasn't there Punt! So how am I to believe this?"

"Hambirrao, are you suggesting we are lying to you?" Moro Punt's voice rose.

"No. I am merely suggesting that I smell a conspiracy to deliberately keep the Yuvraj away from Raigad. Tell me Punt, was the Yuvraj informed of the King's illness?"

Moro Punt fumbled for an appropriate response, but found none.

"I do not think he was," Hambirrao answered his own question. "Had he been informed the day the Chhatrapati fell ill, he would have been at the King's bedside at the time of his demise, and then all your schemes would have failed. Is that not true?"

"The Queen ordered us not to inform the Yuvraj," Anaji Punt made a feeble attempt at a counter-argument.

"Since when does the Queen dictate protocol while the Chhatrapati and the Mukhya Pradhan are both alive and present in the capital?"

Moro Punt's face showed his exasperation. "Hambirrao, do you not agree that Prince Sambhaji is temperamentally ill-suited to be King? That he is short sighted and short tempered?"

"That may be because the Chhatrapati never gave him an opportunity to prove himself."

"The Yuvraj went over to the enemy camp, Hambirrao! That act itself should be enough to disqualify his rights as heir!"

"Yet the Chhatrapati welcomed him back and retained his title of Yuvraj," Hambirrao said firmly. "That act should be enough to qualify him as the rightful heir."

Moro Punt and Anaji Punt gaped open-mouthed at the Commander as he stood up, towering over them. "I will not fall for your petty schemes," he said and clapped his hands. Two armed guards entered the tent.

"Escort the ministers to their chambers and keep them under watch. Prepare to move at sunrise tomorrow. We ride to Panhala to join Yuvraj Sambhaji!"

True to his word, Hambirrao Mohite marched to Fort Panhala with his entire force and the two apprehended Ministers in tow. Given the support of the Commander of the Army, Sambhaji's claim to the throne was now unassailable. He made Panhala his base and summoned as many armed units as he could to the fort. He also took control of Rajapur, and mobilized provisions for his army. In a month his preparations to take over Raigad were complete. He marched from Panhala, first to Pratapgad, where he paid his respects to the family deity, Goddess Bhavani, and then proceeded to Raigad.

When Sambhaji arrived at Fort Raigad six weeks after taking control of Panhala, no one dared oppose him. A force of ten thousand was permanently stationed at Pachad village, at the foothill of the fort. Sambhaji killed Khem Savant, the Chief Officer at Pachad, and took over his force. The fort itself was quiet. The gates were opened for the Yuvraj and he entered with his men.

Once inside the palace, Sambhaji quickly removed his father's men and moved his own into key positions. Moro Punt, Anaji Punt and Kanhoji Bhandvalkar, the Killedar of Raigad, were arrested. Prince Rajaram and Queen Soyarabai were placed under house arrest, watched by Sambhaji's men. Suryaji Kank and Somaji Naik Banki, both arrested in Panhala, were executed; so was Banki's son. Bapuji Bhaurao,

Suryaji Kale, Malsavant and many more were executed as well.

Sambhaji appointed Pilajirao Shirke, his father-in-law as Head of the Raigad Guard. A force of ten thousand was placed under him. Balaji Avji was given temporary charge of the administration, pending fresh appointments.

Having removed all conspirators, and surrounded by men faithful to him, Sambhaji Raje was now firmly in control of Raigad and the administration.

THE IMPERIAL MUGHAL DURBAR, 14 MAY 1680

"Important news has arrived from the Deccan, Your Majesty," Asad Khan, the Mughal Wazir announced after glancing at the communiqué which had just arrived. "Seeva is dead."

Asad Khan's words were greeted by more than an audible buzz as the courtiers expressed surprise at the news. Aurangzeb's face showed no expression. "Seeva will get what he deserves. He will sink into the pit of hell," he said once the court was quiet again. "Give no importance to the death of a mere zamindar. Proceed with the court's business."

Asad Khan bowed and took up the next matter at hand.

Though he had ordered the court to ignore the news of Seeva's death as insignificant, Aurangzeb could not help but think about him. For over two decades he had waited to hear this news. Seeva… the one man in the far reaches of the land who had defied the Mughal Empire, was finally dead. How he had hoped that one of his own officers would arrest or kill him. But all he had heard was news of defeat and plundering of Mughal lands. Seeva had frustrated him for years like no other. And now he was dead. At last, he could fulfil his own desire to subdue the Deccan.

Abruptly, Aurangzeb ordered an end to the court proceedings and rose to leave. He went straight to his chambers and knelt to pray. Though ego prevented him from saying so, he had to admit to himself and to Allah, that Seeva had been a worthy foe.

Royal palace, Raigad, 27th June, 1680

The mood in the Queens' chambers had been sombre ever since the Chhatrapati had taken ill. His death plunged the womenfolk into perpetual darkness. Soyarabai had busied herself in intrigues with the Ministers and hence had hardly had the time to grieve for her husband. The other Queens mourned day and night, along with the staff. Soyarabai had dreamed of the day her son would be crowned Chhatrapati, but it was not to be. Hambirrao's support to Sambhaji had destroyed all her aspirations and condemned her to a life of solitude and house arrest.

Putalabai, the Chhatrapati's gentle and simple third Queen, was deeply grieved. Having no children of her own, she had no interest in harem politics and had locked herself in her chamber. She had loved and cared for Sambhaji as if he were her own, and had hoped he would take his rightful place on the throne. Having seen her beloved husband consigned to the flames, she had experienced an overpowering desire to join him on the pyre. Yet she had stopped herself, waiting for Sambhaji to return. Now that he was back and in control of the capital, she was at last free to join her husband.

Sambhaji entered his step-mother's chamber to find her in the traditional garb of a *sati*[84], with vermillion smeared on her forehead. Putalabai sat in a corner, awaiting him, looking far older than her years. Her face was drawn, her eyes sunken, with dark circles under them. It tore at Sambhaji's heart to see her thus. He bent to touch her feet. Putalabai placed both hands on his head and blessed him as tears flowed down her cheeks.

"The Goddess has been kind," she said. "You shall rule wisely, as did your father."

"Mother, do not leave me like this," Sambhaji said in grief.

"I have nothing left to do in this mortal world, Shambhu. I must join your father. Do not stop me."

"Why does everyone I love, leave me? First my mother, then my grandmother and my father. Now you too, are leaving."

"Do not grieve for me, Shambhu. You have more important things to think about. You are King now."

Sambhaji stayed with Putalabai for a while, but could not watch when she willingly surrendered herself to the flames.

Three weeks later, Sambhaji ascended his father's throne, to the cheers of his Ministers, Officers, Commanders and subjects. As he gazed at those gathered in the royal durbar hall, every head was bowed in obeisance. Sambhaji Raje thus became the second Chhatrapati of the Maratha Swarajya.

---

[84] Women immolated on their husband's funeral pyre

The last six years of Shivaji's life, though less well known, are certainly not short of drama. Shivaji is a sovereign ruler now and we see him conduct himself as one. He is also a significant political power in the Deccan.

The Legend begins with Bahirji Naik's report of Maratha raids in Khandesh. Letters from the English Councils in Surat and Mumbai are our only sources of these raids and my description is essentially taken from them (Ref 3).

By 1674, Shivaji had established control over most of the western coast, save the Canara district, and it was but natural that he would try to annex Canara at some point. He agreed to a temporary treaty with the Mughal Subadar Bahadur Khan, merely to safeguard his fief from a Mughal invasion while he was away. Bhimsen, in his *Tarikh-i-dilkasha,* gives an account of the events leading to the treaty, as well as Aurangzeb's reaction on being told of it (Ref 37). English letters of this period give conflicting accounts of the treaty. The terms are mentioned in *Basatin-us-salatin* (Ref 50). *Maasir-i-Alamgiri* (Ref 39) mentions that Bahadur Khan was given a promotion, titles, robes of honour and cash rewards, while Sambhaji was granted a mansab by the Emperor.

The meeting between John Child and Shivaji is adapted from Child's own letter (Ref 3), in which he says, 'He diverted himself a little by taking in his hands the locks of my periwig...'

Relations between Shivaji and the English remained perpetually strained for two reasons. First, the English kept demanding reparation for damages incurred by Maratha raids on their factories in places like Rajapur and Dharangaon. Shivaji's reaction to this was that he could not be held responsible for damages to their factories in enemy territory. From the accounts of their meetings and events surrounding this debate, it does seem that Shivaji's administration was reluctant to pay up for any damages and tried every means to avoid doing so. Even when Shivaji did sanction payments, it was in lieu of customs duties or in kind. He did however, give *kauls*[85], guaranteeing safety of English factories in some regions. The second reason for discord was the matter of the Siddi of Janjira, which shall be discussed a little later.

The description of the siege and capture of Phonda, is adapted entirely from English factory letters (Ref 3). With the annexation of Canara, Shivaji had taken Phonda Fort, Ankola, Shiveshwar, Karwar, Kadra and Gokarna, and pushed the southern boundary of his kingdom as far as the Gangavali River. He now commanded the entire west coast, thus effectively ending Adilshahi trade from that direction, especially compromising Bijapur's supply of Arabian horses. John Fryer, who visited Karwar toward the end of 1675, mentions in his account: '…for all he has blocked up their ports, which may prejudice them for the future; an irreparable damage (Arab steeds being the life of their cavalry)…' (Ref 21).

Shivaji's eventual refusal to honour the treaty and the resultant fallout with the Mughal, is detailed in *Tarikh-i-dilkasha* (Ref 37) and in English factory letters (Ref 3). Writes

---

[85] Official letters

Bhimsen: '…he arrogantly asked them as to what power they had, that they were asking him to sign a pact of friendship. He added that they should leave the place, otherwise he would insult them…' (Ref 37). The English factors learned of this breach from the Surat Governor (Ref 3).

Shivaji's rift with the English over the issue of the Siddi of Janjira, can be summarized thus: The Siddi was Lord of Janjira Fort and procured most of his supplies from the mainland opposite. The Marathas repeatedly failed to take the fort, but eventually captured the mainland, thus choking off the Siddi's supplies. He then began plying his vessels between Janjira, Mumbai and Surat, getting his supplies from these ports. Shivaji repeatedly asked the English to prevent the Siddi's ships from docking at Mumbai, which they were initially inclined to do since the Siddi's men were a nuisance anyway. But the Siddi, having failed to get adequate help from the English and Portuguese, accepted Mughal overlordship. He thus became General of Aurangzeb's Armada, gaining Mughal clout in the process. The Mughal Governor of Surat then pressurized the English President, who in turn wrote to the Mumbai Council, asking them to allow the Siddi to winter at their port. This negated Maratha efforts at Danda Rajpuri, infuriating Shivaji. The preceding account is collated from the English factory letters (Ref 3).

It must be mentioned here that while earlier it was Siddi Sambul, who was the Abyssinian Lord of Janjira, he was replaced later by his brother Qasim, after an internal struggle between the two. Most accounts however, merely refer to them as 'the Siddi' and fail to mention the name of the Commander. Hence, at times, we are unsure which brother was involved in specific incidents.

Details of the Adilshahi civil war between the Pathani and Deccani factions are gleaned mainly from *Bastin-us-salatin* (Ref 50) and *Tarikh-i-dilkasha* (Ref 37). Though my description of the events is imaginary, the facts are taken from these manuscripts.

Our source for Moro Punt's counter-guerilla operation in Jawhar and Ramnagar, is from the English factory records (Ref 3).

Netoji Palkar's return to Shivaji and subsequent reconversion to Hinduism is mentioned in *Jedhe Chronology* (Ref 15) and in an English letter from Rajapur to Surat, dated 24 July 1676, which says: 'Shivaji has lately returned to him a subtle fellow by name Netoji, who has been ten years in the Mughal's court, turned Moorman, but now remade a Hindu.' (Ref 3).

It does seem strange that, despite his earlier experience, Bahadur Khan concluded a second peace treaty with Shivaji in the latter half of 1676. Says Bhimsen: 'Bahadur Khan came to friendly terms with Shivaji, who despatched four thousand horsemen for the help of the Mughal...' (Ref 37). Did Shivaji bribe the Mughal Subadar? Sabhasad says that some presents and gem-studded ornaments were sent to Bahadur Khan (Ref 36). He does not explicitly say it was a bribe. A letter from the English Council at Mumbai, dated 16 Jan 1678 says: 'Bahadur Khan was corrupted by Shivaji...' (Ref 3). From Shivaji's point of view, the purpose was as straightforward as the first time – he needed to safeguard his rear from Mughal attack while he marched to Karnatak.

Shivaji's campaign in Adilshahi Karnatak is a masterstroke in planning and flawless execution. What were his motives in annexing these southern lands? Well, first it was a fertile and rich territory; that in itself would have been reason enough. But apart from earning the Maratha Swarajya valuable revenue, its conquest compromised Bijapur's revenues, thus compromising the Adilshahi treasury. Only a year earlier, Shivaji had annexed Canara, completing his hold on the west coast. The conquest of Karnatak would secure his hold on the east coast as well, effectively ending the Adilshah's access to coastal trade. Early in Shivaji's career, it was Muhammad Adilshah's obsession with conquering these very lands in Karnatak, which had caused him to neglect Shivaji's activities and helped him grow in power and stature. But after the Adilshah had annexed the lands, he could not secure his administration and military hold on them as he had to divert his attention north to the Mughals and to Shivaji. Thus, Karnatak remained a poorly guarded and administered territory of the Adilshahi, providing another valid reason for its invasion.

But above all, was probably Shivaji's own assessment of the political scenario of the period. He realized that the days of the Adilshahi were numbered and sooner rather than later, Aurangzeb would descend on the Deccan to swallow it. If he (Shivaji) could establish a foothold in the South by annexing Karnatak, he could lay a claim to Adilshahi lands before Aurangzeb. Besides, extending his realm to the eastern coast would give the Maratha rulers of the future an avenue to extend the field of battle, in future wars with the Mughals. The only drawback seemed to be that the Karnatak region was far removed from his holdings in Maharashtra. But with great foresight, he had annexed the Koppal region, which at least partly connected his old dominions with Karnatak. Quite understandably, Sabhasad calls Koppal a 'doorway to the South'.

Shivaji's genius is there for all to see in the way he planned the campaign and laid the ground in advance. The Mughal was pacified with a treaty, thus safeguarding his rear. Bahadur

Khan, now free from his worries about the Marathas, concentrated his efforts against Bijapur, thus ensuring that the Adilshah would remain busy with him while Shivaji went about his conquests in Karnatak. Niraji Raoji was sent in advance to the Qutubshah to garner his support for the campaign. Madanna, the Hindu Prime Minister of the Qutubshah, was tactfully persuaded to agree to a treaty with the Marathas. This move safeguarded Shivaji's rear while he was in Karnatak, while mobilizing much-needed funds for the campaign. Thus, when he arrived at Gingee, Nasir Mohammed was ready to hand over the fort to him, and Sher Khan in the South, had no hopes of succour from any quarter. After such detailed preparation, Shivaji's victory and success in the campaign was pre-ordained.

The precipitating factor may have been the arrival of Raghunath Hanmante and his brother Janardan, who had resigned from Vyankoji's service. Sabhasad says they left his service on account of differences (Ref 36), while Chitnis says Raghunath was dissatisfied with Vyankoji's indolence (Ref 8). Whatever the reason, once these two knowledgeable administrators joined Shivaji; they rendered him valuable advice which helped in conceptualizing the entire campaign.

Shivaji's march to Bhaganagar (Hyderabad), was quite unlike his usual marches, which were always rapid, without long halts and well concealed. The following will give the reader some idea of the speed of his travel – he covered some thousand-odd kilometers in five months, before finally reaching Bhaganagar. He made no attempt to conceal his location. Everyone knew where he was at all times. What was kept secret was his real motive and destination.

Shivaji travelled a wide arc, first going south in his own lands and then turning east along the Doab, between the Krishna and Tungabhadra rivers. Hambirrao marched ahead of him to prepare the ground. He annexed lands along the way and silenced possible enemies before the King followed, thus ensuring his safety. The entire route has been reconstructed beautifully by Mehendale (Ref 27), his chief sources being *Jedhe Shakavali*, English records, *Dagh Register* entries and some Marathi documents (*Peshwa Daftar, Marathyanchya Itihasachi Sadhane*). Various sources have given the strength of Shivaji's force, but of all these the estimate recorded in the minutes of the English Council meeting at Fort St. George (Chennai), seems to be the most reliable (Ref 3). This source places Shivaji's man-strength at 20,000 horse and 40,000 foot.

Sabhasad is our main source for the events in Bhaganagar itself (Ref 36). He tells us that Shivaji had issued explicit orders to his men, not to harass the locals and purchase supplies peacefully from the markets. He further says that a few miscreants were beheaded. Shivaji's courteous message to the Qutubshah, (You are my elder brother... you should not come forward...), Madanna coming forth to receive him, the grand welcome that Shivaji received in the city, are details obtained from the *Sabhasad Chronicle*. I have created my own narration of Shivaji's grand procession from Sabhasad and Kincaid's descriptions (Ref 24). My description of the actual meeting between the two rulers has been created from Sabhasad, and from an account of an unknown Dutchman who was an eyewitness (Ref 3).

The exact terms of the treaty between Shivaji and the Qutubshah are not known. But some idea of the clauses can be obtained from the following sources: English letters from Fort St. George (Ref 3), the account of Martin, the French Chief at Pondicherry (Ref 45), Jedhe Chronology (Ref 15) and Sabhasad (Ref 36). If one evaluates these terms, it is immediately apparent that the Qutubshah did not stand to gain much from this alliance. Shivaji does not seem to have agreed to hand over captured territory to him. Why then did the Qutubshah agree to such unfavourable terms?

There appears to be one sole reason – his Prime Minister, Madanna. From the day Madanna was appointed to that high office, he strove to increase Hindu dominance in the administration and at the court. He managed to appoint many of his own kin in key positions in the government. Shivaji's fame had already spread far and wide, making him a hero to Hindus across India. In Shivaji, Madanna probably saw the hope of resurrecting the Hindu religion in the South, and hence tried his utmost to convince his own ruler to welcome the Maratha King. Abul Hasan Qutubshah was an indolent pleasure-seeker and did not bother himself with the troubles of running his own kingdom. His only worry in inviting Shivaji was his own safety, as he feared Shivaji would double-cross and kill him. But when he received reasonable assurance from Shivaji's diplomat, Niraji Raoji, that the King wished only for friendship, he did not object any further.

Our main sources for the incident at Srishailya (Shrishailam), are the Marathi chronicles. Both the *Sabhasad Chronicle* (Ref 36) and *91 K Chronicle* (Ref 48), describe Shivaji's stay at the shrine in detail. Had Shivaji really decided to offer his head to the Lord? Probably not. But it is likely he was influenced spiritually. There comes a time in every person's life when one is compelled to say, 'This is it; I wish to go now'. Shivaji was, after all human, and his life had been no ordinary one. It is easy to understand how years of struggle, politics, warfare and killing would have affected his mind. The *91 K Chronicle* mentions: 'He decided to offer his head to the Lord. Weapons were removed. Raghunath Punt and the Senapati kept a vigil day and night...' If this account is to be believed, Shivaji's declaration that 'he wished to offer his head' must have been serious enough to worry his people.

The main sources for the events at Gingee, siege of Vellore, visits of the foreign embassies to Shivaji's camp, and of the rout of Sher Khan, are the *English letters* (Ref 3), *Martin's Journal* (Ref 45) and the *Marathi Chronicles* (Refs 8, 36, 48).

Details of Vyankoji's (Ekoji) visit to Shivaji's camp are obtained from *Martin's Journal* (Ref 45), Shivaji's letters to Vyankoji (Ref 14), *Sabhasad Chronicle* (Ref 36), *Tarikh-i-dilkasha* (Ref 37), *Jedhe Chronology* (Ref 15) and from the letters of Nellore Ramanna, the Hindu envoy of the English, who was present in Shivaji's camp at the time (Ref 3). According to Ramanna, Vyankoji arrived at Shivaji's camp with an escort of 2000 men, and Shivaji went forth to receive him. Jedhe, Martin, Sabhasad and Bhimsen say Vyankoji suspected that Shivaji would imprison him and hence he fled from the camp. Shivaji himself says in his letter: 'It was not befitting my position and reputation that I should seize you; so I gave you leave to go to Tanjore' (Ref 14; English Translation in Ref 27). Ramanna says in his letter: 'Shivaji waxed very angry and had him begone.' The *Jedhe Chronology* records that Shivaji annexed Vyankoji's estates after this meeting (Ref 15).

Martin provides us a brief account of Shivaji's camp: 'The camp of Shivaji was without pomp, without women; there were no baggages, only two tents but of simple cloth and very scanty, one for him and the other for his Prime Minister' (Ref 45).

That Shivaji prohibited slave traffic in the newly conquered territory is proven by a kaul from Shivaji to the Dutch dated 26 August 1677. A translation of the letter appears in Ref 25.

Vyankoji's war with Shivaji is recorded by Martin (Ref 45), English letters from Fort St. George (Ref 3), the *Sabhasad Chronicle* (Ref 36) and by Shivaji himself in his letter to Vyankoji (Ref 14). The brief passage in this book which narrates contents of this letter is adapted from Mehendale's translation of the original letter (Ref 27). An entry from the *Fort St. George Diary* says that Shivaji returned a large part of the estates which he had earlier confiscated and that Vyankoji paid him a large sum of money in lieu of the same (Refs 3, 4). The *Jedhe Chronology* too, records that Vyankoji concluded a treaty with Shivaji (Ref 15).

The incidents regarding Jamshed Khan's attempted treason and proposal to Shivaji, are mentioned in an English letter from Rajapur, dated 3 April 1678. Mehendale however, opines that this story cannot be trusted as it is not corroborated by any other source (Ref 27).

The Belavadi incident is described in the *Chitnis Chronicle*, *Sabhasad Chronicle* and *91K Chronicle* (Refs 8, 36, 48). An English letter from Rajapur to Surat, dated 28 February 1678 says: 'Shivaji is at present besieging a fort, where he has suffered more disgrace than ever he did from all power of the Mughal or Deccanis, and he who has conquered so many Kingdoms is not able to reduce this woman Desai' (Ref 3). From these sources one ascertains that it took Shivaji a month or so to reduce the small mud-fort defended by a woman and her garrison. I find that difficult to believe, especially as Shivaji had a large army at his disposal. That the delay was caused by Shivaji's diversion to Bijapur on receiving a communication from Jamshed Khan, is entirely my own surmise.

The Afghan mutiny after Siddi Masud took over as Regent, has been described in detail in *Basatin-us-salatin* (Ref 50) and

Tarikh-i-dilkasha (Ref 37). About the untold misery inflicted by the Pathan soldiery upon Bahlol Khan's family, Bhimsen writes: 'If they could treat their own clansmen thus, one can imagine how they oppressed other people.' Sarkar gives a lively account of the mutiny based mainly on these two sources (Ref 41, 42).

The fall of Vellore Fort after a siege of fourteen months is described in the *Jedhe Chronology* (Ref 15), *Martin's Journal* (Ref 45) and in an English letter from Fort St. George, dated August 1678 (Ref 27).

The Karnatak campaign was probably one of the most significant of Shivaji's career, because its benefits far exceeded the mere collection of valuable revenue. In fact, says Mehendale (Ref 27), the most important benefit was reaped after Shivaji's death, when Aurangzeb invaded the Deccan. Gingee withstood a siege of seven years, thus saving the Maratha kingdom from extinction. Shivaji's dominions in Karnatak stretched the Mughal lines far and wide, thus making them susceptible to Maratha counter-attacks, ultimately shattering them. The Mughal Empire never recovered from Aurangzeb's protracted invasion of the Deccan, paving the way for the Maratha Empire in the next century.

The Khanderi campaign stretched from August of 1679, well up to February 1680. Our main sources for these events are the English letters (Ref 3). My descriptions of the naval battles are adapted from accounts in Refs 27, 28, 32, 38.

Sambhaji's defection to Diler Khan is recorded in the *Jedhe Chronology* (Ref 15), *Martin's Journal* (Ref 45), a Surat Council letter (Ref 3), the *Sabhasad Chronicle* (Ref 36), the *91K Chronicle* (Ref 48), *Tarikh-i-dilkasha* (Ref 37) and Basatin (Ref 50). From these sources it does appear that Sambhaji had differences with his father, though the exact reasons for his defection are not clear. It is entirely my surmise that Sambhaji suspected his father wanted Rajaram to be his successor.

Basatin, Tarikh, the *Jedhe Chronology* and the *Marathi Chronicles* (Refs 8, 15, 36, 48, 50), are our sources for the Bhupalgad campaign. From available sources, it does seem that the fort garrison did not offer a fight to Diler Khan's forces, and the reason for this appears to be Sambhaji's presence in the enemy camp. The *Chitnis Chronicle* states: 'The garrison was perplexed on seeing their King's son and did not open fire for fear of hurting him; they fled during the night' (Ref 8, 46). Tarikh and Basatin state: 'Seven hundred men were taken prisoner and were set free after mutilating one arm each' (Refs 37, 50). The *Chitnis Chronicle* also states that Shivaji then ordered all other garrisons to open fire without hesitation and not to surrender the forts. This clearly shows that Shivaji put his kingdom, his beloved Swarajya, above his own son's safety.

Maasir-i-Alamgiri records that Aurangzeb ordered the demolition of temples in Rajasthan, ordered the broken fragments of idols to be cast in the steps of the Jama Masjid, and that he re-imposed the *jizya* tax (Ref 39).

The political and military mess following Masud's ascension to Regentship, as well as Diler Khan's campaign against Bijapur in second half of 1679, are mainly sourced from *Basatin-us-salatin* (Ref 50). Shivaji's arrival at Bijapur on Masud's invitation is corroborated by Shivaji's letter to Vyankoji: 'We assembled the entire army and went in person with the cavalry near Bijapur' (Ref 14, English Translation Ref 27). Masud's refusal to allow Shivaji to enter Bijapur with 5000 men, Shivaji's eventual cancellation of his plans on Moro Punt's advice, and the elaborate intrigues between

Diler Khan, Prince Muazzam, Hakim Shamshuddin and Malik Barkhurdar, are all adapted from Basatin.

Details of Maratha raids in Mughal territory are adapted from Basatin, *Mutakhab-ul-lubab* (Excerpts in Ref 27) and English letters (Ref 3). Shivaji's misadventure while returning from the loot of Jalna, and the battle with Ranmast Khan, is described by Sarkar (Ref 44). Shivaji's letter to Vyankoji (Ref 14) mentions the battle with Ranmast Khan as follows: 'While we were marching on horseback toward fort Pattagad with that wealth, Ranmast Khan, Asaf Khan, Zabit Khan and five or seven such officers with eight or ten thousand troopers came in the way. We chastised them, captured horses and elephants and arrived at Fort Patta' (English Translation in Ref 27).

Diler Khan's inhuman raids and devastation in the Tikota-Athani region is detailed in *Basatin-us-salatin* (Ref 50). From available sources it does seem that Sambhaji was disgusted with Diler's cruelty and so decided to return to his father. An English letter from Mumbai, dated 1 January 1680, states the same (Ref 3). Both Basatin and *Tarikh-i-Dilkasha* (Ref 37) say that Shivaji tried to conciliate Sambhaji by sending his men to meet up with the Prince in secret. Shivaji himself says in his letter to Vyankoji: 'We employed various means to bring him back. He too realized that in the Empire or in the Badshahis of Bijapur and Bhaganagar, things will not be done to his liking. So, in response to our letter he came and met us, I conciliated him as is proper in family affairs' (Ref 14, English Translation in Ref 27).

Sambhaji's character is not just a matter of great intrigue, but also great controversy. There is no doubt that he was a very brave and competent soldier and General, perhaps paling only in comparison to his illustrious father. Without doubt, he was also devoted to his kingdom. But was he as good a politician as Shivaji? Was he as far-sighted, cautious and wise in administrative matters? I am inclined to think not, though this is open to debate. As Sabhasad says, Sambhaji certainly seems to have had differences with Shivaji's Ministers and Administrators (Ref 36). Some details of his interactions with the Ministers and Soyarabai have been obtained from *Parmanandkavyam* by Kavindra Parmanand's son Devdutt, and grandson Govind (Ref 17). As I have mentioned earlier, I have tried to portray Sambhaji according to what I make of him, steering clear of controversy.

Another contentious issue is the charge that Shivaji was poisoned by Soyarabai. Since there is no documented evidence for this, I have chosen to ignore the matter altogether. However, it must be noted that the English records (Ref 3) make a mention of letters received by the Fort St. George Council from Shivaji, on 14 May 1677 and 25 May 1677, requesting a supply of cordial stones, Maldives coconuts, and Bezoar stones, all known to be counter-poisons or antidotes. Why did Shivaji request these, not just once but twice? A Dutch letter dated 23 October 1680, refers to a report from Golconda, that Shivaji may have been poisoned by his second wife (Ref 14).

My dramatization of events surrounding Shivaji's last illness, his death, and the aftermath, is based mainly on the *Marathi Chronicles* (Ref 8, 36, 48). Shivaji's despondency over Sambhaji's behaviour and defection, his meeting with Sambhaji on the latter's return, the proposed division of Shivaji's kingdom, the description of his last meeting with his Ministers, are all adapted from the *Chronicles*.

The cause of Shivaji's death remains shrouded in controversy. Both Sabhasad and Chitnis say the King was stricken with *jwar* or 'fever', while the *E.K. Chronicle* states that he died of *navjwar* (literally 'new fever'). Was it some new kind of illness that was not understood by the King's Vaidyas? A letter from the Mumbai Council dated 28 April 1680 states: 'It is now 23 days since he is deceased, it is said of bloody flux, being sick 12 days' (Ref 3). Modern historians have generally accepted that the cause of his death was bloody dysentery (was it Typhoid?). The date of Shivaji's death is given in the *Jedhe Chronology* (Ref 15).

Shivaji's death is briefly mentioned in *Maasir-i-Alamgiri* (Ref 39) thus: 'News came from the Deccan that Shivaji after returning from a journey, dismounted from his horse, twice vomited blood in the excess of heat and sank down into the pit of hell. *Muntakhab-ul-Lubab* states: 'The author has found the chronogram of his (Shivaji's) death in the words *Kafir ba-Jahannam raft* ('The infidel went to hell')' (Excerpts and translation in Ref 27).

The *Marathi Chronicles* (Ref 8, 36, 48) and *Parmanandkavyam* (Ref 17) are our sources for the events following Shivaji's death, with some facts emerging from English letters (Ref 3). From available sources, it does appear that Shivaji did not express any desire to meet Sambhaji before his death. Had he done so, it would have been impossible for anyone to deny him. But the fact that Sambhaji remained at Panhala throughout Shivaji's illness implies that Shivaji had, in all probability, not sent for him. It also seems that Shivaji had not named his successor. Had he done so, it would have been impossible for the Ministers to deny Sambhaji that right, especially since he was the Yuvraj or Crown Prince.

That the Ministers chose to make Rajaram the successor while keeping Sambhaji restrained at Panhala, would indirectly imply that the Ministers were merely taking advantage of the fact that the King had not named a successor. They would, of course, have obtained ratification for their actions from the eldest Queen (Soyarabai). Besides, since Rajaram too, was the King's son, they were not committing treason.

Chitnis says that Balaji Avji refused to write a letter to the Killedar of Panhala, instructing him to arrest Sambhaji, and offered to ask his son to write it. The fact that Sambhaji (or his men), accosted the 'spy' who delivered the letters to the Killedar, and then forced him to divulge the details of events at Raigad, is mentioned in two Chronicles: *Marathi Rajyachi Choti Bakhar* and *Ch. Shahu Maharajanchi Bakhar* (Ref 47). *Parmanadkavya*m mentions that Hambirrao imprisoned Moro Punt and Anaji Punt (Ref 47).

The fact that Sambhaji gathered troops on Panhala and mobilized provisions from Rajapur, is mentioned in an English letter from Rajapur, dated 19 April 1680 (Ref 3).

The *Jedhe Chronology* (Ref 15) gives us the dates of Sambhaji's visit to Pratapgad and eventual return to Raigad. An English letter from Rajapur, dated 26 June 1680 states: 'Sambhaji Raja is at Rairi' (Ref 3). A letter from Surat dated 12 July 1680 states that Anaji Punt was not killed but imprisoned; and that the kingdom was now 'stable' since Sambhaji has been declared King (Ref 3). *Parmanandkavyam* (Ref 17) says that Sambhaji consoled Soyarabai and Putalabai, whereas Chitnis says he accused Soyarabai of poisoning his father.

The date of Sambhaji's ascension as the second Chhatrapati of Maratha Swarajya is given by the *Jedhe Chronology* (Ref 15).

As we come to the end of this trilogy on Chhatrapati Shivaji's life and times, it perhaps behoves me to add a brief note about what happened to the main characters who peopled this history after the coronation of his eldest son, Sambhaji as second Chhatrapati of the Maratha Swarajya.

Sambhaji's rule was a short one, from 1681–1689, before he was captured by Emperor Aurangzeb's officers, and then later tortured and executed. His half-brother Rajaram, was crowned Chhatrapati after him. Sambhaji's eight-year rule was marred by conflict, with both the Mughals, as well as with the other political stakeholders of the time.

Moro Punt Pingale was removed from the high office of Mukhya Pradhan. He was arrested and imprisoned, but later released. He continued to serve the administration till his death a couple of years later. His son took over the office of Mukhya Pradhan.

Anaji Punt was also arrested, and later released. He too, continued to serve the administration.

A second conspiracy was hatched against Sambhaji in 1681. Though details of that drama are not clear, some sources name Anaji Punt, Soyarabai and Hiroji Farzand as the chief conspirators. This second attempt too, failed. Anaji Punt and Hiroji were (according to some chroniclers), executed.

Soyarabai, Shivaji's second wife and Queen for most of his reign, died a year after Sambhaji's coronation. She did not live to see her own son, Rajaram, crowned Chhatrapati, the end to which she had devoted her life. The cause of her death remains unclear.

Shivaji's Senapati, Hambirrao Mohite, continued to serve Sambhaji in the same capacity. He was killed during a battle with the Mughal forces in 1687.

The Adilshahi Sultanate perished in 1686, when Aurangzeb marched against Bijapur in person. Sikander, the last Adilshah, staved off the Mughal onslaught for a year before finally surrendering his city to the Emperor.

Shortly thereafter, Aurangzeb annexed the Qutubshah's kingdom through an internal conspiracy. Madanna and Akanna were executed. Abul Hasan, the last Qutubshah, was imprisoned and sent to Daulatabad Fort, where he died in captivity in 1699.

Aurangzeb himself remained in the Deccan till his death in 1707, aged 88. He never returned to his capital. His war with the Marathas had lingered over two decades and resulted in the irreversible weakening of the Mughal Empire, which was financially devastated. The Maratha Swarajya survived Aurangzeb, growing into an Empire that covered a large part of India, and a mighty political force.

Bibliography

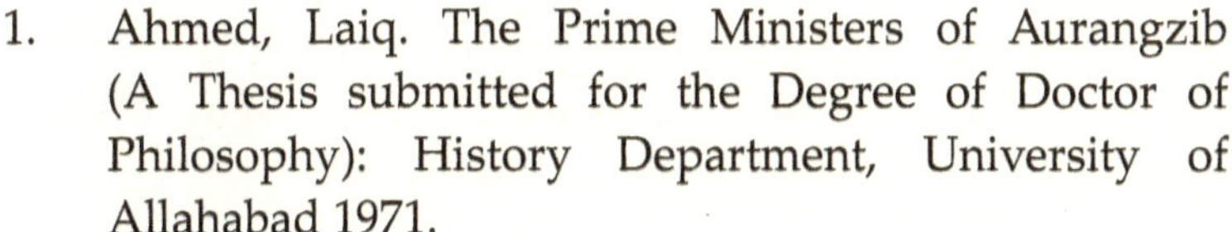

1. Ahmed, Laiq. The Prime Ministers of Aurangzib (A Thesis submitted for the Degree of Doctor of Philosophy): History Department, University of Allahabad 1971.

2. Amatya, Ramchandrapant. Ed. Kulkarni, Dr. A.R. Ajnapatra (Modi-Marathi-English): Diamond Publication 2007.

3. Anon. English Records on Shivaji: Shiva Charitra Karyalaya 1931.

4. Bal Krishna. Shivaji the Great (Vol I, Parts I & II): D.B. Taraporevala Sons & Co. 1932.

5. Bendre, V.S. Govalkondyachi Qutbshahi (Marathi): Bharat Itihaas Samshodhak Mandal 1934.

6. Bernier, Francois. Ed: Smith, Vincent A. Translated by Archibald Constable. Travels in the Mogul Empire, AD 1656-1668: Low Price Publications 1994.

7. Chile, Bhagwan. Famous Forts in Maharashtra: Shiva Sparsh Prakashan 2011.

8. Chitnis, Malhar Ramrao. Ed: R.V. Herwadkar. Shri Shiva Chhatrapatinche Saptaprakarnatmak Charitra (Marathi): Venus Prakashan 2000.

9. Cooper, Randolf G.S. The Anglo-Maratha Campaigns and the Contest for India: The Press Syndicate of the University of Cambridge 2003.

10. Cousens, Henry. Bijapur - The Old Capital of the Adil Shahi Kings (A guide to its ruins with historical outline): Archeological Survey of Western India 1889.

11. Eds: Apte, D.V. Divekar, S.M. Shiva Charitra Pradip (Marathi): Bharat Itihas Samshodhak Mandal 1931.

12. Ed: Foster William. The Embassy of Sir Thomas Roe to the Court of the Great Mogul 1615-1619 (As narrated in his Journal and Correspondence): Hakluyt Society London 1899.

13. Eds: Khare, G.H., Kulkarni, Govind Tryambak. Aitihasik Farsi Sahitya: Aurangzebchya Durbarche Akhbar (Persian Original with Marathi Translation): Bharat Itihas Samshodhak Mandal 1976.

14. Ed: Kulkarni, Dr. Anuradha. Shivachhatrapatinchi Patre (Marathi): Param Mitra Publications 2011.

15. Ed: Kulkarni, Dr. A.R. Jedhe Shakavali-Karina: Diamond Publication 2007.

16. Eds. Majumdar, R.C. Chaudhari, J.N. Chaudhari, S. The History and Culture of the Indian People: The Mughul Empire: Bharatiya Vidya Bhavan 2007.

17. Ed: Shivde, Dr. Sadashiv. Translated by Ayachit, Dr. S.M. Parmanandkavyam (Marathi): Vishwamitra Prakashan 2010.

18. Ed: Sovani, Avinash. Aitihasik Shakavalya (Marathi): Shabdavedh Prakashan 1998.

19. Eraly, Abraham. Emperors of the Peacock Throne: Penguin Books 1997.

20. Eraly, Abraham. The Mughal World: Penguin Books 2007.

21. Fryer, John. A New Account of East India and Persia in Eight Letters being Nine Years Travels: London 1698.

22. Gribble, J.D.B. The History of the Deccan Vol I & II, Rupa and Co 2002.

23. Joshi, Major Mukund. Dakshin Digvijay: Manodaya Prakashan 2007.

24. Kincaid, Dennis. Shivaji The Grand Rebel (An Impression of Shivaji. Founder of Maratha Empire): Rupa Publications India Pvt. Ltd. 2015.

25. Kruijtzer, Gijs. Xenophobia in 17th Century India: Leiden University Press 2009.

26. Manucci, Niccolao. Translated by Irvine, William. Storia Do Mogor or Mogul India. John Murray for the Govt. Of India 1907.

27. Mehendale, Gajanan Bhaskar. Shivaji: His Life and Times: Param Mitra Publications 2011.

28. Mehendale, Gajanan Bhaskar and Shintre Santosh. Shiva Chhatrapatinche Armaar (Marathi): Param Mitra Publication 2010.

29. Pagadi, Setumadhavrao. Chhatrapati Shivaji: Continental Prakashan 2014.

30. Palsokar, Col. R.D. Shivaji the Great Guerilla: Nataraj Publishers 2003.

31. Parmanand, Kavindra. Ed: Sadashiv Mahadev Divekar. Shri Shivbharat (Sanskrit original, Marathi translation): Shabdavedh Prakashan 1998.

32. Pendse, Dr. Sachin. Maratha Armaar (Marathi): Merven Technologies 2017.

33. Pissurlencar, P.S. Translated from Marathi by Parvate, T.V. Portuguese-Mahratta Relations. Maharashtra State Board for Literature and Culture 1983.

34. Pindye Jayram. Translation by Desai, Rajaram Damodar. Parnal-Parvat-Grahanakhyam (Sanskrit text with Marathi translation): Sadashiv Mahadev Divekar 1923.

35. Purandare, Babasaheb. Raja Shiv Chhatrapati (Marathi): Purandare Prakashan 2008.

36. Sabhasad, Krishnaji Anant. Ed: Dr. Y.M. Pathan. Sabhasad Bakhar (Marathi): Snehvardhan Publishing House 2007.

37. Saksena Bhimsen. Translation by Sarkar, Sir Jadunath. Ed. V. G. Khobrekar. Tarikh-i-Dilkasha: Government of Maharashtra 1972.

38. Samant, Dr. Shrinivas. Vedh Mahamanavacha (Marathi): Deshmukh and Co. 2012.

39. Saqi Mustaid Khan. Translated to English by Sarkar, Sir Jadunath. Maasir-i-Alamgiri (A History of the Emperor Aurangzib-Alamgir): Royal Asiatic Society of Bengal 1942.

40. Sarkar, Sir Jadunath. History of Aurangzib Vol III: M.C. Sarkar and Sons 1921.

41. Sarkar, Sir Jadunath. History of Aurangzib Vol IV: M.C. Sarkar and Sons 1930.

42. Sarkar, Sir Jadunath. History of Aurangzib Vol V: M.C. Sarkar and Sons 1924.

43. Sarkar, Sir Jadunath. House of Shivaji: S.N. Sarkar 1940.

44. Sarkar, Sir Jadunath. Shivaji and His Times: Orient Longman 1973.

45. Sen, Surendra Nath. Foreign Biographies of Shivaji (Extracts and Documents relating to Maratha History Vol II): Kegan Paul Trench Trubner & Co. Ltd.

46. Sen, Surendranath. Siva Chhatrapati (Extracts and Documents relating to Maratha History Vol I): University of Calcutta 1920.

47. Shivde Sadashiv. Jwaljwalantejas Sambhaji Raja (Marathi): Diamond Publications 2001.

48. Vakeniwis, Dattaji Trimal. Ed: V.S. Vakaskar. Shri Shiva Chhatrapatinchi 91 Kalmi Bakhar (Marathi): Venus Prakashan 1962.

49. Various. Shivaji Nibandhavali: Bharat Itihaas Samshodhak Mandal 2014.

50. Zubairi, Muhammad Ibrahim. Translated to Marathi by Parasnis, Narsinghrao Vitthal. Ed. V. S. Bendre. Busatin-us-Salatin (Vijapurchi Adilshahi): Mumbai Marathi Granthsangrahalay 1968.

ACKNOWLEDGEMENTS

The completion of *The Legend*, brings me to the end of an incredible journey extending over more than a decade. The overwhelming sense of relief at having accomplished the impossible is tinged with some sadness as I realize that I will not be a part of this riveting story any longer.

Before I conclude the trilogy, I must thank all the people who have been with me on this roller-coaster ride. As always, my family deserves first credit, not just for supporting and encouraging me, but also for putting up with my absence while I was lost somewhere in the mid-17th century.

My close friends continue to be my first critics, offering valuable advice to improve my writing.

I am ever grateful to the entire team at Leadstart, without whom, my books would not have reached my readers. Special thanks are due to my Editor, Chandralekha Maitra, whose meticulous efforts have improved the quality of my narration immensely. Working with her has been an absolute pleasure and has made me a far better writer in these past years.

My mentor, guide and teacher, Mr. Gajanan Mehendale, deserves all my respect, gratitude and more. Ever since I first approached him for help years ago, he has proverbially 'carried me' throughout this journey. His teachings and advice, as well as his constructive criticisms, have helped me navigate rough waters and reach the shores of success.

It would not be an exaggeration to say that without him, it would have been well nigh impossible for me to complete this trilogy. It is the mark of a truly evolved human being to help someone to this extent, without expecting anything in return.

I would also like to acknowledge the role, albeit indirect, of my other mentor, Shri Babasaheb Purandare, who recently left this mortal world. Had it not been for his inspiring books, stories and lectures, I would probably never have embarked upon this journey. His writings have always, and still continue to be, the chief inspiration for my work. I offer him my sincere respect and gratitude.

Over the course of the 12 years that it has taken me to write this trilogy, I have read and referred to hundreds of books, papers and manuscripts, and heard and watched an equal number of lectures and films on the subject. I wish to thank the authors and creators of these works, as they form the basis of my own books. Throughout the process, though writing historical fiction, I have tried my best to remain true to documented history and these works have helped me accomplish that.

Finally, I wish to thank my readers, without whom the entire exercise would be fruitless and meaningless. Over the years I have been overwhelmed by their responses, emails and reviews on popular websites, which have not only encouraged me to do better, but have also given me a deep sense of satisfaction and accomplishment. I hope to live up to their words and expectations in my future projects.

300 BRAVE MEN

BOOK I: 1641–1660

The incredible story of Chhatrapati Shivaji Raje Bhosale, legendary warrior-king, guerrilla fighter, brilliant tactician and clever diplomat. But above all, a remarkable man.

The Indian sub-continent is ruled by three tyrannical Sultanates – the powerful Mughals in the North, and the Shia Adilshah and Qutubshah in the South. The very idea of freedom has been wiped from the minds of the native population, suppressed for centuries. As incessant battles rage between the Sultanates, Maharashtra, once a prosperous and peaceful land, has been reduced to a wasteland.

In this dark era, the sixteen-year-old son of an Adilshahi jagirdar rises to declare: *I shall not serve, and neither shall my people!* With the dream of a free State and an identity for his people burning in his heart, he dares to rebel against the powerful Sultan, Adilshah. He begins with nothing...no army, no weapons and an empty treasury. Yet he achieves what no soldier, chieftain or king has ever achieved in defiance of imperial rulers.

LORD OF THE ROYAL UMBRELLA

BOOK II: 1661–1674

Land of the Marathas

Shivaji Bhosale's struggle against imperial powers continues as massive Mughal armies repeatedly descend upon his tiny fiefdom. Emperor Aurangzeb recognizes the dangerous threat of the Mountain Rat and resolves to finish him off, once and for all. He sends Shaista Khan, his maternal uncle, with a large army, but Shivaji, in a daring night raid, attacks the much-decorated Mughal General, cutting off his fingers. Turning his attention to Sultan Adilshah, Shivaji systematically expands his holdings in the Konkan. Along the coast, the British, Portuguese and Abyssinians also find him a serious obstacle to their coastal interests.

Infuriated, the Mughal Emperor sends Jai Singh and Diler Khan to the Deccan with another large army. Jai Singh proves to be the toughest challenge Shivaji has faced. He is finally subdued and receives Aurangzeb's firmaan to surrender a large part of his fiefdom and serve in the Mughal army. In a final insult, Shivaji is compelled to visit Agra and bow before the Badshah. However, the ingenious Maratha, foiling all attempts to assassinate him, escapes, leaving the Emperor seething in impotent fury.

Shivaji then embarks on the re-conquest of his lost forts and territories. Finally, in 1674, in defiance of imperial rule, he crowns himself King of the Marathas. After more than 350 years of enslavement, the Marathi people have their own *Chhatrapati, Lord of the Royal Umbrella.*

We are always keen to look at interesting new content across genres. Please mail submissions to: **submissions@leadstartcorp.com**

Proposals should include:

1. Synopsis

A summary of the book in 500 – 1000 words. Please mention the word count of the manuscript.

2. Sample chapters / Poetry

A couple of chapters from the book; these need not be in order, just send the best two chapters of the book. Or a few poems if the same is a collection of poetry.

3. A Note About The Author

An interesting note about yourself (about 200 words).

4. Additional Information

- Target audience
- Unique selling proposition
- List of illustrative content (if any)
- Other comparative titles
- Your thoughts on marketing the book

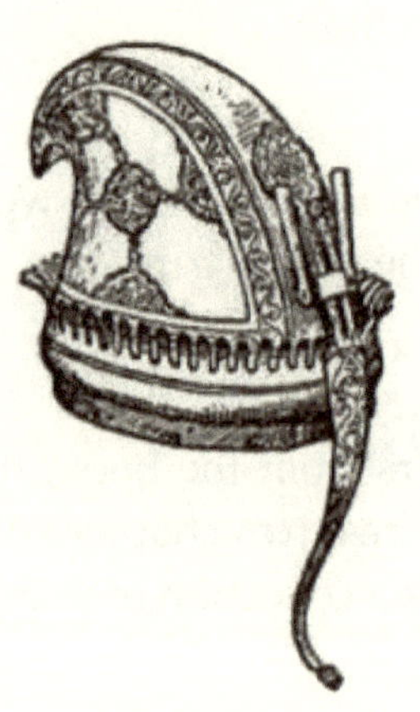

www.ingramcontent.com/pod-product-compliance
Lightning Source LLC
Chambersburg PA
CBHW031450160726
47994CB00005B/1956